I0451925

ASTRID DARBY & THE EYE OF RA

ELEANOR PROPHET

An imprint of Diogenes Club Press

Worldly, Whimsical, and Weird Books

www.diogenesclubpress.com

Dallas, TX

Copyright © 2012 by Eleanor Prophet

All rights reserved. This book, its logos, symbols, images, and likenesses are copyrighted by Author name. No part of this work may be reproduced in any media or format without prior written consent of copyright holder except for limited selections intended for journalistic review.

DC Dreams, an imprint of Diogenes Club Press
8619 Reva St. Dallas, TX 74227
www.diogenesclubpress.com

The characters and events in this book are fictional. Any similarity to real persons, living or dead, is coincidental and not intended by the author.

ISBN: 9781622010059
Library of Congress Control Number: 2017955888

CHAPTER ONE

Our expedition came upon a small village on the outskirts of Moscow. The cold was dreadful, and I feared for the health of our frailer fellows. I was reluctant to enter the village as it appeared to be uncivilized or, at the very least, unsophisticated, but the nearest city was kilometres away, and the cold had rendered our engine inoperable. The steam turned as quickly to ice as it hit the freezing air, and the wind made it impossible to maintain speed. We were forced to hire a sleigh and driver to haul our equipment over the icy terrain, and we were all in desperate need of a warm fire and a stiff drink.

Upon reaching the village gates, it became immediately apparent that there was something decidedly odd about its denizens. They seemed unusually jubilant at our arrival and overly acquiescent to our needs. We were immediately directed to a small inn in the centre of the village. I was pleasantly surprised by its agreeable accommodations.

The innkeeper was a jovial, portly fellow called Luka, and his wife, Duscha, was soft-spoken and suitably attentive without making herself a nuisance. We dined well on lamb pelmeni and course, strong vodka before Duscha directed us to our suite. It was obvious we were the inn's only guests, and I realized the villagers must indeed have been pleased by the arrival of a party of seven gentle fellows; tourism is unlikely a thriving commerce in the minuscule, out of the way village. Subsequently, I marvelled at the necessity of maintaining an inn at all, regardless of its size, and a clean, well-managed one at that.

Nestled in the crisp, newly laundered linens of the soft, warm bed in the suite I shared with the Lady Elisabeth Weston, I allowed my earlier suspicions to dull and eventually fade. I soon discovered this sense of security was premature. I awoke in the depth of night to a foreign noise in my room. I became instantly alert; the expedition fellows are close acquaintances, but I was hard-pressed to trust our feminine virtue to the swarthy sleigh driver Lord Benedict had hired out of the city.

I saw nothing in the darkened room, and after a few moments, I began to believe I had imagined whatever had awakened me. However, I was unable to shake the distinct sense that we were being watched. A sudden glint in the corner of the room confirmed my suspicion. I rose from the comfort of my bed to examine the metallic object that had caught the reflection of the pale moonlight through our bedroom window.

To my surprise it was, in fact, a fly on the wall, though such a fly I have never seen. The design was impeccable; the tiny clockwork was sleek and well crafted. Though nearly silent, its soft humming must have been what had interrupted my slumber as it passed over my sleeping person. As I reached for it, it darted away as quickly as the creature in whose image it was cast. After a few moments of stalking it around the chamber, I determined I would be unable to catch it by hand, and I was loathe to risk damaging it by attempting to swat it out of the air. I needed reinforcements. I did not wish to disturb the Lady Elisabeth whilst sneaking about in the night, but I suspected a disrupted beauty sleep would be infinitely preferable to remaining alone with the bug. I made haste to our provisions.

How right I was. When I returned, it was to a horrifying scene. The poor Lady Elisabeth was engaged in a very close encounter with our tiny night-time intruder. Though the clockwork had yet to attack, it was hovering in dangerous proximity to the Lady's aristocratic nose. "Stay still, Lady," I ordered softly, and she seemed inclined to comply, though she may merely have been too shocked by the unexpected visitor to respond.

Ensnaring the bug was easier than I had anticipated; young Xander's fishing net proved sufficiently successful. Again, however, I found myself lulled into a false sense of security. The automaton had no shortage of tricks up its proverbial sleeve. The clever little thing was well up to the challenge of escaping my net. To my astonishment, the bug was equipped with, not only an uncanny sentience, but a tiny, oscillating blade that shredded my young cousin's net to ribbons in mere seconds. The like of it I have never seen.

The Lady dove for cover in anticipation of an attack, but the clockwork seemed disinclined to exact revenge upon my person. Though I had been its captor, it had eyes only for the Lady Weston. It did not appear to have any intent to harm my companion, but as she moved experimentally around the chamber, it followed as a Spaniel follows its master, never moving more than several centimetres away.

"What is it, Astrid?" Lady Elisabeth whispered. Unlike many of her peers, the Lady is not prone to hysteria; it is one of the numerous qualities I admire in her. I was pleased to note there was no panic in her voice.

I shook my head. "I'm not sure. It looks like an automaton."

"What is it doing here?"

I pressed my finger to my lips. I suspected, if the tiny clockwork bug could produce a moving blade from its metal exo-skeleton, it was likely equipped with a listening device of some kind. I became quite certain after a few moments of watching the creature circle the Lady that someone was controlling it remotely. Luka, perhaps? I thought this unlikely. The innkeeper was kindly and did not seem bright enough to have constructed such a sophisticated machine. I felt equally certain that Duscha was not our puppet master.

The implications of this were perplexing and disturbing.

Attempting to keep myself at the fly's back, I motioned the Lady to return to her bed and sought the assistance of our mechanic and electrician, Mr Reinhart. Unfortunately, as the Lady's betrothed, Lord Benedict insisted upon accompanying Mr Reinhart, young Xander and me back to my chambers. Thus, being the only member of the party left out of the night-time escapade, excepting of course the swarthy driver who had no part in our expedition aside from our safe passage to our awaiting airship in St Petersburg, Mr Murdock, our endlessly capable yet infuriatingly meddling guide, joined the skirmish.

The Lady Elisabeth appeared to be asleep upon our return, and the automaton hummed over her bed like a tiny sentinel. I allowed the gentlemen to examine the creature. Xander in particular seemed highly impressed, though I was hardly surprised; the lad has always had a keen fondness for mechanics, which I attribute to my dear, departed Nathaniel. But I digress. Lady Elisabeth was not, despite initial appearance, asleep. In fact, I am sure she found it quite impossible to sleep in the presence of the intruder. Lord Benedict, being of quick temper and sadly lacking in the poise and grace his intended had displayed thus far, was highly irate and demanded Mr Reinhart swat the fly out of the air at once.

Mr Reinhart, possessing a curious nature and passionate interest in science and all its innovations, most emphatically refused. Luckily, Reinhart, being a former student of my late Mr Darby, had come prepared for such an event. He carried a compact, electro-static generator, the function of which I can only assume was to emit a brief, powerful shock that disrupted the mechanical controls within the tiny creature. Blue lightning arced from the spherical metal wand and unceremoniously zapped the bug from the air. Its humming effectively silenced, it lay on the end of Lady Elisabeth's bed like a small, benign tinker toy.

Reinhart was very keen to examine the bug up close, but the question of who had sent it remained in the forefront of my mind; I am a woman of action and resolve, not science and supposition. I had little interest in what the bug did; I wanted to know why and for whom. However, it had been a long and trying day, and the incident had only succeeded in reminding my weary

body how badly it craved a refreshing night's sleep. Order restored and our
privacy ensured, for Mr Reinhart had kindly left his device with me in case of
a replacement bug, the Lady and I returned to our beds to enjoy several hours'
uninterrupted sleep.

It was not to be, however. At dawn, the village came to life, and I was
awakened by the shouts of children calling to each other on their way to school.
With a groan, I rose from bed, hoping at least for a decent cup of strong, black tea

"Mrs Darby?"

to chase away the early morning fatigue.

"Cousin?"

As usual, the Lady appeared perfectly rested, impeccably coiffed and
unbearably cheerful compared to my likely rumpled, weary and grumbling mien.

"Astrid!"

I paused, startled at the interruption, my forgotten quill poised and dripping
small beads of black ink over the pages of my memoir. Alexander Knightly, my
young cousin and most trusted associate, stood in the doorway to my study, still
dressed in the tan frock-coat and brown corduroy suit he'd worn on a tour of
Lord Ignatius Fairway's acclaimed aviation exhibition at the Centre of Scientific
Innovation and Speculation earlier that day. I assumed Xander's disapproving
expression indicated he had been attempting for some time to tear my attention
from my journal.

"I beg your pardon, cousin. I did not realize you were there." I returned my
quill to the small ink-pot beside the blotter, pushing the thick, leather-bound
tome aside. "What is it then?"

"You have received a telegram." He moved hesitantly into the large, wood-
panelled study; Xander had never gotten used to the luxury of Darby Manor and
even less so the ability to move freely through its splendid halls. I had no such
qualms, despite our similarly humble beginnings, and his less than speedy foot
annoyed me.

6

"Yes, yes, come in, Xander," I ordered irritably. "Who is it from, then?"

"It's from Rake & Gage. They urgently request an audience in London."

I raised my eyebrows, holding out my hand to take the parchment. When he neared me, I realised young Knightly was rocking back and forth on the balls of his feet in an anxious fashion. I frowned at the undignified behaviour.

"What is the matter?"

Xander immediately stilled, suddenly cognisant of his movement. "Sorry, cousin, it's just—well, Rake & Gage is England's top manufacturer of the government's military defence systems."

"Yes, I am well aware of that, Xander, but you don't see me bouncing where I sit." I peered over my square-rimmed spectacles at him.

He hesitated, looking away for a moment. "Well, they are known to employ the best engineers and scientists. I only thought..."

I smiled. "Ah, ambitious, are you, my young cousin? I hear they are recruiting assistants this time of year. Are you hoping to fill one of the vacancies?"

Xander looked aghast. "Certainly not! I am perfectly happy with my present employment and accommodations; you know how I feel about returning to the city."

"Indeed, cousin, so why the unrestrained excitement?"

"Astrid, don't you remember anything from Nathaniel's lectures?"

I pursed my lips at his scolding tone, suppressing a smile. "Of course not, Xander. You know I am not interested in such things. I attended merely to humour my dear husband; surely you must know I paid absolutely no attention to his blathering."

Xander chuckled at this, for he had known me long and knew me well. "I beg your pardon, cousin. How foolish of me; you are a woman of action and resolve, not science and—"

"Supposition, yes. Now if you'd be so kind as to let me in on what it was I missed in Mr Darby's lectures that is so important as to have you practically flying out of your trousers."

"I beg your pardon! I most certainly am not flying out of my trousers. They are quite soundly fastened and will remain as such—" When I rolled my eyes at him, he paused and redirected. "Rake & Gage is rumoured to have commissioned Dr Sebastian Cross, one of England's most acclaimed physicists and inventors, to invent a mysterious new defence system, the nature of which they have been extremely secretive regarding thus far. It is to be revolutionary, at least according to the Society of Mechanics and Automata Inventors. He was the creator of one of the original directed energy beams, the Crystal Wave. It was dismantled, obviously, when its true destructive nature was discovered, but it was a masterpiece of physics." He pressed his hands together, his eyes burning like blue flame. "Dr Cross was one of Mr Darby's heroes. He always wanted to meet him before—well, the tragic event of August 25th three years ago."

I bowed my head in a moment of silence for my late husband and returned my gaze to my eager cousin. "Well," I said in a softer voice, "perhaps you will have the chance. Nathaniel would be honoured you remembered."

Xander smiled sadly, and I directed my eyes to the telegram, skimming it swiftly.

Dear Mrs Darby STOP Your attendance is urgently requested in London at the offices of Rake & Gage STOP This is a matter of extreme importance and security STOP Please respond at your earliest convenience STOP Signed Mr Maxwell Cole Executive VP Rake & Gage END

I peered at the missive a moment. "Xander, kindly respond to Mr Cole. I will be arriving in London in—" I removed a small, gold pocket watch, a gift from my late husband on our second anniversary, from my lapel pocket, glancing at its opened face. "Approximately two hours, provided we can catch the late airship travelling to the city this evening. I shall expect strong, black tea and chocolate biscuits upon my arrival. You may accompany me on the journey."

Xander nodded politely, but I suspected he was suppressing a grin; his pale, blue eyes twinkled in merriment. "Yes, Mrs Darby," he replied smartly, spinning from the room in a flurry of tan coattails.

I sighed, peering mournfully at my abandoned journal. The epic recounting of our adventures in Russia would again have to wait. *It is just as well*, I thought. Thwarting an evil inventor was not nearly as exciting when he was a hormonal fifteen year-old employing his automatons to kidnap women only to release them, utterly unharmed, three hours later. He hardly even put up a fight, and he treated the Lady Elisabeth quite pleasantly, by all accounts. I believe she still occasionally writes to the lad.

* * *

The car that awaited us when we disembarked in London was emblazoned with the Rake & Gage crossed keys, and a tall, overly thin man in a smart,

8

charcoal-grey suit stood beside it, as perfectly contented as if he'd nothing better to do than idle away at the airship port at ten in the evening. He bowed to young Xander and me, motioning us inside the spacious back seat. He did not speak to us, but he gave us an appraising sort of look as if to determine whether his time had been well spent. I was not especially concerned with his determination and turned my attention to the sights of London as they skimmed past our window.

Beside me, Xander was practically vibrating with excitement. The zeppelin flight had done little to calm his nerves, as he had developed a distinct distaste for dirigibles of any sort since my late husband's fatal accident. He had managed to suppress the unseemly quivering from earlier and appeared to be quite in possession of himself for the time being. I envied his enthusiasm at times; it seemed like ages since I had felt the spark or passion for the job. Perhaps I had grown weary from too much of the same. When one is an adventurer, the novelty of foiling evil schemes, espionage and mad science is soon to wear off. I had not realized how I missed the thrill of the job until I had taken my young cousin into my employ.

There were times when I would easily trade the wisdom of experience for the keenness of youth.

It was wisdom, not keenness, however, that had won me my reputation, and so I gave Xander a cautionary look as we arrived at the monolithic metal and glass structure that housed the offices of Rake & Gage Defence Contractors. The taciturn driver beckoned us inside brass doors twice the height of a man and into a darkened lobby. Our heels clicked smartly on the shining, mirrored floors, and a glass lift took us to the topmost level.

Maxwell Cole's office was at the end of a long corridor on the thirteenth floor. The night-lights of London twinkled outside the glass walls, making it seem as if we were walking along a bridge in the sky towards a floating room. Xander appeared quite uneasy, and I was uncertain if I appreciated the effect.

Our driver and lately guide knocked once on Mr Cole's door. "Enter," a voice called from within.

When the heavy door swung open, a tall man in a sleek, expensive, black, pinstripe suit stood up from behind the desk to greet us. He had shortly cropped black hair liberally streaked with grey and a thin, elegant goatee.

"Mrs Darby," he said, shaking my hand vigorously, relief written on his thin, patrician face. "And this must be young Knightly."

"Yes, sir." Xander gave the older man a quick, tidy bow.

"I am Maxwell Cole. This is Junior Vice President Edgar Thorne." Cole gestured towards the man standing silently beside his desk with his hands clasped behind his back. He was shorter, squatter, and, unlike Cole, he appeared displeased to see us. He gave a slight frown before rearranging his features into a neutral expression and nodding curtly to us. His suit was dark brown and custom tailored, but he did not wear it well; he shifted uncomfortably, as if the suit were scratchy or too warm in the fire-lit office.

Cole gestured to the chair across from his desk, and I seated myself primly, folding my hands into my lap and striking an expression of professional interest. "Mr Harlow," Mr Thorne spoke up in a clipped voice. "Perhaps young Mr Knightly would enjoy a tour of our facilities."

The driver nodded, turning to Xander. "This way, Mr Knightly," he said in a deep, drawling sort of voice, speaking for the first time since we had come into his company.

Xander glanced at me, and I nodded. He was not unused to being dismissed by clients in such a fashion, and I suspected he was far keener to explore the offices and laboratories than sit quietly whilst I conducted business. When Xander and Mr Harlow had disappeared, stepping back into the night sky, I turned my gaze to my potential employers, clearing my throat politely to indicate I was prepared to listen to their proposal.

"Thank you for coming on such short notice," Mr Cole said. I noticed Mr Thorne scowl and slide into the chair next to mine, turning it towards me as if to watch my every move.

"It was no trouble. I do hope you have the tea and biscuits I requested."

Mr Cole smiled fractionally. "Yes, of course. I am a man of my word. Mr Thorne, if you'd please." Mr Thorne looked exceedingly disgruntled by this command, but he rose and moved into a sub chamber of his superior's office, returning moments later with a tea service.

"Ace," I said, accepting the plate of chocolate biscuits and scones from Mr Cole and adding a lump of sugar to the strong, aromatic bergamot tea. "Now. On to business. What is it that I can do for you, Mr Cole?"

He sighed heavily, weighing his words with care. "As I stated in the telegram, this is a matter of the utmost urgency and security. Your strict confidence is required before I may proceed with an explanation of the situation."

"I assure you, Mr Cole, my word is my bond. My reputation for discretion is unblemished."

"I have heard said, Mrs Darby," Mr Cole agreed. "However, as this is a matter of national security, Rake & Gage requires further assurance of your silence." He slid a parchment across the desk towards me, and I picked it up, my eyebrows travelling upwards. "We do not mean to imply that we do not trust you, Mrs Darby. It is merely our company policy to acquire an agreement that our meeting this evening will remain off the record. You understand the debacle that could ensue should the media get wind of this situation."

"Of course, Mr Cole. Naturally, I understand your position. You'll allow me a few moments to study the document?" It was a standard confidentiality agreement, but the last stipulation caused me to raise my eyebrows once again. "Mr Cole, I am compelled to inform you that, as per your request, neither I nor anyone I might employ in this matter will approach the authorities regarding this meeting or any subsequent meetings. However, if I am approached by our government or any of her subsidiaries regarding this contract, I am both legally and honour bound to provide them with any information I may possess that they may consider pertinent."

"That is quite unacceptable," Mr Thorne began heatedly, but Mr Cole held up his hand to cut him off.

"I understand, Mrs Darby. We would not presume to require you compromise your delicate sensibilities." He sighed again, and I could see the strain around his eyes and in the tightening of his thin mouth. "I regret we may be unable to remain mum on this situation for very long. I fear it is only a matter of time before we are quite thoroughly exposed."

"Maxwell, I don't think—"

"It is alright, Edgar," Mr Cole said, cutting off his subordinate again and eliciting a deep, impotent scowl. "I trust, once we have explained, our reasons will become clear, Mrs Darby."

I signed the agreement with a flourish, sliding it back across the desk towards Mr Cole. "I am most confident that they will, Mr Cole. If you please, then."

"Maxwell, I must again object to this course of action," Mr Thorne piped in.

"Yes, yes, Edgar, I heard and noted your objections the first several times you voiced them," Cole said impatiently, frowning slightly at the interruption.

"I only hope to persuade you that this…woman's integrity is questionable at best. She is a mercenary. How can we be assured she will not run directly to the media the moment she leaves this office?"

"I beg your pardon, Mr Thorne," I interjected mildly, tamping down on

11

my indignation; causing a scene was hardly conducive to a smooth business transaction. "My integrity has been tried and tested many times over. If you require more than my signature on an official, legally binding document to be certain of my fidelity, I have a number of recommendations and referrals from past satisfied clients including royalty, aristocracy, government and military from all over the world. I have completed hundreds of assignments to the highest standards of excellence and expect this assignment to be no different."

"Mrs Darby comes highly recommended, Edgar," Mr Cole added. "I am quite confident she is the best person for the job. Now, that aside, Mrs Darby, we called you here to recover an object that has been...misplaced."

"Misplaced?"

"Well, you see..." Cole inhaled heavily, and I understood that his position was dire indeed. Though I had little patience for hemming and hawing, I sat quietly, waiting for him to continue. He gathered his bearing, meeting my gaze with steely green eyes. "As you may have heard, being a woman of culture and erudition as it were, Rake & Gage has commissioned Dr Sebastian Cross to invent a new, state of the art, military defence system."

"I have heard as much," I replied as he had paused a moment, peering at me, and seemed to be waiting for my confirmation. "In fact, young Knightly was just explaining that Dr Cross is a most well-known physicist deeply admired by the late Mr Darby."

Mr Cole nodded grimly. "Yes, Dr Cross is most esteemed and his invention most ingenious. You see, then, why it is quite alarming that both he and his apparatus have, inexplicably, gone missing."

"Espionage?"

Mr Thorne scowled. "Defection," he responded darkly.

"We fear the worst," Mr Cole admitted. "Dr Cross required only a small lab with one assistant he hand-picked from outside the firm. None of our employees were welcome inside the laboratory, including myself and Mr Gage. We received periodic updates on his progress every other week, and he seemed to be nearing completion of the prototype. His last update was expected on my desk today, but it was never delivered. I checked with the courier—a young intern from the university, very steadfast—and discovered the papers had never reached the tube deposit. Thus, despite Dr Cross' strict orders, I sent my assistant, Waverly, to check in on him. When Mr Waverly arrived, it was to find the lab empty. Dr Cross and his apparatus were gone, as well as his assistant."

"Any signs of a struggle?" I asked, leaning forward in my seat. "Has anyone been able to locate this assistant?"

"No, nothing. Everything was gone. His assistant is one Dr Joseph Ramsey. I had not previously heard of him, but Dr Cross refused to take anyone else. I understand they have been working together for many years. Cross does not trust many people."

"They likely had it planned all along," Thorne growled, his back stiff and his knuckles white where he gripped the arms of his chair. "Use our resources and materials to construct the blooming prototype and vamp it right out from under our noses."

"Mr Thorne!" Cole scolded in astonishment. "Please, mind your language. You are in the presence of a lady."

I was sure I heard the shorter man mutter derisively under his breath, but I ignored him pointedly, returning my gaze to Mr Cole. "Is it possible one of your competitors lured him away?"

Cole nodded mournfully. "It is possible. Competition for military contracts is fierce. If one of the other defence firms got wind of the project, they may have contacted Cross and made him an offer."

"Could one of your employees have leaked information to one of your competitors?"

"Mrs Darby, our employees couldn't have done this," Thorne told me coolly. "We trust them implicitly. If anyone leaked information, it was Cross. Or that upstart Ramsey."

"Perhaps. Or perhaps something more sinister is afoot. Do you have any reason to believe the doctor was kidnapped?"

"Kidnapped?" Thorne exclaimed. "This is a business, Mrs Darby, and real life, not a work of fiction. That is simply preposterous."

"Mr Thorne, please control yourself," Cole cautioned, but he too appeared unconvinced. "Mrs Darby, industrial espionage of this magnitude is unheard of. I find it far more likely to believe the doctor left of his own accord and entered into the service of one of our competitors."

I nodded. It was clearly not the time to speculate on the possible reasons for the doctor's and his assistant's disappearance. However, one of the best known verities is that the gut, in which I now felt a distinctive sensation liken to gnawing, is the part of the body most sensitive to unconfirmed certainties. As a woman of action and resolve as opposed to science and supposition, I was not usually given to such far-fetched notions, but as an adventurer, I have come to regard them as noteworthy if unreliable. I was confident the truth of the matter would come to light soon enough.

"As you like, Mr Cole. Am I to understand my charge is to locate the missing doctor and his assistant?"

"In a manner of speaking." Mr Cole was looking uneasy again, and I had the distinct impression he was a man quite comfortable being ruthless and quite uncomfortable with anyone knowing about it. "Our concern is the apparatus, Mrs Darby. You must understand our position; we have been given the prodigious task of providing our military with a revolutionary defensive strategy. It would be catastrophic should she then learn that we have allowed the apparatus to disappear right from under our noses."

"Ah, yes," I replied, amusement in my tone. "It becomes apparent why you have contacted me. You wish me to locate the apparatus and bring it back here to you before anyone finds out you ever misplaced it."

"Just so. With the utmost secrecy and alacrity."

"Naturally. I can do this for you, Mr Cole." I seized a parchment and quill from his desk, penning my required compensation with a flourish and sliding it across the table to him. "This is in addition to any expenses that I may accrue in the course of the charge. Are these terms acceptable to you?"

Mr Cole peered at the parchment, and I saw his lips tighten slightly. "Is this your usual fee, Mrs Darby?"

"Dependent upon the nature of the commission, sir. As this is a case of the utmost urgency and security, a supplemental fee has been applied. In addition, should I be found to be providing this service to you under the very nose of our esteemed military, there is likely to be a penalty for aiding and abetting a conspiracy to keep your potentially disastrous situation under wraps. You understand my position I am sure, Mr Cole?"

He considered a moment, his eyes darting from me to my proposal as if measuring my merit against the likelihood of my violating our confidentiality agreement and alerting the authorities should he fail to accept my terms. I endured his scrutiny patiently, meeting his gaze with a bland expression. Mr Thorne strained to read the parchment, but Cole twitched it away from him, ignoring any protest he may have made. I had the most emphatic impression that Thorne was dying to leap to his feet, red-faced, and exclaim, 'that's outlandish, sir!' Or, at least, I imagined it was something he might be likely to do, and I had to take a deep, steadying breath to suppress a snigger.

After a long moment, Mr Cole laid the parchment face down on the surface of his oak desk. I noticed, for the first time, that it was so polished I could see his reflection. A man who keeps a desk so clean and smudge-free that his reflection is nearly flawless upon its surface is a meticulous and unforgiving man. I could see this in his eyes despite the congeniality with which he had regarded me thus far. I wondered to what extent he would go to ensure my silence; as far as I was concerned, I had little to gain by sullying the firm's reputation and in turn my own as a trustworthy and reputable adventurer. However, he was clearly not a man who bestowed blind faith.

"Mrs Darby, I will accept your terms on one condition," Cole announced finally, pressing his fingers together on top of the parchment.

"Yes, Mr Cole?"

"I require that you undertake this assignment alone."

"Alone? I beg your pardon, Mr Cole, but I employ a team of highly skilled mechanics and navigators to accompany me on my assignments. I am afraid I would not be nearly as effective without their assistance," I protested, sitting up in my chair in surprise.

"Nevertheless, that is my condition. I have decided to trust you, Mrs Darby, as you come highly recommended. However, the more people find out about our situation, the more difficult it will be to keep it mum. I expect you will locate Dr Cross and return our property with minimal fuss and unnecessary staff," Cole explained sternly, and the affable, somewhat deferent man was gone, replaced now by the ruthless businessman I had sensed beneath the surface.

I am not a woman susceptible to intimidation, and I met his glacial gaze with calm dignity. "Mr Cole, I am afraid that is quite out of the question. I will agree to fore-go gathering my usual associates, but I must insist upon the aid of young Knightly. He is my personal assistant, quite capable of performing the functions of any number of labourers and skilled mechanics and as faithful as any man could be. I require him by my side."

Cole sighed quietly, taking another moment to consider me. "Very well. I will allow Mr Knightly's attendance."

"I am grateful, sir. Now, as negotiations are closed, I require a gander at the doctor's laboratory."

Thorne inhaled sharply through his nose, then heavily out again in a long-suffering sigh. "Is that really necessary?" he demanded tersely. "We have already searched the lab. Dr Cross and his apparatus are most obviously not there. We would merely be wasting valuable time we do not have."

"Begging your pardon, Mr Thorne, but I realise Dr Cross is not in the laboratory," I replied, my voice climbing a register in my irritation. "However, if I am to, as they say, get to the bottom of his disappearance it is necessary for me to retrace his steps. As you are a junior vice president and not a detective or adventurer, there is a great likelihood that you have passed over some important clues that may assist us in discovering where he and his apparatus have gone. If you are concerned about wasting valuable time, sir, I suggest you abstain from contradicting my methods in future."

Thorne's eyes widened, and his face darkened to a ruddy shade of red, but Cole cut him off as he sucked in a breath, preparing to retort. "Mrs Darby, you'll excuse Mr Thorne; our laboratories are state of the art and highly secured; we are reluctant to permit outsiders entry."

"With all due respect, Mr Cole, it was you who requested me and hired me for this assignment," I reminded him. It had been ages since I had worked for corporate executives, and I suddenly remembered why I usually avoided them. They were impossible. They often spent more time hindering me from performing the job for which they had hired me than providing pertinent information and necessary access. "If you intend to encumber my efforts to locate your missing weapon, please inform me now, and I will spend less time actually endeavouring to achieve success."

A small crease appeared between Mr Cole's eyebrows, but I did not concern myself with his irritation. Negotiations were over, and the time for being gracious was at an end. I was charged with a job, a job I intended to complete with satisfactory results, and I would not stand for the foolish men impeding my progress with their silly corporate boys' club antics. Cole took a deep breath through his nose, but he did not puff it out as had Thorne. As he exhaled slowly, steadily, the crease vanished by degree until his face was smooth and unlined again. Calming himself then; it must have been irksome for him to be dressed down by anyone, least of all a woman.

"Very well," he said stiffly. "I will escort you to the laboratory. Mr Thorne, if you would kindly locate Mr Harlow and Mrs Darby's young assistant so they may join us?"

Thorne, still red-faced with impotent fury, nodded and rose inelegantly to his feet. When he had stormed from the office into the glass corridor, Mr Cole turned to me, his eyes shrewd.

"Mrs Darby, I want to be very clear. I will not tolerate impudence from my hired help."

I raised my eyebrows at him. "Mr Cole, if I may be perfectly frank, you are not in a position to admonish me. You are familiar with my achievements and understand that I am the only one to whom you can entrust this task." My voice was low and calm, though aggravation was pumping hot in my veins. "That being the case, I suggest you keep your imperiousness to yourself. I have every intention of completing this job to your absolute satisfaction as I have completed many jobs before this. I expect to be treated with dignity and respect, not as a common underling, and I expect that you will not stand in my way when I make requests, regardless of your delicate corporate sensibilities. As you are not capable of performing this job yourself and are unable to enlist the aid of the authorities, I am the best you have, and you will treat me as such. I have no interest in quarrelling or delving into matters that do not concern this particular case. My ambition is simply to find your missing scientist and his project; I have no need to divulge your corporate secrets to the media or your competitors. I have nothing to benefit from that. You, on the other hand, will greatly benefit from my success. Hence, it is in your best interests to work with me instead of obstructing our mutual goal. Is that perfectly acceptable to you, Mr Cole?"

Cole sighed, but this time his frown was contemplative as opposed to affronted, and he finally nodded, offering his hand. "Mrs Darby, I regret my attitude. We are working for a common goal. I will offer any assistance you need in order to accomplish it."

I bowed my head to him, shaking his hand firmly. The tension in the room seemed to dissipate in a puff of smoke, and I carefully concealed my relief behind an amicable expression. "Thank you, Mr Cole. I am at your service."

"Splendid. Come; allow me to escort you to the laboratory. I look forward to hearing your theory of what has become of our missing doctors." He stood, opening his office door and motioning me out into the hallway with an exquisite bow.

"Much obliged, Mr Cole," I said as I swept past him with my head held high. "I am most eager myself."

CHAPTER TWO

The laboratories were located in the bowels of Rake & Gage, far beneath the streets of London. As we descended, the walls became dull, mottled steel, cold and severe in stark contrast to the mirrored floors, shiny brass adornments and glass halls of the lobby and main floors. I felt as if we were slowly plunging into a dark, underground sepulchre, and I moved away from the globular walls of the lift as if the bleakness of the austere surroundings could seep into my skin through the glass. As if he sensed my discomposure, Xander's pale blue eyes found mine. I gave him a wan smile, but when we departed the lift, I breathed a tiny, inaudible sigh of relief.

I am a woman of strong constitution, but I learned long ago, ensconced in a damp, dripping cave in Crete whilst questing for a cursed mask said to embody the spirit of Nemesis, that I have a particular aversion to dank, dark, enclosed places. The vulnerability was one in which I rarely allowed myself to indulge, and I was certain only Xander was aware of it. Indeed, Messrs Cole and Thorne seemed oblivious to my discomfort as they turned into an antechamber with similarly grim expressions.

The corridor dipped into a steep decline, leading us further below ground. It appeared as if we were moving through a metal tube, and I resisted sucking in deep, heaving breaths of air to counteract the tightening in my chest. We passed a number of doors behind which the sounds of sawing, clanking and sparking could be heard. Still we moved deeper and deeper underground.

I wondered how far underground the tunnel went and suspected the most dangerous experiments and inventions were kept furthest from the surface where they could cause the least damage should they go terribly awry as such inventions were prone to do. The air had grown warm in the steel hall by the time we reached a pair of tall, thick metal doors at the end of the corridor. They were dented, curiously, from the inside.

Cole paused a moment, then drew a large, shiny, pewter key from the inside pocket of his pinstripe suit. Instead of being flat, the key was oddly shaped with teeth sticking out from every side of the thick shaft. He spun it clockwise, anticlockwise and clockwise again before the lock disengaged, and he pulled on the heavy handle. The door slid open with a loud, metallic screech, and Xander and I stepped forward eagerly.

The laboratory walls were the same, sterile steel as the hall, but the ceilings were triply tall. There was so much space I could scarcely see the other side of the room from where I stood in the doorway. Beside me, Xander let out a soft, awed breath, and he started forward, his eyes darting every which way. A long table covered in test tubes, beakers, graduated cylinders, bits of coiled copper wire and tools the like of which I have never seen and whose purpose I was hard-pressed to identify stretched the length of one wall.

Gears and sprockets littered the floor in all directions. Sheets of metal were piled up in a corner, and wires and hoses of various sizes were strewn about willy-nilly as if the doctor had picked them up and tossed them arbitrarily away. I noted all of these things absently, having seen a laboratory like this many times before, most recently in Darby Manor.

My dear Nathaniel had had a dreadful habit of collecting bits of scrap, wire, clockworks or anything else he might have incorporated into one of his potty inventions. As such, his underground laboratory had been stuffed to bursting with the equivalent of a rubbish heap. The laboratory had passed to Xander who, despite my insistent nagging and a general leaning toward cleanliness, honoured my late husband and his peers' tradition of confused disarray to the letter. I saw prosthetic limbs, unkempt hair and burning, mad eyes in my poor, young cousin's future, but I did not begrudge him his love of science.

It was upon the centre of the laboratory that my attention was riveted. There, surrounded by bent and twisted springs, coils, gears and sprockets was a huge, shiny, brass mechanical man. It stood as tall as three grown men, and on its right side was a cockpit into which a human could climb, manipulating a series of uncomplicated controls that moved the automaton forward, backward or clockwise. It was a rudimentary machine: a simple clockwork with limited mobility, and I suspected its movements were stilted, uneven and difficult to manoeuvre. Nevertheless, it was a magnificent sight.

Its face was smooth and featureless. In place of its eyes was a single thin, horizontal slit. It had a flat, sloping nose with two large nostrils covered in domed glass behind which the driver could look through a spyglass to see in front of him. Its mouth was a thin crease. Its arms were immobile, likely more for balance than show, and its legs were tall and thick with joints at the hip, knee and ankle.

I turned to look at Mr Cole. "Pray tell, Mr Cole, what is the automaton for?"

He peered up at the automaton's face with a mixture of trepidation and pride.

"It is the latest innovation in border security. These machines can patrol the boundaries of our great nation without the expense and casualty of a traditional militia. This is one of a handful of prototypes into which we intended to install Dr Cross' invention."

Xander had circled the laboratory and returned to our sides, his eyes alight with enthusiasm. "What exactly is it Dr Cross was creating in here, Mr Cole?" he asked, his hands clasped behind his back in a scholarly posture.

Mr Cole considered a moment, as if he were unsure if he wanted to answer the question. "An entirely new and ground-breaking form of defence," he said finally. "It is called the Eye of Ra."

"The Eye of Ra?" My brow furrowed. "What is it?"

"A directed energy weapon," Xander guessed, and Mr Cole peered at him in approval.

"Indeed, dear boy. Are you familiar with Dr Cross' early work on the Crystal Wave?"

"Oh, yes. It was a masterpiece of modern technology."

"In theory, indeed." Cole's dark eyes blazed, and he turned to face Xander squarely. "However, the application was fundamentally flawed. His attempts to create an independent energy source with enough power to continuously alternate voltage in the accelerator were initially ineffective. They were simply too large to be employed in a mobile capacity. Thus, the early accelerators were highly unstable, and once the beam had been successfully discharged, it took far too long to recharge the chamber to be employed in the field. The Crystal Wave was dismantled, but its working theories have been applied to the Eye."

"Has Dr Cross been successful in overcoming the complications in the Crystal Wave's application?"

For a moment Mr Cole's brow furrowed. "It would appear so. The doctor's reports have been...less than comprehensive in regard to the actual application of the theories presented. However, he has made reference to a compact, electro-static generator that has the capacity to continuously charge the magnetic field and fits into the machine's internal chamber."

"Is that possible?" Xander asked, astonished.

"Dear boy, I can only assume that, as the doctor has absconded with his prototype, it is."

The examination of advanced scientific theory seemed to invariably

20

accompany a faint buzzing in my brain as if there were something I was failing to notice or did not understand. This was uncomfortable but not altogether unexpected; I had never had a particular interest in science before my marriage to Nathaniel and since had only succeeded in developing an ambivalent relationship with the field.

That is to say, I enjoyed the comforts science and its ingenuity provided but had little patience or aptitude for the theory behind the application. Thus, I left my more scientifically inclined assistant and employer to their natter and proceeded to move in large, methodical circles around the laboratory, examining the detritus of the doctors' toil.

Mr Thorne followed behind me at a respectful distance, as if he were allowing my inspection with unconcerned affability. I suspected his scrutiny was rather more than that, but I resolved to ignore the irritation and burgeoning dislike for the stocky, disagreeable man and continued with my ministrations. I noticed little out of the ordinary; that is if one considered the implements of mad science ordinary.

Dr Cross had not been particularly neat or especially organised. Quite the contrary; the lab was cluttered and chaotic, though there did seem to be a sort of unidentifiable order to the rubbish scattered about. The corner of the lab farthest from the door seemed to be his primary work area; tools, wires and scraps of metal were lying about in a slapdash sort of arrangement, and a path cutting through the flotsam and jetsam led to a small, cramped space in the centre of the collection that contained a small footstool, a ladder and a chair with well-oiled wheels.

I found a thin stack of papers on a workbench along one wall, but they were merely notes written in a spidery scrawl on the various obstacles Dr Cross had encountered with his original designs. This could be of little interest to anyone who had read his research or was familiar with his experiments, but I tucked it into my thin, worn, leather valise all the same. I have often found that answers can be found in the areas we least expect them, and even notes on a failed and subsequently abandoned project could contain clues.

Thorne scowled as if he intended to protest my removal of the papers, but he said nothing.

A complete walk through of the laboratory had yielded nothing, nor had I expected it to. There was nothing to indicate the doctor had not left of his own volition; the lab appeared to have been utterly abandoned by its master. Project notes, designs, blueprints and formulas were gone as were any personal effects to suggest what sort of men the scientists were, and the materials had been summarily cast off in complete irreverence. Indeed, it appeared as if the doctor and his assistant had collected their belongings, the apparatus and any record of their occupation and simply scarpered.

There was something disquieting about this conclusion, and I paused in the centre of the laboratory, spinning in a slow circle with a furrow on my brow.

Mr Thorne stood a few feet away with his arms crossed, watching me with a look that was simultaneously smug and scornful. I took no notice of this, nor of my cousin and Mr Cole, who were talking animatedly like old chums, peering into the cockpit of the brass automaton. If the doctor and his assistant had taken their things and vacated the lab, why had they overlooked the notes on the Crystal Wave design? It appeared to be the only conclusive evidence that Dr Cross had ever been here at all whilst everything else had been systematically removed. It did not appear as if the lab had been evacuated with any particular haste, and therefore it was unlikely they would have simply forgotten them.

Likewise, there was no evidence that anything untoward had occurred in this laboratory, and had I not found the doctor's apparently trivial notes, I would probably have presumed that Cross, as Cole suggested, had simply deserted his contract with Rake & Gage and defected to one of their competitors. I was unable to accept this conjecture. Something had happened; despite all logic to the contrary, I was certain of it, though it seemed not to have happened in this laboratory. Thus, I saw no reason to linger. "Xander."

The youth peered around the mechanical man, his eyebrows raised. I sensed irritation in his bearing, but I had no time to waste on his curiosity. "Mrs Darby?"

"The hour is late, and I am finished here. I require a warm drink and a good night's sleep before we begin our investigation afresh in the morning."

A look of disappointment crossed Xander's face, but he quickly schooled his handsome, boyish features into an agreeable expression, and he nodded shortly, hurrying to my side.

"I will have Mr Harlow take you to the airship port at once," Thorne announced cheerfully, striding towards the exit.

"That would be most appreciated, Mr Thorne."

I paused a moment to await Mr Cole, who joined us presently. "Have you found anything of interest, Mrs Darby?"

I considered describing my increasing certainty that something was amiss, but I quickly discarded the idea. There was no sense in alarming Mr Cole, and I strongly suspected his confidence in me would suffer should I make such an outlandish assertion at this juncture. "Mr Cole, by all appearances your theory that Dr Cross and his assistant have absconded is entirely correct. I expect I will find more to the point when I visit his residence first thing tomorrow morning."

Mr Cole looked sufficiently satisfied and nodded as he bowed us out of the laboratory. The walk back to the lift was as oppressive and unsettling as the last, but this time my mind was occupied with the mystery of the doctors' disappearance. Xander, well attuned to my moods by now, kept Mr Cole engaged in their continuing discussion of the automaton's state-of-the-art design. Mr Thorne radiated tacit disapproval at his superior's candour with my young cousin, but Mr Cole was unabashed.

While both Xander and Mr Cole seemed keen to prolong their banter, it was with relief that I bade the gentlemen farewell. Mr Harlow was already waiting outside with the car, and I was grateful to Mr Thorne for the speedy accommodations, whatever his reasons behind it. The trip to the airship port was silent. I was not yet ready to share my suspicions with Xander. Though Mr Harlow was equally quiet and behaving as if we were not in the passenger seats at all, I was hesitant to speak freely in his company.

It was not until we were seated on the airship that Xander spoke, his pale, blue eyes sharp. "You found something in the lab, cousin." I extracted the stack of papers from my valise and handed them to him. For a moment, he peered at them in apparent confusion. "These are Cross' notes on the Crystal Wave. They can be found in part in any scientific journal related to directed energy in the last several years. I don't understand." He scanned them further, as if searching for a clue within the words.

"I was mystified myself. By all appearances, the doctors utterly abandoned the lab. There was no trace of their personal effects but these discarded notes." I stood to gaze at the stars outside our window. The airship was moving like a cloud slowly and quietly through the night. After the suffocating steel tunnels of Rake & Gage, the vastness of the sky was a welcomed sight. "It occurred to me that the doctors seemed in little haste to leave the lab, and so meticulous was their exit that I found the forgotten notes quite out of place."

Xander considered. "Yes, I see your point, cousin. There was every sign the doctors took their time emptying the lab of their effects."

"Thus, it seems unlikely these notes were merely left behind, eh, cousin?"

"Just so. What is your hypothesis, then?"

I frowned slightly, exhaling a deep sigh. "I am quite at a loss, to be frank. Perhaps they were considered too insignificant to trouble with, or perhaps they really were simply overlooked."

"But you have a different theory?"

"I have...a feeling." I sat back down beside my cousin, gathering the papers from him and glancing down at them with a look of concentration. "Though I have no reason to think so, I am quite certain something terrible has happened to these doctors."

"You don't believe they went over to one of their competitors?"

"I do not."

"Astrid, here I thought you were not a woman of supposition."

I met his amused look with a stern frown. "I make no supposition, cousin. I am merely willing to entertain the possibility that there is something more to this disappearance than meets the eye. I anticipate a more thorough understanding of what has happened here when I have had the opportunity to explore the doctor's residence."

"May I join you?" Xander's eyes shone.

"I am afraid, my dear cousin, that you will be needed elsewhere tomorrow morning."

His eyebrows shot up. "Oh? And where might that be?"

"I expect that, by nine tomorrow morning, we will have secured meetings for you with the head developers at both Airtech and Steam Brothers defence contractors. If Dr Cross has left Rake & Gage for one of these competitors, perhaps you will find evidence of him."

"Will they meet with me?"

"I am quite certain that, as a student of Dr Sebastian Cross, the most notable physicist of our time, they would be most interested to make your acquaintance."

Xander looked startled. "But, Astrid, they will never believe it."

"On the contrary, cousin. You have the doctor's personal notes on his original design and subsequent experimentations. Who else but a close confidante would be in possession of such delicate papers? Furthermore, the only people to dispute your claim are mysteriously missing. They will have to find Dr Cross to substantiate your contention, and that will be impossible unless he is hiding within their walls."

"Very clever, cousin."

"My dear Xander, I am astonished you would expect any less."

* * *

The following morning found me in my study, sipping strong, black tea and scanning Dr Cross' notes. They appeared to be merely a collection of formulas, designs and symbols that I found impossible to understand. What was the significance? The closer I looked, the more it seemed as if there were none.

I sighed, setting aside a page of elemental equations. Upon the subsequent page was a rough sketch of a small, cylindrical object. I heaved another sigh, certain there was nothing more of interest than in the preceding notes until I noticed a small, cramped scrawl along the margin.

Did you enjoy that Phineas? I blinked, rereading the note several times. Phineas? I understood Cross' assistant was Dr Joseph Ramsey. Who was Phineas? It was not the only note of its kind. I picked up the stack I had already examined and found more scrawls. *You won't try that again, will you?* and *I hope you didn't lose too much of that hair you are so fond of, old friend.*

What was this? I slammed my teacup on the delicate silver tray, hardly noticing the resulting chip in Mr Darby's beloved great-grandmother's antiquated china. I swept the papers up and raced downstairs. "Xander!"

He was already in the parlour when I arrived, hastily gulping down his tea and scones. He was smartly dressed in a coal black suit for his appointments later in the day with the head developers for both Airtech and Steam Brothers. His roguish black hair was combed neatly back from his boyish face, and his eyes were bright.

When I barrelled into the parlour, screeching his name like a mad woman, he looked up, shocked. "What is it, Astrid?"

"Xander, look at this. You have to look at these." I shoved the papers into his hands, bouncing on the balls of my feet.

"What could possibly be contained herein that has you practically flying out of your dressing gown?" He teased, but I pointed urgently at the notes, ignoring his cheek.

"Look at them. Look closely."

He did so, and after a long moment in which I continued to rock back and forth in unrestrained excitement, he looked up.

"This is all rubbish. Why didn't I notice this before? None of these formulas is correct. In fact, several of them would result in an explosive chemical reaction."

I raised my eyebrows. "Really?"

"Isn't that what you wanted me to see?"

"No. You know I wouldn't have known that, but it makes perfect sense now. Look at these. In the margin. The notes." I pointed to them, and Xander inhaled sharply in surprise.

I was surprised when he chuckled. "'I hope you didn't lose too much of that hair you're so fond of.' If someone attempted that fusion, they would certainly create a spark." He raised his eyebrows at me. "Do you think he left these as a joke?"

"Or because he suspected Phineas would steal them and attempt the experiments." I clapped my hands together. "Now we know why he left them. He wanted them to be found. But who is Phineas? Have you ever heard of an associate of Cross' named Phineas?"

Xander's eyes widened. "Yes."

Again, I was startled. "Really? Who?"

"Dr Phineas Cobb. I do not know if he ever worked with Cross, but he is infamous in scientific circles. He was accused of stealing another doctor's designs several years ago, but he was never formally reprimanded since the papers were never found and there was only circumstantial evidence against him. His reputation was ruined, however, and he has been in disgrace and unable to obtain respectable work ever since. I heard he's been working on some secret project for the last five years hoping to re-establish himself in the scientific community."

"Perhaps Dr Cross thought Cobb was trying to steal the Eye designs."

"Perhaps Cobb did steal the designs."

"I don't think so. Cross might be in hiding to protect his project from potential thieves. If Cobb was after Cross' papers, it is probably a safe assumption that he did not find them; he would not have left these. What doesn't make sense is why he left them in the lab. Surely Cobb couldn't have gotten past Rake & Gage's security."

Xander and I were silent a long moment, considering this. "Unless he thought someone from inside Rake & Gage would let him in."

"Exactly. But who?" Before I was able to ponder this idea any further, a car horn honked outside, and I jumped. "What is that?"

Xander rolled his eyes, sweeping up his messenger bag and quickly tucking the doctor's notes inside. "My car, Astrid."

"Oh! Right. Your appointments." I frowned thoughtfully.

"Though they might not be important now."

"Not so. All these papers prove is that Dr Cross suspected Dr Cobb might try to steal his designs. It doesn't prove he actually did; in fact, it seems to prove that he did not. It doesn't get us any closer to understanding what did happen." I sighed. "Well, at least we know now why he left the notes."

Xander smiled. "I'd better go. Good luck, cousin. I'll be home sometime this evening."

I was already wandering towards the winding staircase on the left side of the parlour. "Yes, right. Have a nice time, cousin."

He chuckled and ducked towards the door. "Don't forget to pick up Cross' file on your way to the airship port, Astrid. It's ready at Langley's."

"Oh, brilliant. Thank you, Xander." I was nearly to my chambers when I heard the door slam and the car pull away. My mind was racing with new theories, but the discovery of the sabotaged notes had only succeeded in confusing me more. I knew it was unlikely that Cross would be at home simply waiting for someone to fetch him, but I hoped the journey would yield some answers as to what had happened to the doctors.

My chambers were characteristically messy when I arrived. I could hunt with aborigines in the Australian outback and ride a canoe through the Congo, but I had never managed to keep a tidy home. Thankfully, my departed husband's family fortune had seen to it that Mrs Randall, our sturdy and capable housekeeper, rendered this particular character flaw inconsequential. Unfortunately, she spent her mornings on the first floor, and so I spent nearly fifteen minutes rummaging around in my closet for a pair of clean petticoats. When I had finally located a handsome scarlet day dress and tall, lace-up boots, I stood before my mirror, peering speculatively at my reflection.

I was not unhappy with my appearance, not really. In fact, in general I was quite pleased with the overall effect, but it always seemed as if there was something faintly off about it. My long, curly, dark blond hair was just a bit frizzier than was currently stylish these days, my skin just a shade too pale. I was slightly rounder in the hips and bosom than was fashionable, and the features of my face were simply too uneven to be of the sort of classic beauty I admired in the Lady Weston.

I smoothed my unruly hair with a tonic of Xander's creation—one of his more useful inventions, to be certain—and tied it back in a long, thick braid. With my hair swept back from my face, it appeared even more heart-shaped, my eyes even darker and larger, and my nose even more upturned and button-like.

I had aged well, however, and, now in my mid-thirties, looked like a woman in her late twenties, save for the fine lines around my mouth and the tiny crow's feet around my eyes. I had at first been mortified by these signs of my age but had since learned to take them in stride; I had learned in my years as an adventurer that a young woman was rarely taken seriously, particularly a woman of diminutive stature with pixyish features and perpetually wide and childishly large eyes.

It had only been through hard work and determination that I had garnered the respect I deserved and been seen as something more than the naive and innocent young girl I had appeared to be. The outward evidence of my experience had lessened the burden.

Thus, it was with a brisk, satisfied nod that I spun away from the mirror. Several more minutes of searching for my favourite black gloves ensued, and when I finally reached the parlour, I heard a honk outside signalling that my own car had arrived. The driver was a portly, jovial fellow named Mills whom I had specifically requested for his superb manners and cheerful disposition. I was pleased to see he was waiting for me at the door with a characteristic smile.

He appeared unsurprised by my harried countenance, and he bowed me into the backseat with a polite greeting. "Where to today, Mrs Darby?"

"The airship port, if you please, Mr Mills." I tucked my skirt around me primly, settling comfortably against the seat. "Oh, and I'll need to stop by Langley's on the way."

Mr Mills was accustomed to my needs, and he steered expertly towards the familiar destination. The stop at Arthur and Harold Langley's private investigation firm yielded a disappointingly thin file on Dr Sebastian Cross and a promise to provide a thorough background on both doctors Joseph Ramsey and Phineas Cobb as soon as possible. I spent the short airship flight to London scanning Cross' file.

It was a brief elucidation on the doctor's education, achievements in the field of physics, past employers, etcetera. The only apparent blight on his unsoiled record was the death of his sixteen-year-old daughter, Anastasia, in a freak laboratory accident ten years ago. There was little information regarding this accident, but it was speculated that she had died in some sort of explosion.

This was not altogether unheard of when one is in the business of inventing dangerous and unstable directed energy weapons, and so, though it was terribly unfortunate, I passed over it quickly. Since Anastasia's tragic end, the doctor had no living relatives in the country. His wife, a much younger woman from a wealthy merchant family, had died fifteen years prior of an incurable heart condition and had not lived to witness her daughter's premature death.

According to my steadfast and dependable source, Dr Cross had been married once before whilst still attending university. The young woman, a fellow student and scientist, had given birth to a son, Gideon, who was now nearly forty and living in America. Gideon's mother had, sadly, died in childbirth, and Dr Cross had had to raise his son to adulthood alone.

How very desolate his life must have been, I lamented, but there was no more time to dwell on the doctor's heart-rending history. The airship had landed gracefully in London, and I joined the other travellers as they left the vessel and moved towards the tubes or the cars waiting outside the port.

* * *

Dr Cross' home was a small, unassuming brick flat in Kensington. Though I expected no answer, I knocked firmly on the front door, waiting only a few seconds before glancing around to ensure I was unobserved and trying the knob.

To my amazement, the door opened easily, and I bent down to examine the jamb. It was splintered inexpertly, and I suspected whomever had forced it open had done so hastily and with little effort to conceal the burglary. I crept inside, listening intently for any noise. I heard none.

The sun's early morning rays filtered in from the half-drawn curtains in the parlour, and I could see instantly that someone had thoroughly ransacked the room. Furniture was unceremoniously upturned, broken glass littered the floor, and torn scraps of paper lay scattered all over as if someone had tossed them in a fit of temper on top of the rubble. I reckoned they probably had; unless the intruder had been intent only upon the most complete destruction, which I supposed was a genuine possibility; whatever they had been searching for had been well-hidden.

I had not expected to find the doctor at home, but I had even less expected to discover the evidence of treachery. I paused a moment to collect my bearings, straining my ears for the slightest indication the burglar was still in the flat. For a moment everything was quiet, eerily so, as if the house itself was suspended in a state of shock over the devastation.

A soft, barely audible crash from deep within the house startled me.

I drew a small, pearl-gripped pistol from my valise, moving cautiously towards the noise. I passed through a short, narrow hall that lead to the back of the flat, but none of the small, cramped and cluttered rooms yielded any signs of life. They all looked to be in the same state as the parlour.

My heart raced in my chest, but I peered carefully into each room. Another noise guided me forwards to the last door in the hall, and I opened it slowly, wincing when it creaked ever slightly.

I did not stop to consider what I was doing. I was a woman accustomed to taking care of myself in any number of situations, and I had on many occasions walked headlong into danger with little concern for the possible consequences.

The door opened to a descending staircase, and I could hear someone down there, rummaging around. Though it was likely the careless intruder, continuing his efforts to locate his elusive treasure, I moved towards the sound, my blood pumping in excitement.

I sensed there were answers to be found below, and I did not intend to wait to contact the authorities to find out who had broken in and what they were after.

My inferior size and experience sneaking around had made me light of foot, and I crept down the staircase as silently as possible, finally ducking with my gun poised at the ready when I was able to see past the low ceiling into the basement.

It was Dr Cross' laboratory, I saw straight away, and it contained the same implements as the lab at Rake & Gage. It had received the same treatment as the rest of the house. I did not immediately see anyone inside, but the sound of shuffling footsteps drew my eyes towards the far end of the room.

CHAPTER THREE

Bent over a desk along the east wall was a tall, slim man in an unexceptional and carelessly rumpled tan suit. He was a relatively young man, approximately my age, with dishevelled, over-long dark hair that looked windblown or as if he had lately ran his hands through it in frustration. He did not appear to be armed. In fact, he did not appear to be doing anything untoward, despite being surrounded by the ruin of the lab.

I could see only his profile, but I could tell his brow was furrowed in concentration. He pushed his spectacles further up his nose as I watched him and bowed lower over the desk, rubbing his chin as if he were examining a troublesome formula or very small writing. I presumed he probably was; I had seen the doctor's notes and had first-hand experience reading his spidery, cramped scrawl.

He appeared to be so absorbed in whatever he was reading that he did not notice me approach him until I spoke.

"Stop right there. What are you doing?"

He spun so quickly, he nearly toppled over the desk chair someone had shoved hastily aside. When he saw the gun aimed at his chest, he gasped, throwing his hands up in the air in alarm. "Oh–I–oh!"

His eyes were wide behind his square-framed spectacles, and I noticed immediately that he did not have the roughened look of a criminal or burglar. In fact, he had the soft, boyish features of a man unfamiliar with toil and unsavoury living conditions. He was bookish, intelligent looking despite the comical gape on his mouth, and his clothes, though wrinkled as if he'd been sleeping in them and had forgotten to change them the previous day, were well-cared for and of better quality than the average thief's.

I frowned at him. "Who are you? What are you doing here?"

"I'm Dr Joseph Ramsey!" he exclaimed in a rush, as if afraid I might shoot him before he had finished speaking.

I paused in astonishment, my gun hand faltering a moment. "Ramsey? Dr Cross' assistant?"

"Yes!"

"You're supposed to be missing."

He lowered his hands at this, bemused. "Who are you?"

"Astrid Darby."

"Astrid Darby? Who says I'm missing?" He frowned at me, his dark, green eyes darting from my face to my gun. "Can you lower your weapon? It's really very difficult to concentrate."

"Not until you tell me what you're doing here."

He continued to eye the gun warily, but he seemed to have regained his composure. He squared his shoulders resolutely. "I was looking for Sebastian."

"You don't know where he is?"

"No. He was gone when I arrived at the lab yesterday. Everything was gone."

"I know; I've been there."

"But who are you?"

"I'm a private investigator. I was hired by Maxwell Cole to find you and Dr Cross."

"But I'm not missing."

"Yes, we've established that. Why didn't you contact Mr Cole when you realised Cross was gone?"

"I—well, it's not like Sebastian not to be at the lab when I arrive. He is always there earlier and stays later than I do. When I saw our things were gone, I knew something was wrong."

His posture was tense, as if he was fighting the compulsion to pace as he explained. He rocked slightly forwards and back, struggling to hold my gaze and avoid looking at the pistol.

"Where do you think he went?"

"He wouldn't have abandoned our contract with Rake & Gage without telling me. Or, at least, I thought he would not. I came to find him, but he wasn't here."

"Was the house like this then?"

"No."

"Did you do this?"

"No! It wasn't like this yesterday, and I didn't do it!" He scowled at me, but I motioned for him to continue impatiently. "As I said, he wasn't here, so I spent the day trying to find him."

"You didn't?"

"Obviously not." He pushed a hand through his hair distractedly, tousling it further so it looked as if he had just stepped out of an exceptionally fierce gust of wind. "When I got back here this morning, the house was like this. Honestly, can you put the gun away now? It's making me very nervous."

"Oh, yes. Quite sorry." I shoved the gun into my valise, but I kept my hand on the grip in case he was not as innocent as he appeared and was overcome by a compulsion to attack me. "Do you have any idea where he might have gone?"

"How do I know you aren't working for the people who did this?" Ramsey demanded, suddenly very defiant now that there was not a weapon aimed directly at him.

"Would I have asked you if I'd done this?" I rolled my eyes.

"Maybe. To throw me off what you are up to."

"Don't be absurd. If I knew what happened to Cross, I wouldn't have had to come here looking for him, would I?"

"Perhaps you missed something the first time."

"Honestly, do I look like I could have carried him off somewhere?"

"Well, you do have a very large gun."

I sighed. "Very well." I dug in my valise for a moment and handed him my credentials. "Here are my papers."

When he still looked dubious, I rolled my eyes again.

"Look here, Dr Ramsey, if you want to find your missing colleague, I am the only one who can help you."

He frowned at me for a moment then sighed in resignation. "Yes, I suppose you're right. I found this." He swept his hand towards the desk, and I saw a leather-bound book opened to the last few pages. I assumed it was this that he had been examining when I had snuck up on him. "It's Sebastian's journal."

I bent at once over the volume as he had been doing when I caught him, and I frowned at Cross' familiar handwriting. It did not appear that the doctor had written in the journal every day. Dr Ramsey flipped back a few pages, pausing on an entry written a few weeks prior.

April 3rd

I am unsettled.

This evening I was approached by an unfamiliar man in the Square a few blocks from my home. At first glance, he appeared to be a gentleman like any other who stroll the Square like myself on clear, brisk evenings, and I paid him no heed.

When he neared me, however, I saw he was not what he had seemed from afar. Though he wore a finely tailored suit, there was something decidedly sinister about him.

He was shorter than me by several inches, but I was instantly apprehensive. He did not leer or threaten like a common criminal. Instead, it was merely his presence that was so intimidating. His face was scarred, as if someone had taken a dull blade to his cheek, and when he removed his hat to bow, I saw he was completely bald, as if no hair had ever grown on his head.

His smile was grotesque—like a shark about to swallow its prey--and when it became clear it was, indeed, myself upon whom he was focussed, my heart nearly leapt from my chest as if it were too terrified to see my body through this ordeal.

He knew about the Eye. In fact, it seemed as if he knew everything about it. He would not tell me his name, but I suppose it is best that way. It is not as if I can contact the authorities about him.

I do not know how he knows the things he does. It was as if he had read my latest progress report, and I am most terrified that he did. Could someone within R&G be a spy? Maxwell assured me all his employees are above reproach, and I trust Joseph nearly as much as I trust Gideon, but how else could he have known the things he did?

Are there traitors in our midst, waiting to strike when the time is right?

The man was after the designs. He offered to buy them, and when I refused, he became angry and frightening. I feared he would attack at any moment, and my frail, old body would have been no match for him. I was saved only by a couple strolling past us who paused to see what was happening. Though I suspect the man would have neither difficulty nor qualm in harming the couple and me, he made no move to stop me when I turned tail and fled. I am certain it will not be the last I see of him.

I fear my old friend Phineas sent him. It would be just like him to use intimidation tactics to steal designs that do not belong to him, and the man must be in league with another scientist. Surely, he is not the sort of man who is capable of interpreting or applying advanced physics theories. The implications of this are even more horrifying. Could Phineas have gotten to one of Maxwell's trusted people? He could not have known how far we have come otherwise. Phineas is a brilliant scientist, but he could not have merely guessed what stage of completion we have reached.

I dread what will happen to me when I have completed the prototype, but I am afraid my fate will be graver still if I do not. My employer is terrifying, but I have kept the true nature of the Eye a secret.

Only Joseph knows its true power. I trust the boy implicitly, but could my enemies, terrorists or nationalists have gotten to him? He has never shown much interest in politics. On the contrary, he has always been quite oblivious to such matters. He seems to be completely unaware of the unrest all around us. But everyone has a price. No, I will not believe it. His attitude has never changed, and he is as unwavering as ever.

I am afraid there are snakes in the grass all around me, waiting for the moment the Eye is complete. I have begun to fear my own shadow. I am sure the man is lurking around every corner. I no longer take my walks in the Square in the evenings, and I never leave my home after dark even to visit my favourite places or take a meal in my favourite restaurants.

There is no one I can trust. No one but my dear Gideon.

"Melodramatic," I muttered softly, turning the page to the next entry, dated several days later.

"He has always been effusive, but it seems he wasn't just paranoid this time," Dr Ramsey put in with a frown. "He is, after all, missing."

April 10th

The prototype is nearly done. It requires only the power source to sustain it. I have hesitated to complete it. I have been stalling production, giving Joseph busy work so he will not become suspicious. I cannot continue to divert him, but I am too afraid to allow it to reach its final stage.

I have sabotaged my own masterpiece. I have removed its heart, and I feel as if a part of me has been removed with it, but I want to continue living more than I want to see my life's goal fulfilled.

Does that make me unfaithful to my science? Physics is my truest love. What have

I left without it?

April 20th

It is time. My Eye must be completed. I can stall my employer no longer, and Joseph is not a fool. He has been noticing my distraction for weeks, and he has begun to ask questions.

The man found me on the tube again last night as if he knew, but that is impossible, isn't it? Not even Joseph knows I need only install the heart. The man did not speak to me, and I was infinitely grateful for the rush hour traffic.

I ran from him, but I do not think he meant to speak to me, not really. I think he meant only to remind me that he can find me anytime, anywhere, and he has not gone away.

I have no choice. I must destroy the Eye or take it where no one can ever find it.

"That was two days ago," Dr Ramsey said in a gruff voice, slamming the volume on the last entry. His face was grim.

"Yes, I gathered." I sighed deeply, considering this new information. "Where did you find this journal? Was it on the floor?"

"Yes. It looked as if someone had looked inside and tossed it away. They must have been looking for something else. I found it behind the desk. "

"You think they were looking for the designs."

"I'm sure of it." His eyes slid away a moment, staring blankly at the far wall past my head. "I only pray Sebastian was gone before they arrived. I shudder to think what they might have done to him otherwise."

"Where would he have gone?"

"I found something else, as well."

"What is it?"

He offered a folded parchment, and I plucked it hastily from his fingers. "He must have written to his son," he explained in a subdued voice. "It's a letter."

Dear Father,

I was deeply concerned by your last letter. I warned you when you began this project that the people are not ready for what you have created. The world is full of wicked, cruel men and politicians who would use it to tear everything asunder to achieve their own ends. You know why I left England, and I implore you to do the same.

My home is modest, but it is comfortable, and I miss you terribly. Leave this life. Leave the simmering hatred and the constant fear. Do not allow yourself to become the instrument of the terrorist nationalists who care nothing of taking the lives of the very people they claim to be saving.

Stop working for the government who provokes their ire and gives them an excuse for their actions.

We can live a quiet, peaceful life here. Together we can destroy the deadly abomination you have created and begin a new, better life. It has become too dangerous for you to remain in England, and I beg you, leave now before it is too late.

In such times of tension and unrest, there is truly no one you can trust. I have enclosed a train ticket from Chicago to Denver, and I will meet you there if only you will heed my suggestion.

Please, Father, come to America. There is no more time to waste. Please write back and give me your word.

Your son,

Gideon

I stared at the letter for a long moment then slowly returned my gaze to Dr Ramsey, who was watching me expectantly. "Did you find the ticket?"

"No. I haven't had a chance to look; I had just found the letter when you arrived."

"Did Dr Cross ever mention the man who approached him to you?"

He sighed deeply. "No." His voice was almost whisper soft and full of regret. "He never revealed any of his suspicions to me, but it's all beginning to make sense. For the last several weeks, he has been...despondent. He would not let me see any of his designs. It seemed as if the closer we came to completing the project, the more erratic and puzzling he became. He gave me a list of tasks every day, but I did not have any idea why he wanted me to do them. They didn't seem to serve any particular purpose." He scowled, whipping off his glasses to rub his eyes wearily. "Now I know they didn't. He wouldn't answer any of my questions. He would become furious if I persisted and shout at me."

"Perhaps it is better you did not know what was happening," I said in a gentler voice. "You are already in enough danger, being the only other person who has worked on the project. Perhaps he was trying to protect you."

Ramsey spun away, shoving his glasses angrily back onto the bridge of his nose. "Or he didn't trust me."

I moved away from him, my eyes roaming slowly around the laboratory.

"Where did you find the letter?" I crouched beside him, sifting through the debris carefully, searching for the missing ticket. I chanced a glance at him, but he had risen to pace a few feet away, his hands tugging at his hair in distress. "Dr Ramsey, I would be much obliged if you would assist me in searching for the ticket."

He dropped his hands and spun towards me. "Yes, of course. The ticket."

"Did you tell anyone about the project?" I asked when he seemed to have regained his self-possession for the time being. "Anyone at all? A wife, brother, sister, friend, anyone?"

"No! I was sworn to secrecy! I take my oath quite seriously."

"Do you know if Cross told anyone else other than his son?"

"Certainly not. I should think his paranoia was obvious. He guards his projects quite jealously. He's always afraid a rival will attempt to steal his plans."

"Cobb. He mentioned him in the journal."

"Phineas Cobb. Yes. You've heard of him?"

"Cross left some notes for him in the laboratory at Rake & Gage."

"Notes? What notes?"

"They appeared to be formulas and experiments from the former Crystal Wave designs, but they'd been sabotaged. He left notes in the margins as if he intended Cobb to find them and attempt the experiments."

"Sebastian left them in the lab?"

"Yes. Didn't you notice them? There weren't well hidden."

"No, I didn't notice them. I only noticed the Eye and the designs were gone. It was enough to be getting on with at the time. I did not search to see if he left anything behind; he has always been extremely meticulous. It never occurred to me that he might have forgotten anything. I was quite distraught when I realised he was absent; I wanted to get out of the building and find him as quickly as I could before someone saw me or found out what had happened."

I paused. "Did anyone see you?"

"I don't know. I was early, so most of the employees were not yet there. I

38

didn't see anyone else, but that doesn't mean they didn't see me."

I nodded, rising to my feet. I picked half-heartedly through the remnants of the ruined lab, but there was no sign of the train ticket or the designs. In fact, there was little more of interest than the remains of scientific journals, scarcely recognisable tools, piles of broken containers and jagged, razor-sharp strips of metal. Whoever had razed the laboratory had been very conscientious. "Dr Cobb is a friend of Dr Cross?" I asked, stopping to glance over at Dr Ramsey, who wore an expression of deepest meditation as he sorted through the mess.

"Friend?" Ramsey scoffed, sitting back on his haunches amidst a pile of discarded copper wire. "Perhaps once. I understood Sebastian was at university with Phineas. They were rivals all through school and through their careers. They competed for contracts, and Phineas was always trying to persuade Sebastian's assistants to leave him and work for Phineas. I think he hoped they would bring Sebastian's designs with them."

"Did he ever approach you in that capacity?"

"No." Ramsey's mouth twisted in distaste. "He's a swindler, but he's not a fool. My loyalty to Sebastian is absolute. He had already fallen into disgrace by the time I began assisting Sebastian."

"For stealing another scientist's plans."

"Yes, allegedly." His lip curled. "There was no solid evidence to convict him."

"But Cross believed he'd done it."

"Oh, yes. Sebastian despised Phineas, whatever he said about him. He was always worried he had spies lurking around to steal his plans. It took him a year before he trusted me enough to work for him, and even then he wouldn't let me see any of his designs."

I spun around to examine his face. "Do you think Cobb is responsible for this?"

Ramsey considered a long moment, his eyes flickering from indignant to pensive. "I honestly don't know, but…he is a scientist. He is underhanded and deceitful, but I do not know if he would go so far as this. He is usually far more devious than extreme."

"Could he have hired someone to do it for him?"

Ramsey shook his head slowly from side to side. "I honestly don't know. I am not well-acquainted enough with Phineas to understand what he is capable of doing, Miss Darby."

"Mrs Darby."

"Begging your pardon, Mrs Darby. In addition to stealing Dr Miranda Trousseau's steam engine designs, Phineas was accused of hiring saboteurs to pose as assistants and servants to many of his competitors. I cannot attest to the validity of the allegations. He was never formally charged with anything. There are a lot of people who would be keen to get their hands on this design; it is sure to make Sebastian famous."

"Has he talked about his son, Gideon?"

"Yes, all the time. They are very close, and I understand they've written to each other almost twice a week since he moved to America."

"Has Cross been to see him since you started working for him?"

Ramsey did not have to think long about this. "At least once a year for the last five years. He is usually gone for a few weeks at a time, and I'm given paid leave."

I nodded briskly and strode towards the stairs. "Ace. Thank you, Dr Ramsey."

"What are you doing?" he demanded almost sternly, hopping to his feet to follow me.

"The ticket isn't here."

"What does that mean?"

I paused and turned to face him. He had advanced quickly, and I had to tilt my head back to meet his scowling gaze. "I don't yet quite know. If he's gone, do you think it's likely he would have gone to see his son?"

"Certainly. And the ticket is gone. That is what you think he's done? Gone into hiding?"

"Well, I don't rightly know, Dr Ramsey. I know as much as you do at this point. Likely less, as you have the advantage of having known the good doctor for a number of years. What do you think?"

Before he was able to respond, I turned on my heel and climbed the stairs to the hall.

"Wait," Ramsey ordered belatedly, bounding up the stairs to fall into step beside me. "Where are you going?"

"I am going to check his room and see if any of his clothes or personal items are missing." When he didn't make any move to leave me to this search, I sighed.

"Perhaps you can be of assistance."

Dr Cross' bedroom was a large, wood-panelled room on the west side of the hall. It had received much the same treatment as the lab, though there was considerably less broken glass to sort through. I moved directly to the wardrobe, but it had been turned out and its contents strewn across the room. The master bath was similarly demolished. I returned to the young doctor to find him standing in the middle of the room, looking around at the disorder with dismay.

"Right, then, this is futile," I announced shortly.

"I am most regretful, Mrs Darby."

I waved my hand in dismissal at his words and started for the door. "Again, thank you for your assistance, Dr Ramsey. You've been exceedingly accommodating."

"Where are you going?" he demanded a second time, and as before I faced him impatiently.

"To the airship port, naturally."

"For what?"

"To find out if Dr Cross purchased a reservation for a flight to America, of course."

"Oh. Yes. Yes, I see. Of course." This time he was quick, and he didn't allow me to get to the door before he stopped me again. "I am going with you."

"I beg your pardon?"

"I want to go with you."

"I am an adventurer, Dr Ramsey, not a cargo train. I do not have a storage compartment for hangers-on."

His face was earnest. "Please. I can't just sit back and let someone else find him. He's my mentor and my friend. I know him better than anyone. I can help you."

I studied him for a long moment. I suspected he was determined to see this through to the end, and any refusal would be a wasted effort. I sighed and nodded wearily. "Very well. Come along then."

* * *

The airship port was bustling with mid-day travellers when we arrived, and we jostled through the throng to the ticket booth, ignoring the outraged shouts of the people we passed. The man at the counter was a lacklustre youth with pallid, pock-marked skin and a bored expression beneath the dark blue hat perched precariously atop his bushy, blond hair. He did not spare us a glance as we approached him. "Help you?" he asked in a disinterested voice.

I glanced at Dr Ramsey, who had raised his eyebrows at me expectantly, clearly waiting for me to exert some sort of influence over the young man. I had just such influence tucked safely in my valise, but I attempted a subtler line to commence negotiations.

"We need to know if a Dr Sebastian Cross made reservations within the last few days, if you please, sir," I said politely. "He would have been travelling to America."

The youth's bland expression didn't falter. "Can't tell you that, madam. Against regulations, you know."

"It is extremely urgent that we find out!" Dr Ramsey growled, leaning towards the young man.

The ticket agent did not appear at all impressed by his bluster.

"Yes, it is a matter of the utmost importance," I added smoothly, drawing a shiny, brass badge from my valise with a small smile. The young man perked up fractionally, eyeing it cagily for a moment before he seemed to decide it was unworthy of his attention.

"Sorry. Can't help." His eyes flicked away in dismissal, and Ramsey looked at me with a deep frown. I smiled serenely at him. I slid a bank note across the counter, and the youth's attention was suddenly undivided. "Who was that you said? Cross?"

"Sebastian Cross, if you please."

"Ah, yes, let me just have a look here." He turned to riffle through a small card box behind the counter.

I grinned pleasantly at Ramsey, and he responded with a strained smile.

The youth turned back in mere moments. "Here it is. Dr Sebastian Cross. He booked a flight to New York City yesterday at 2:15 p.m."

"Did he make the flight?" Ramsey asked, the smile vanishing from his face as if it had never appeared. A shame. It had been a very agreeable smile.

"I wouldn't know, would I?" the young clerk replied with a derisory frown. "I just sell the tickets, don't I? I give the passenger list to the flight attendant like

I'm told."

"Is he here?"

"'Course he's not. Not back yet, is he? It's very long way to New York City and back. Everyone knows that."

Ramsey sighed, and I looped my arm casually through his, smiling gaily at the clerk.

"Thank you for your most gracious assistance, sir," I said cheerily to the youth. "You have been very obliging."

"Right. Anytime, miss."

Ramsey grumbled, but I steered him firmly away from the booth.

"What now?" he demanded despondently, allowing me to lead him towards the waiting car.

"I am going to pay a visit to Dr Phineas Cobb."

When I realised he was no longer beside me, I turned back, pausing with a hand on the car door. He remained where I'd left him, staring at me, looking utterly flummoxed.

"Well?" I called, rolling my eyes. "Are you coming?"

He sprang into motion, bounding towards me. "Yes!"

* * *

For a scientist in disgrace, Phineas Cobb lived remarkably well. His home was large and brightly white with delicate red latticework around the windows and a wrap-around balcony that over-looked a thick copse of trees. The cobblestone walk was short, leading to a wide, gleaming red terrace that looked to have been recently painted.

In fact, it had. A small sign posted along the railing read, Wet paint.

Ramsey did not seem to notice this small detail. He was striding with single-minded determination towards the similarly pristine front door, and he hardly noticed when I gently guided his hand away from the railing as he climbed the front steps. He spared me a quick glance when he had reached his destination and pounded on the red door.

The summons was answered almost at once, as if the occupants of the house had been expecting visitors. A tall, thin young man with slightly pink cheeks and tidy, shortly-cropped, coppery-red hair peered out at us from around the door.

"Yes? Can I help you?"

"We're here to see Dr Phineas Cobb," I said politely. "Is he in?"

"Doctor!" The young man shouted over his shoulder, and I flinched slightly at the display of poor manners. "There's a lady and gentleman here to see you!"

Brisk footsteps echoed through the handsomely fashioned vestibule, and a man in a crisp, white lab coat appeared in the doorway. He was tall and broad, built more like a soldier than a scientist, though he seemed to have gone soft around the middle as he'd aged. His short, stiff dark hair was combed severely back from his sharp-featured face. He had a dark, ruddy complexion and was in need of a good shave, but his smile was wide and pleasant. He looked much older than Ramsey and me, but he'd aged well. His face was unlined, still pleasing, and he carried himself with an air of practised confidence.

When his chocolate brown eyes fell on Dr Ramsey, however, his smile faded instantly and a hard, arctic look overtook his features. "Ramsey."

Ramsey's expression was no warmer. "Cobb."

"Dr Cobb, I am Astrid Darby," I interjected courteously, offering my hand.

Dr Cobb's mouth tightened around the edges, but he turned his gaze to me and took my hand with a self-assured grip. "To what do I owe this dubious pleasure?" he drawled dryly.

Ramsey narrowed his eyes at Cobb, his entire body coiled in tension as if he expected the larger man to spring. Cobb returned his glare with equal hatred, but neither spoke.

"Dr Cobb, we are investigating the possible disappearance of Dr Sebastian Cross."

Cobb's dark eyebrows rose coolly. "Sebastian is missing?" There was no deception in his voice, but nor did there seem to be any genuine surprise.

"He certainly appears to be. He has not been seen for a few days." I was very close to violating the agreement I'd made with Mr Cole, but under the circumstances, I suspected the risk was worth the reward; a modicum of truth is the foundation of every successful deception.

"Are you a police officer?"

I smiled. "A private investigator. I was hired by Dr Cross' son when his father failed to answer his correspondence. I understand you two were friends?"

Cobb's eyes darted to Ramsey. "Friends?" he repeated snidely.

"Rivals, then," I said with a cheerful grin.

He sneered. "We are hardly in the same league, madam, I assure you."

Ramsey's features were rigid with fury. "That's undeniable. You stole Miranda's plans and hired that rat fink Sweeney to sabotage Stanwick's synchrotron. You are a fraud, not a scientist."

I was startled by his ferocity; I had taken him for a far meeker man.

Cobb, however, was glacial. "You have no evidence to substantiate any of those outlandish accusations, Ramsey."

"Just so, as Sweeney mysteriously disappeared after the explosion and no one ever saw Miranda's plans again."

Cobb's glare could have frozen a large body of water. "What is this about?" he snarled. "Are you suggesting I had something to do with Sebastian's disappearance? I am a scientist, not a kidnapper."

"You won't mind if we look around, then?" I asked genially.

For a moment I was certain he would refuse and the call would come to naught. He continued to glare between Ramsey and me with intense indignation.

Then he pursed his lips and gave a jerky nod. "This intrusion is highly affronting, but I have nothing to hide. You may look around, if only to have you out of my home as quickly as possible. I have little time in my day to squander on baseless allegations. I have important work to do." He tilted his head at Ramsey. "But he is not welcome."

Ramsey sneered, but I ignored him.

"Very well," I said.

"Nicholas!" Cobb's young assistant popped his head around the corner. "Show Dr Ramsey to the parlour. Madam, this way if you please."

I nodded to Ramsey. He looked as if he wanted to argue, but I cut him off with a sharp look and followed Cobb towards his laboratory. His body was taut with irritation, and he was silent as we descended a flight of stairs.

His lab was larger than Cross' by nearly three times and as well-equipped as the one in Darby Manor. He motioned me inside with a flippant sweep of his arm and stood, scowling, watching me as I flitted about examining the shelves and tables with ostensible detachment.

I suspected if the Eye was hidden in this laboratory, I would have no way of identifying it. I was gambling on the element of surprise; if he had had a hand in Cross' disappearance and the designs were here somewhere, it was likely he would not have thought to hide them.

Though I knew I would be hard-pressed to ascertain the difference between plans for a particle accelerator and a homemade biscuit recipe, I was positive I would recognise Cross' scrawl at once.

"What is it you are looking for exactly, Ms Darby?" Cobb asked, moving towards me the moment my hand fell on a stack of parchments.

I smiled. "Oh, nothing in particular, Dr Cobb. I find in my line of work, the most expedient path to determining what has occurred is to first determine what has not."

His brow knitted together at this, but he did not restrict my exploration. If he did have anything to hide, he had done it well. I found nothing out of the ordinary. In fact, the laboratory, unlike others of its kind, was remarkably tidy.

The shelves were well-ordered and the long, steel counters along the walls were neatly arranged for optimum efficiency. I found this interesting; Cobb had thus far defied nearly every characteristic I had come to expect in a scientist.

The centre of the room was less immaculate. Amidst various instruments and tools was a large, metallic skeleton. At first glance it appeared to be a miniature zeppelin, somewhat egg-shaped and made of light titanium.

Beside it was a cylindrical brass engine with a series of knobs, valves and dials, and a long hose that lay coiled like a snake on the floor around it. Its hatch was open to reveal the boiler chamber, and it looked as if Cobb had been working on it when we had arrived; coal still smouldered in the chamber as if it had been recently doused with water, and thin wisps of steam issued from a collection of small, thin pipes that protruded like tiny appendages on its brass body.

I wondered vaguely whom had originally designed the apparatus.

I glanced at Cobb. His expression had undertaken a radical change. He was smiling crookedly, peering at the dingus with pride. "What exactly are you working on here, Dr Cobb?"

"It's a flying machine."

I leaned towards the skeleton, running a finger delicately over one of the metal ribs. It was smooth and almost silky to the touch. "What sort of flying machine?"

His dark eyes lit up in enthusiasm, and it seemed the rancour between us had been soundly quashed by my interest. "It will revolutionise the automobile industry. A flying machine for everyday use that is as common as the average steam car. Once it's complete, people will be able to abandon their inconvenient auto-motives and simply fly to work."

I raised my eyebrows. "That sounds very interesting, Dr Cobb. Do you think it will catch on?"

He stroked a hand lovingly along the side of the skeleton. "Oh, certainly. Imagine never having to take the tube or fight the early morning traffic on the thoroughfares. One could avoid it altogether and just fly right over it all."

"Very ambitious, doctor, but what happens when the air is as congested as the streets?"

Cobb stiffened and gave me a disapproving look. "My dear lady, it is quite apparent you have no eye for the future."

My lips twitched in amusement, but I nodded gravely in concession. "So you're not working on a weapon, then?"

"A weapon? Wherever did you get that idea?"

I shook my head in mock bemusement. "I just heard said somewhere. Perhaps I was mistaken."

"My dear, I am a respectable scientist, not a mad inventor like your friend Ramsey. I prefer to devote my time to inventions that improve the conditions of the world, not destroy it."

"Please forgive my blunder, Dr Cobb." I smiled sheepishly. "I'll have to learn to place less confidence in idle gossip in future."

Cobb nodded smartly, as if I were finally speaking some sense. "Sebastian was working on a weapon?"

His tone was blasé, and he raised his eyebrows innocently. "Come now, doctor, surely you have heard of his contract with Rake & Gage."

He placed a finger delicately to his pursed lips. "Hm. Now that you mention it, perhaps I do remember reading something about it. Not that I paid it much mind. I am quite busy these days and haven't had much time to devote to gossip." He looked mildly interested. "What sort of weapon was it?"

I tittered airily. "I really have no head for science, Dr Cobb. That was my late husband's field."

His eyes narrowed fractionally, and the superficial innocence slipped for an ephemeral instant before he smiled indulgently. "It is not for everyone."

I sensed my welcome was dangerously close to wearing. "Well, thank you for your time, doctor. It's been most enlightening. I hope the intrusion wasn't too significant a strain on your valuable resources."

Cobb gestured gallantly to the door, and I preceded him up the stairs. "The pleasure has been entirely mine, Mrs Darby." When he spotted Dr Ramsey waiting in the foyer with young Nicholas, however, his mouth turned down in distaste. "Well, perhaps not entirely." He shot Ramsey a dark look, but he gave me a small, courteous bow. "I expect you'll not need to repeat the pleasure in future."

"I expect not, Dr Cobb. I feel most confident that we will locate the good doctor in no time at all. Good day to you." I joined Ramsey at the door, smiling merrily.

"Perhaps you should check the local asylums," Cobb drawled. "I hear the 'good doctor' has gone quite mad in his old age, building weapons and such." Dr Ramsey stiffened, but he remained silent. Cobb smiled malevolently. "Ramsey, it's been a pleasure as always, but I shan't say I'll look forward to when we meet again."

"I assure you the sentiment is quite mutual," Ramsey growled. "Good day, doctor." When we were outside, he heaved a long, frustrated sigh. "Did you learn anything?"

"Just that he is working on a ridiculous flying machine," I replied brightly, striding towards our waiting car. "And he says Cross is mad."

"A flying machine? What sort of flying machine?"

"Well, I really have no idea how it's supposed to work, but he believes it will replace the steam car."

Ramsey's eyebrows shot up as he bowed me into the car. "Really?" He considered a moment and climbed into the seat beside me. "I wonder from whom he stole that design."

"Funnily enough, I thought precisely same thing. It was all of little interest to me. I am concerned with the Eye at present. There was no sign of it." I sighed. "Not that I would have recognised it. By all appearances Cobb is quite guiltless."

Ramsey scowled. "He is hardly guiltless. I should have described the apparatus to you. I didn't expect he'd actually let you into his lab."

"Yes, well, I was looking for the designs. I thought I would at least recognise

Cross' writing."

"There was nothing?"

"No. If anything is there, he's hidden it well enough. He wouldn't exactly have allowed me to search his entire flat. I had to content myself with what I was given. He isn't a very good suspect. All we have to go on at the moment is Dr Cross' suspicions and some unconfirmed accusations of fraud."

"He's involved with this somehow; I know he is," Ramsey grumbled, glaring out the window.

"That very well may be. In fact, I'm quite certain he has something to do with all of this. I just don't know what, and I didn't find anything."

We rode in silence to his flat in Kensington, mere blocks from Cross' home. When we arrived he made no move to exit the vehicle. He turned to me with an unhappy expression. "So, what now?"

I paused, considering him a long moment. At length I replied, "I'm going to follow our best lead."

"Which is?"

"Gideon Cross."

"Sebastian's son?"

"I know of no other."

"But he's in America."

"Yes, he is."

"You're going to send him a telegram?"

"No." I tilted my head at him archly. "I suspect if Dr Cross has gone into hiding, he will not be keen to confirm his whereabouts to a private investigator hired by the very people from whom he is hiding." He opened his mouth, but I added with a smile, "Begging your pardon, Dr Ramsey, but nor do I expect he would confirm them to you. He did, after all, make the arrangements without alerting you to his plan."

Ramsey seemed to deflate, and I understood his mentor's lack of faith troubled him. When he glanced back into my eyes, his jaw was rigid. "Can I go with you?"

"To America."

"Well, it isn't as if I have a job anymore, is it? Sebastian is missing and the plans and prototype are gone, not to mention Rake & Gage is still under the impression that I am also missing."

I sighed. "Be that as it may—"

"Please, Mrs Darby."

The earnest look had returned, and I found I was disinclined to rebuff him. Curious, but I supposed if I was to locate Dr Cross and the stray apparatus, Dr Ramsey, the only other person to have seen the Eye and its designs, in addition to being Dr Cross' closest associate, could prove invaluable. "Very well. Meet me at the airship port in four hours. Don't be tardy. I have neither the time nor the inclination to stand around an airship port all day waiting for strays."

"I shall be quite prompt, Mrs Darby."

"I shall see you then, doctor."

CHAPTER FOUR

I was infinitely grateful to Mrs Randall for her unerring attention to detail. My favourite black travelling dress was freshly laundered and hanging in the forefront of my over-sized closet. My fine, ivory luggage sat in a neat pile at the foot of the bed as if my faithful housekeeper had known I was planning a journey.

It was a very good assumption; I often travelled in my work, and pre-planning likely saved her additional toil in her leisure hours. I was not bringing my lovely ivory luggage for this trip, however. It had been a gift from my dear husband many years ago, and I was very fond of it.

The American frontier was, by all accounts, a barren, dirty place, and I doubted the light, delicate, paisley brocade could survive unscathed.

Thus I packed my sundries into a large, worn, brown leather case and was dragging it down the stairs when the front door swung wide and Xander strode into the entryway.

"Oh, hello, cousin," I greeted with a smile. I was anxious to share my discoveries with him and had been extremely disappointed to find him still out when I'd arrived home. "Did you learn anything interesting at your appointments?"

He dropped his rucksack on the floor, his blue eyes bright and eager. "Yes! Loads of things. I was taken on a tour of the laboratories and saw the latest technologies. None were as inspired as the Eye of Ra, but they were dead fascinating anyway. At Airtech, there was a pair of wings that fit over the arms and can carry a man hundreds of feet into the air. Barmy, if you ask me, but brilliant."

"Did anyone suspect you weren't who you claimed to be?"

"No. They weren't fussed. They barely asked about Cross. They were more interested in showing off and trying to persuade me to take an internship in their labs. They didn't even ask to see my credentials."

"I see," I replied stiffly, shoving my case against the wall with more force than was necessary to move the relatively light object.

"Come now, Astrid, you know I'm perfectly comfortable with my present situation. I have my own laboratory here, and I would go spare stuck up inside all day without all the excitement. Besides, you'd be lost without me."

I smiled. "That I would, cousin. You are quite indispensable." I motioned him to join me in the sitting room where Mrs Randall had thoughtfully laid a tea service. "Was there any sign of Cross?"

"No, none. I inquired about the latest defence strategies, and neither of the head developers seemed keen on the idea of a death ray."

I chuckled, pouring boiling water into his cup and offering him a biscuit. "I'm not particularly surprised at that. I am most uncomfortable with the idea myself, the more I learn about them."

We took our tea in companionable silence, but several times I saw Xander's sharp eyes flicker towards my suitcase. I gloated a little into my cup, certain he was simply dying to ask about it. He glanced at me cunningly, and I knew he was only humouring my fondness for dramatic effect.

"Astrid, for what have you packed?" he asked casually several moments later.

I grinned. "America."

"America?"

"Wyoming, to be exact. The wild west."

"What for?"

"Well, when I arrived at the doctor's house this morning, I found someone else had already been there. They had torn it completely apart looking for something—the designs, we assume."

When I paused, he prompted, "What does that have to do with America?"

"I found some journals and a letter in his laboratory." I described the information I'd gleaned from Dr Cross' papers, and as I did, Xander's eyes widened by degree until his entire face had lit up in surprise. "It seems most likely that Dr Cross is on the run and has hidden out in Wyoming with his son, Gideon. He booked a zeppelin flight to New York City yesterday afternoon."

"Brilliant! We've never been to America. I'd better start packing."

I smiled sheepishly at him. "I'm sorry, Xander. I will not require your assistance on this particular journey." When his face fell, I reached across the table to touch his hand. "I have something here that necessitates you remain."

"I'm not going with you? But what will you do?"

"I will have accompaniment."

His brow knitted together. "Who? I understood Cole forbid you to contact our usual associates."

"I will be accompanied by Dr Joseph Ramsey."

His face took on just the expression of dumbfounded shock I had expected, and I beamed in satisfaction.

"Ramsey?" Xander asked, spluttering slightly. "Dr Cross' assistant?"

"The same."

"But I thought he was missing!"

"Not so. I met him at Cross' home. He was already there looking for Cross when I came upon him. He arrived as usual at the lab yesterday morning to find it abandoned. Cross had not informed him of his plans to abscond with the prototype. When he was unable to find him at his home, he spent the day searching for him and had returned this morning at nearly the precise moment I had chosen to investigate the residence. It was Dr Ramsey that showed me the journals."

"Did he have any insight?"

"He is quite at a loss, I'm afraid. Cross did not invite him into his confidence the weeks leading up to his disappearance. This has come as a complete shock."

"Do you suspect he has anything to do with what happened?"

"I highly doubt it, unless he is a very skilled deceiver. He seems terribly distraught, and I believe he is in earnest." I bit into a blueberry scone and chewed for a long moment before adding, "Dr Ramsey accompanied me to the home of Dr Phineas Cobb."

"Cobb? You went to see Phineas Cobb?"

"I certainly did. He graciously allowed me into his laboratory."

"Did you find anything?"

"No. I am quite sure he would not have done if he was hiding the doctor therein. It's reasonable to assume I would not have recognised the Eye had it been in plain view, but I saw no signs of the plans or anything out of the ordinary." I paused with a thoughtful expression. "However, I still strongly suspect he is somehow involved. It is my working hypothesis that Cobb sent the man to intimidate Cross into giving up his plans, and, becoming so paranoid, Cross smuggled the prototype to America."

Xander inclined his head. "That is the most likely conclusion at this stage."

"Which brings me directly to why you are needed here. Whilst I am away, you will be keeping an eye on Cobb. I will require a comprehensive account of where he goes and whom he sees at all times. There is something more to this than Cross simply fleeing the country. Someone hired that man to terrorise him, and it's likely to be someone close to the project or someone who has a contact within Rake & Gage. I requested Cobb's file from Langley's, so pay particular attention to his past associates. Send Cole a telegram and request a list of anyone into whose hands Cross' progress reports may have passed, including the couriers and executives. See if any of these correspond to Cobb's list. There is a connection somewhere."

Xander was nodding, and I felt satisfied he would handle the investigation magnificently in my absence. "Yes, I can do that."

"You may have to seek the assistance of a relief party for the surveillance. Use Janek; he never asks questions, and he's quite gifted. It isn't directly related to the assignment at this juncture, so I don't think we'll be violating the terms of our contract. Just the same, don't tell him anything, and we won't mention it to Cole."

"Understood, cousin. I will make every effort to complete the task on my own, but should I prove incapable, I will be very discreet."

Outside, a brief, blaring horn signalled that Mr Mills had arrived to return me to the airship port. I dabbed delicately at the corners of my mouth with a soft, ivory handkerchief and stood.

"Right then, I'm off. Should you need me whilst I am away, I am afraid I'll be quite unreachable. I will send word when I have arrived in New York."

Xander stood as well to escort me to the car. "Good luck, cousin."

"If all goes well, I shall return with the doctor and his apparatus in short order."

"I certainly hope so. The alternative is absolutely ghastly."

"I am in accord, Xander. The implications are rather grave. Let us pray our hypothesis is sound. Good day, cousin. I expect I will see you again before long."

* * *

Dr Ramsey was pacing anxiously on the platform when I arrived at the airship port a short time later. He had, I noticed with approval, combed his unruly hair back from his face and changed out of the rumpled tan suit. He looked rather smart in dark grey and much more appropriate a travelling companion.

54

"Mrs Darby!" he greeted keenly when he spotted me, hurrying to my side to relieve me of my burden. "You are precisely on time. I have purchased tickets for the eight o'clock flight. I expect we'll be boarding directly."

"Thank you, Dr Ramsey."

He was correct. Moments later we were aboard the gleaming white dirigible with the other passengers.

I was mildly surprised the late flight was so heavily occupied, but Dr Ramsey and I found two comfortable seats in the back facing the long windows and stowed our luggage beside us to discourage any stray passengers overhearing our discussion. We were silent, listening to the din of people settling in for the long flight. When we heard the engines hum to life, Ramsey glanced at me anxiously.

"Have you learned anything else since we last spoke?"

I shook my head. "Only that Cross did not defect to Airtech or Steam Brothers, not that we expected he had. My assistant, Xander, is continuing the investigation whilst we are away."

"Cobb?"

"In a manner of speaking. He is our primary suspect in the matter of who hired the man who approached Dr Cross. There is also a question of how the man knew everything he did about your project. We're cross-referencing anyone who may have come into contact with the progress reports with Cobb's past and present associates. We're hoping a connection will become clear if there is one to be found. In the meantime, he'll keep surveillance on Cobb's house and make note of anyone who comes and goes. Hopefully something will be learned in our absence. Xander is highly competent, and I trust he will have worked something out by the time we return.

"My theory is that the man who approached Cross is the very one who ransacked his house in search of the designs, probably on Cobb's orders. It is possible Cobb bribed one of the couriers at Rake & Gage to bring him the progress reports, which would explain how the man knew so much. As Cross booked a reservation to New York, I suspect he made it out of the country before the burglary, probably taking the designs with him, hence the extent of the destruction."

Ramsey sighed. "I dare hope that you are correct about that."

"We have no reason to believe he did not make his flight. Fear not, Dr Ramsey. We will find your doctor yet. I am most confident we are on the right path."

Silence fell between us for a long moment, and we watched the stars drift past our window. Around us, the passengers were similarly quiet, lulled by the slow, peaceful movement of the airship. Several people were settling in with blankets and pillows to sleep away the long flight.

I suspected I would soon feel my eyelids droop; the gentle motion of the dirigible nearly always soothed me into slumber, and when I am on an adventure, a decent night's rest is not always an absolute. I often availed myself of the long hours in which I was forced to bide my time in conveyance to catch a well-earned kip.

I was not to idle away the hours on this particular flight in a doze, for Ramsey spoke from beside me.

"If you'll forgive the intrusion, Mrs Darby, does Mr Darby approve of you travelling across the Atlantic with another man?" He looked troubled, but I deduced that he was merely distracting himself from the disquieting circumstances rather than fretting over my husband's approval.

I chuckled. "I expect, even were Nathaniel alive, he would not be overly disturbed."

"Oh, he's—" Ramsey faltered awkwardly.

"Yes, I am a widow, Dr Ramsey. My Mr Darby died three years ago."

"I'm so very sorry."

I sighed, peering wistfully out the window. "Yes, it was quite tragic. My husband was an adventurer, as well, you see. He had been in Madagascar questing for the lost journals of an archaeologist who'd made some interesting discoveries in the Ankarana Caves on the island. His air balloon was attacked over the India Ocean by rival mercenaries hired to ensure the journals never reached the public. The balloon went down. He and his assistant, Terrance Wartman, were lost at sea, as were the journals."

Ramsey had risen during my exposition, peering pensively out at the ocean far below. When I'd finished speaking he backed away from the window, looking slightly green.

"That's—that's dreadful," he said in strained voice, dropping heavily back into his seat.

"Indeed." I shot him an amused look. "Never fear, Dr Ramsey. There appear to be clear skies ahead this evening, and I am unaware of any malevolent pursuers."

* * *

This prediction proved sound. When we touched down safely in New York City many hours later, it was in the earliest hours of fledgling morning. Though the sky was as dark as pitch, New York was not asleep. It glittered with bright street lights and illuminated signs, and people milled around the streets as if they had not a care in the world or any particular place to be. Though I had nodded off for the last few hours of the journey, fatigue still hung heavy on my mind and body.

Dr Ramsey looked none the better; his eyes were sleepy and bloodshot, as if he'd awakened too soon from a well-needed sleep. Likely he had. The doctor had the look of a man in desperate need of a warm bed and several hours' uninterrupted rest. He also, I noted, studying his lean frame from under my lashes, appeared in need of a few hearty meals. He was sullen and quiet. I raised my eyebrows at him.

"You look as if you would benefit from a few more hours' sleep, doctor."

This assertion, too, was exactly right. The following morning, when Dr Ramsey found me in the hotel cafe, he was brighter-eyed, even if he still appeared grim and anxious. The dark hollows under his eyes had faded, and there was colour in his cheeks. He smiled faintly when he slid into the chair across from me.

"Good morning, Dr Ramsey."

"Good morning, Mrs Darby."

"Coffee?"

"Yes, thanks." He took it black, and as he sipped, the tightness around his eyes lessened marginally. He sighed contentedly. "So what is on the schedule this morning?"

"I booked us a flight to Chicago. From there we'll have to take a train to Colorado."

"A train? But that will take days."

"Undeniably. Unfortunately there are no airship ports west of Chicago. Under the circumstances, it's the best we can do."

This sigh was gloomy. "Brilliant."

"Eat your breakfast, Dr Ramsey. Our flight leaves in one hour."

"Right."

* * *

Unlike Dr Ramsey, whose interest in the case was personal, as opposed to professional, I had slept quite soundly the previous night, and I did not sleep on the flight to Chicago. The sun was brilliant outside the wide windows, but Ramsey seemed not to notice. I leaned against the curved wall, peering out at the land below while my companion kipped.

There were mountains in the distance, still tipped in snow despite the warming season. The scenery held my attention only briefly; I had had the pleasure of exploring exotic destinations around world, and I found myself disinterested in the relatively mundane landscape beneath us.

I sighed, dropping lightly onto the bench across from Dr Ramsey. I was unaccountably restless, and I reasoned there was a dark recess of my mind that was concerned for my young cousin, left alone to investigate a fraudulent doctor and a mysterious, threatening stranger.

Xander was perfectly capable of conducting the investigation and minding himself, as he had proven in countless circumstances. However, he was still young yet, barely twenty, and I felt a sisterly sense of responsibility towards him.

Xander was my cousin, Eleanor's, boy. She and I had been as close as sisters growing up. We shared a neighbourhood in the merchants' quarter of London as well as Grandmother Eleanor's name, though she, being several years older, had the honour of sharing a first name with the formidable matriarch. My father had been forced to settle with bestowing the coveted name as my middle and not without consternation.

I, however, was quite pleased with the outcome of the family naming tradition and happily shared my mother's sister's given name.

Whilst I had left our humble upbringing for the opulent life of a wealthy scientist and adventurer's wife, Eleanor had married a fisherman. She had been happy, nevertheless, and when young Xander was born, I had been named his godmother, though I had been a blushing youth in my early teens and had no sense of what this might mean at the time.

He had been a mere boy of six when his father had been lost at sea in a terrible storm, and when he was fourteen, his mother, my dearest and closest friend, had taken ill and died, leaving her son to mine and my husband's care. I never regretted the course of events, despite my apparent lack of motherly instincts, and he had become like a younger brother of whom I was exceedingly fond.

I could not have been prouder when he'd chosen the life of an adventurer over that of a scholar, but I still often worried over him, however needlessly.

I endeavoured to immerse myself in the light-hearted works of Miss Jane Austen, which had always succeeded in distracting me from the long, tedious hours of inactivity in the past, but the all-too familiar words did little to soothe my agitation on this occasion.

My eyes flickered to Dr Ramsey, but I turned my attention back to the pages of the dog-eared paperback. My concentration wouldn't cooperate, however, and I found myself staring blankly at the same paragraph for several moments before I gave up altogether.

As if it had been my inclination all along, I found myself studying Dr Ramsey as he dozed in the seat across from me. He looked different in slumber, unassuming and almost vulnerable. His jacket lay over his lap, though he still looked as pleasing as he had earlier in the day when he'd joined me for breakfast with his shirt tucked seamlessly into dark trousers and his tie neatly knotted around his throat. His glasses were hanging slightly askew from his nose, and his hair was characteristically mussed; he was in need of a good haircut.

His lips were slightly parted with his breath, and I now noticed they were thick, well-formed and almost sensual. He had tucked his arms tightly over his chest as if to protect himself in sleep, and I reached over, compelled quite without reason to gently remove his glasses.

He stirred slightly and muttered inarticulately, but he did not wake. There were slight indentations on the bridge of his nose where the glasses perpetually settled, but without them he looked less like a mad, sleep-deprived, absent-minded scientist and more like a young, roguish man.

I considered him in interest, cocking my head to the side as if to study him better. When he had been awake, alert and bespectacled, he had struck me as the scholarly type, tedious and unexciting, passionate about little but his work. This seemed a wholly inaccurate description now, and I wondered if I had been aware of its fallacy all along; he had been fierce with Cobb and so determined to find his mentor that he was pursuing him doggedly across an entire ocean.

I was beginning to suspect it had been my own preconceptions that had tempered my opinion of him. Perhaps I was seeing him clearly for the first time since I had made his acquaintance as a too-long lock of hair strayed over his forehead and stirred gently with his breath.

With some trepidation I realised I found him attractive. Perhaps it had been too long since I'd taken a lover. My marriage to Nathaniel had been arranged by our parents, a mutually beneficial agreement for all parties, and though we had not been in love with each other in the romantic sense, we had shared a deep affection and fondness for each other that had carried us well through the ten years before his death. I had been faithful to my husband all those years but since had on occasion enjoyed a number of men.

There had been a widowed Italian diplomat many years my senior who had plied me with wine, music and all the experience of a man accustomed to romancing younger women; a young, lithe, Egyptian archaeologist with smooth, dark skin and powerful, confident hands; a tall, blonde Australian guide with whom I had shared many nights in front of campfires across the outback; and a Ministry of Defence agent with whom I had often crossed paths on our various assignments, amongst others. Since Nathaniel, I had never been with another scientist.

Dr Joseph Ramsey, no matter how rakish and attractive he appeared at the moment, was precisely the sort of man I was especially keen to avoid. Physicists who built death rays and were on the lam from their potentially treacherous employers were not my ideal choice of lover. I greatly preferred men of action, adventure and romance to men too focussed on their work to remember to comb their hair properly.

Ramsey stirred again, as if he sensed my stare or my thoughts, and opened his eyes. They were dark green, as I'd noticed before, with flecks of brown, and looked foggy with his lately slumber. He blinked, training a confused gaze on me, and I blushed slightly, embarrassed at having been caught watching him.

I didn't look away, despite my embarrassment, for I felt a sudden twinge in the lower regions of my belly. He was peering at me through hooded, intense eyes, and for a moment I pictured him above me, breathing raggedly, peering at me in just the same way.

When he spoke, it was in a husky voice, and I exhaled sharply. However, when I focussed on his words, I was shaken abruptly out of the brief, heated fantasy.

"Mrs Darby? Where are my glasses? I can't see a thing."

I chuckled somewhat breathlessly and, realising I still held his spectacles in my lap, returned them hastily. He wiped them reflexively on his jacket and replaced them on his nose. He blinked a few times, and his eyes slid back into focus.

I breathed an almost audible sigh of relief when he was transformed once again into his former self, the mundane scientist for which I had taken him. I still could not shake the images that had momentarily captivated me, however, and I avoided his eyes.

His brow furrowed, and he cocked his head at me. "Are you quite all right, Mrs Darby? You look a bit flushed."

"Oh, I–" Flustered by the newly awakened fascination, I struck around for a suitably composed response. "I didn't mean to wake you."

His smile was baffled. "No, you didn't." He was silent a moment, his eyes trained on my face. "Are we nearly there?"

My answering smile was somewhat tight. "Just, I think."

I stood, moving towards the window, grateful for an excuse to turn away from him and gather my bearings. Below us, I saw only barren wilderness, but if I looked closely enough, I thought I could see a city skyline on the far horizon.

"It should be only another few hours."

He did not respond, but I waited a few more breaths just the same, watching the skyline move slowly closer. Sure the heat of my cheeks had finally subsided, I turned back to him, and when I did, he was leaning back in his seat, eyeing me the way I imagined he would a very complicated formula.

This did nothing to settle my nerves, but I was at least satisfied that I had smoothed my features into an appropriately bland expression.

"What shall we do in the meantime, then, Mrs Darby?" he asked in a quiet voice.

Though I was certain there was no illicit meaning to his words, my pulse quickened, and I struggled to keep my voice light when I replied, "Whatever you like, Dr Ramsey."

He smiled. "Why don't you tell me about yourself? I would very much like to know how you came into your line of work."

I shrugged, thankful for the distraction he'd again unwittingly provided. "It came to me, in a matter of speaking. My late husband was a scientist, you see, and often lectured at universities across Europe. I usually accompanied him on his travels, and we became quite close to Stuart Whatley, a professor of archaeology at Oxford. When I was twenty-two, Professor Whatley invited Nathaniel and me on an excavation in Egypt. His class had discovered the tomb of a Pharaoh in which they found several dozen grams of an unidentifiable metal."

"What was it?" Ramsey leaned forward eagerly.

"It was hitherto undiscovered. Nathaniel tested the metal, finding it to be highly radioactive, and contained it for later research in his own lab. However, the site was set upon by thieves, and the material, along with the other discoveries from the tomb, were stolen. Nathaniel and I were just returning from a pleasurable visit to the pyramids when the attack occurred. Our friend, Professor Whatley, was injured trying to stop the thieves and had to be taken to a local infirmary. Nathaniel and I waited until the thieves had left the camp and followed them."

Ramsey looked aghast. "Your husband allowed you to accompany him on such a dangerous errand?"

I chuckled, settling back comfortably in my seat to enjoy the reminiscence. "Nathaniel and I had been married two years by then, doctor, and I assure you he knew better than to attempt to stop me doing anything I'd set my mind to. We waited in the dark all night while the thieves celebrated their plunder, and when they were finally asleep, Nathaniel and I snuck into their camp and stole back the items they'd taken."

He seemed wholly engrossed in the tale. "Did they catch you?"

"Oh, yes. We were quite inexperienced at that sort of thing at the time. Luckily, Nathaniel had with him a prototype of the hand-held shock gun he'd been working on before we'd left for Egypt, and he fought the thieves off whilst I escaped with the artefacts. I stole one of their horses and rode it back to the excavation site. Nathaniel met me an hour later, a little worse for wear after his fight, but his eyes were lit with exhilaration from our adventure." My own eyes slid away wistfully, and I smiled.

"Before we had time to celebrate our victorious reunion, however," I continued, "the thieves had caught us up. We fled on the stolen horses with the thieves in hot pursuit. Well, luckily for us, by then Whatley had alerted the local authorities to the debacle. Just when we were sure the horses could go no further and we would have to stop for a rest in the barren desert, we met with a cavalry of the Cairo police. They captured the thieves, and we returned the recovered artefacts to the university.

"Of course, our story became quite well-known, and, upon hearing of it, a number of private individuals and libraries began contacting us to render similar services. After the incident in Cairo, Nathaniel had developed rather a taste for adventure, and thus we began our careers as adventurers for hire. After his tragic death, instead of retiring into the life of a wealthy socialite widow," I shuddered theatrically, "I continued our life's work with my young cousin, Alexander

Knightly."

"That is really quite a fascinating tale, Mrs Darby."

"Indeed my life has been far from ordinary."

He rose from his seat then, a slight furrow on his brow. "Mine has been quite the opposite. Rather unexciting, really." He stared out the window at the sights below. "I think I am beginning to develop a taste for adventure. Perhaps it's exactly what my life has been missing all these years."

I smiled, joining him at the window. "Dr Ramsey, you build death rays. I would hardly call that commonplace."

He chuckled. "I suppose not, but I have spent most of my life in classrooms and laboratories. I've never really seen the world. I feel as if I'm just waking up and looking around for the first time."

"Don't speak too soon, doctor. You still haven't had a taste of danger yet. Let us endeavour to keep it that way."

Ramsey smiled. "Do you doubt my mettle, Mrs Darby?"

"On the contrary. I am certain you would perform splendidly under pressure. I am simply optimistic that our journey will end in success and not grievous bodily harm."

"You make it sound as if you are quite familiar with that."

"Dr Ramsey, you would be astonished to learn how often even the most straightforward of tasks can turn perilous when you least expect."

* * *

Our stop-over in Chicago was brief, merely long enough to catch a meal at a bustling cafe, and we caught a train to Denver, Colorado late that evening. Though Dr Ramsey had gotten a few hours rest on the zeppelin, it was with great relief that I bunked down in my small compartment for the night to catch several long hours of sleep.

I often found that I slept uneasily on locomotives, waking often as the tracks became bumpy and irregular, unlike dirigibles that glided almost effortlessly through the clouds and lulled me into gentle, undisturbed sleep. I did not share my young cousin's disquiet aboard the airborne vessels, despite the manner in which my late husband had met his tragic end.

This night, however, I was suitably exhausted, and the uneven motion of the train had no affect on my repose. Thus, when I awakened the following morning,

I was thoroughly refreshed. Dr Ramsey was already awake and sitting alone in the dining car, reading a newspaper.

"Good morning, Mrs Darby. Did you sleep well?"

I smiled. "I did indeed, doctor. And you?"

"Oh, yes. I have never spent the night on a locomotive before. I found the motion quite soothing."

"Did you? I myself usually find it difficult to rest on a train. I prefer a smooth ride. However, I was reasonably comfortable last night."

"The conductor estimates we will be in Denver by tomorrow morning, provided the weather remains clear and we don't have to make any unscheduled stops."

"That will have to do." The young, bright-eyed waitress paused beside our table, and as we placed our orders, I noticed a tall gentleman with neatly combed blond hair, smartly-dressed in a tan suit, join us in the car. He took a seat beside the opposite window, peering out at the passing scenery.

After a moment he glanced over at us, smiling. "Good morning. I wonder if I might borrow your newspaper; that is, if you are finished with it."

His accent sounded distinctly Welsh, and I briefly wondered if he was a travelling salesman; an over-stuffed brown rucksack lay at his feet as if he had been loath to leave it behind in his carriage.

"Certainly," Ramsey replied, scooping the forgotten newspaper from the table. The gentleman met him halfway and smiled gratefully.

"Thank you, sir."

Ramsey nodded, returning the smile, but he seemed distracted when he returned to the table. "What will we do when we get to Denver?"

"They don't have many cars this far west," I responded over the top of the fresh, steaming coffee the waitress had just delivered with a shining smile. "We may be forced to rent a wagon."

He looked crestfallen. "Are you quite serious?"

I raised my eyebrows, amused. "Dr Ramsey, have you ever left London?"

He frowned indignantly. "Of course I have. I have visited Paris and Milan and Rome..."

"Dr Ramsey, the American frontier is still largely unpopulated and underdeveloped. You won't find a tube or airship here. People travel by horse and carriage and train." I grinned at him. "I thought you were looking for adventure, doctor."

He chuckled. "So I am."

"You'd best enjoy the train whilst you have the chance. When we reach the west, there will be no hot baths or dining cars."

"I think I can handle it, Mrs Darby."

"We'll see, doctor."

We spent the day companionably, getting to know each other in the bright observation compartment as we watched the frontier pass by through the large, wide windows.

By tacit agreement we did not discuss the Eye or the circumstances under which we'd met. He told me of his childhood, growing up in London the only son of a family of five girls. His father was a wealthy barrister and had expected him, as his only son, to join the family firm and continue its legacy.

However, the young, precocious child had been more interested in the study of atoms and energy than the practise of law so had disappointed his father when he'd been accepted to Cambridge to study physics and chemistry.

Ramsey had not been deterred by his father's disapproval and had gone on to obtain his doctorate and participate in studies and research that would later grant him the position of assistant to one of the world's leading physicists.

He had never been married, had never had time to be married, he'd asserted, as he had begun work for Dr Cross nearly directly out of university five years ago.

He lived in Kensington, near Dr Cross and his own family. He talked about his work, his love of science, and his eyes lit like Xander's when he'd become particularly impassioned by some fact or theory.

I was quite mesmerised by this. Had I ever thought him mundane and uninteresting? How foolish I had been. Dr Ramsey was a man of great passion, and my insides had begun to stir as they had on the airship.

I found myself watching his mouth with rapt attention as he spoke. I wondered fleetingly why I had not been so moved when my own husband's eyes had burned in such a way and his tone took on an almost manic edge of obsession. I reasoned that it must have happened so often in the ten years we'd been married that I had simply grown accustomed to it.

Dr Joseph Ramsey was entirely new and exciting. He listened with equally spellbound attention to my recounting of my many adventures, though I suspected, unlike me, he was actually paying attention to my words and not drifting off into fantasy.

I described adventures in Russia, Greece, Rome and the African Congo, Australia and Ireland. I told him of the artefacts I'd recovered and the strange individuals I'd encountered. He was fascinated, delighted and envious of the things I'd seen and experienced. His eyes widened and smouldered and brightened with my tales, and I felt giddily like a young girl paid praise by a boy she fancied.

We took dinner in the dining car again and drank wine with zest, elated by the thrill of new friendship. We were on our second bottle of port wine, giggling like young children over my reminiscence of a hilarious mishap in Nathaniel's laboratory involving a mouse and a radioactive peanut when he slid his hand across the table, covering my own.

His eyes had become suddenly serious, and my pulse leapt with the contact. "Do you miss your husband, Mrs Darby?"

I grew quiet, startled by the sudden shift in conversation. His dark green eyes were gentle, and I found myself quite captivated. "Often," I admitted.

"Did you love him?"

I considered this question a long moment. I was surprised he would ask such a personal question, as his enquiries had been hitherto extremely polite and reserved. I suspected it was the wine that had loosened his tongue.

I was uncharacteristically candid in my response, likely suffering from the same lack of inhibition.

"Nathaniel and I were very fond of each other, but we were not in love. Our marriage was arranged when I was just nineteen. Our families were friends and business associates, and it was an ideal arrangement. We were lucky to have gotten on as we did. It was very painful to lose him."

"You were very lucky." His face was suddenly dark and sullen. "My father tried to force me to marry the daughter of one the partners at his firm when I was twenty-three. She was dreadful. Loud, conceited and ill-tempered. Not to mention in love with another man."

I raised my eyebrows. "What happened?"

"Well, I spent the weeks leading up to the wedding deciding the best fashion in which to flee without being disinherited. I had concluded the only plausible solution was to blow up my laboratory while I was inside and hope I was only marginally disfigured. The proceeding hospital stay would surely extend past the scheduled date of the wedding."

I laughed. "She must have been awful."

"Indeed she was. Luckily, just as I had planned to light the match, my father received word that she had run off and eloped with a fish merchant's son. So, I was saved the heartache of an unwanted wife and hideous disfigurement."

I smiled. "I didn't realise you had a sense of humour, Dr Ramsey."

"There are all sorts of things you don't know about me, Mrs Darby." He winked, surprising me again and eliciting an odd swooping sensation in my chest. Then his face returned to its former solemnity. "I'd prefer if you'd call me Joseph. We're friends now, aren't we?"

I looked down demurely and smiled up at him from under my lashes. "Yes, we're friends now."

"Am I being too forward?"

"No. There's no one here but us, is there? I am a lady of experience, Joseph. There's no need to be overly proper."

He looked momentarily vexed. "I am a gentleman, Mrs Darby."

I chuckled. "So you are, but you may still call me Astrid."

"Astrid." He grinned widely, and his eyes slid out of focus. "I believe I am in need of the loo." He pushed to his feet rather unsteadily and wobbled, catching the back of his chair to regain his balance.

I grinned at him, rising hurriedly to wrap a firm arm around his waist. "I think you may have imbibed a bit too much, doctor."

He snickered and dropped an arm heavily over my shoulders. I swayed slightly under his weight, but we moved slowly towards his compartment.

"I think you may be right. I don't normally drink. It's quite pleasant, though, now that the room has stopped spinning."

I shook my head in amusement. "Come, Joseph. I think it's time to retire."

"Yes, perhaps it is."

Joseph's compartment was across from my own, and I slid the door open with difficulty, straining under his graceless form. "Here we are."

"Thank you." He spun abruptly to face me, and I stumbled backwards. He caught me with unexpected haste, and I gasped, unsettled by the sudden proximity of his face. I could feel his breath stirring the fine, loose hairs on my forehead, and I gazed up at him raptly. "You have very pretty eyes, Astrid. Like midnight."

I smiled, feeling breathless and dizzy, but when he leaned closer with unfocussed eyes, I pulled back, pressing a hand lightly to his shoulder. "You're quite intoxicated, Joseph. Let's get you inside."

He blinked, his face suddenly dismayed. "Oh, I...Oh. Yes. I'd better go."

I smiled at him, but he still looked troubled. He released me, but the train lurched, and he stumbled backwards into his compartment, his mouth comically agape. I giggled as his arms pin-wheeled, desperately searching for purchase, and he found it, catching my shoulders to steady himself.

He was unsuccessful. His momentum dragged me with him, and we fell against the opposite wall with a unified grunt. He did not look amused, but I sniggered at his shocked expression. At once, I became aware of our bodies pressed indecently close and took a quick step back, trying to ignore the heat pulsing through my body.

He muttered unintelligible apologies, his face scarlet with embarrassment, and I pressed my lips together to keep from giggling. I turned down the thin, scratchy wool blanket on his bed, and he tottered towards it, one hand on the wall to remain upright as he slipped past me. He was careful not to brush my body with his.

He was asleep before his head hit the pillow, and I smiled, tucking the blanket over him and placing his glasses on the small stand bolted to the floor beside his bed. I sighed and brushed the dark hair from his forehead with soft fingers. "Perhaps next time, Joseph."

CHAPTER FIVE

I sipped strong, sweet black coffee in the dining car the next morning, longing, as I often did on long journeys, for one of Mrs Randall's extravagant tea services. I enjoyed coffee on occasion, usually in the evening after a meal, but I preferred tea with my breakfast. I sighed mournfully but decided I was, despite my disappointment in my morning brew, much better off than Joseph this particular morning.

He trudged into the dining compartment, dropping inelegantly into the chair across from me and pressing his fingers to his temples with a soft groan. I hid my smile behind my cup. "How are you feeling this morning?"

"Oh, I have a dreadful headache." His voice was subdued and miserable.

I slid the small, corked vial at my elbow towards him. "Here. Try this tonic. It should help. I ordered you some plain toast and coffee."

"Thank you." He tilted his head back, swallowing Xander's concoction in one gulp, and remained that way a moment, his eyes closed. I took the opportunity to grin but immediately smoothed my face when he sighed deeply, dropping his head to look at me. "I don't drink often."

I nodded, my lips twitching. "I had gathered that."

He mouth tightened into a grim line. "I hope I wasn't out of line last night."

"Quite the contrary, Dr Ramsey. You were very much the gentleman."

"You knew my name before."

"I still know it."

He smiled slightly and nodded in apparent satisfaction then winced in pain. I struggled not to chuckle at his predicament and silently watched him gingerly eating his toast. I wondered if he'd be able to hold it down.

When he'd finished I checked my gold pocket watch. "I expect we'll be arriving in Denver soon."

He nodded, and though he looked pale, he seemed to be improving. He sighed and leaned back, closing his eyes. I noticed the gentleman from the previous morning glance at us over the top his newspaper. He smiled knowingly, and I returned the gesture, cutting my eyes to Joseph to be sure he hadn't noticed our mirth.

He hadn't moved from the table in the dining car when the train rolled into Colorado. I had left him an hour before to pack my valise, and I peered into the dining car, chuckling when I found him there, his head cradled in his arms on the table top. "Joseph."

He looked up, startled. "How long have I been here?"

"About an hour. Are you quite all right?"

He sighed, but he pushed reluctantly to his feet with a groan. "I must have dozed. I'll be all right. Are we there?"

"Nearly. Do you need help packing?"

"No, no, thank you." His movements were sluggish, but he was steady on his feet, and I was confident he would not take ill any time soon. Though he did not permit me to assist him, I hovered in his doorway as he packed his things.

He did not seem to mind my intrusion, but he did not respond to my chatter, merely grunting noncommittally. I gave this up quickly and left him to sit motionless on his bed, staring blankly at the mustard yellow, paisley-covered wall for the final leg of the journey.

As predicted, there were no cars waiting in Denver when we arrived. There was, however, a conveniently located stage coach rental establishment.

Joseph was quiet whilst I completed the transaction.

"We'll need a driver," I insisted, sliding a handful of bank notes across the counter.

"Ain't you never driven a buggy before?" the wizened old man demanded.

"Yes, and I don't intend to repeat the experience."

He sighed irritably and shouted over his shoulder. "Clyde! Get out here."

A young man in a scuffed leather bowler hat stuck his head out from a back room, looking startled. "Yeah?"

"These folks need a driver. Headed to Cheyenne, they are."

Clyde blinked, and I scrutinised him narrowly. He looked capable enough and cleaner than the old man, who had smudges of dirt on his wrinkled cheeks. Clyde surveyed us in interest. "You folks from the Old States?"

"London," I replied shortly, and he nodded as if he'd suspected it all along.

"Right. I reckon I can take you as far as Cheyenne."

"Ace. We'll need to leave at once."

"Take the new road, Clyde," the old man ordered and turned to us. "It's the safest route. They got the Marshals patrollin' the new road. You're less likely to be attacked by red-skins or bushwhackers, but it ain't all even. I hope you're not prone to the motion sickness."

I glanced at Joseph. He was slightly green, but he shrugged.

I nodded at the clerk. "That will do. Thank you, sir."

"Well, get a wiggle on," the clerk ordered Clyde, who jumped as if he'd been whipped and darted into the back.

"How far is it?" Joseph asked meekly.

"'Bout a hundred miles, maybe a little less. Takes about twenty hours if you go straight. I reckon you'll be there day after tomorrow if you drive straight through the day. Ain't nothin' much between here and there. You'll want to stop at the general store on your way out of town."

Joseph grimaced. Clyde emerged from the back several minutes later, carrying a large rucksack. He appeared slightly flustered, and I suspected he was not especially keen to undertake such a journey on such short notice.

I resolved to tip him handsomely when his boss' back was turned. He was tremendously helpful, however, and aided us in gathering supplies for the voyage quite enthusiastically once he realised I was financing the expedition. Thus equipped, we set out towards Wyoming at a comfortable pace, snacking on peppered jerky and sweet bread.

I peered out the window contentedly whilst Joseph leaned back in the padded seat across from me, his legs propped up on the bench beside me with his eyes closed. His own curtain was pulled tight against the sun, and he still looked distinctly off colour.

"I think you need a lie down, Joseph," I told him, and he cracked an eye open.

"What do you think I'm doing?"

"That looks dreadfully unsuitable. Why don't you crawl in the back and have a kip?"

"Madam, I do not 'crawl' anywhere."

I laughed. "Well, aren't you petulant when you are feeling under the weather?

Here, have my pillow."

He scowled without opening his eyes. "I'll be fine. Don't fuss."

"As you wish." I opened the carriage door, and his eyes flew open.

"What are you doing?"

"I'm going to sit with Clyde."

He grumbled inarticulately, but he settled back in the seat, closing his eyes.

Clyde looked started when I opened the carriage door. "Stop the carriage, if you please, Clyde."

"Ma'am?"

"It's a lovely day, and I wish to sit in front with you."

"Yes, ma'am." He tugged on the reigns, and the carriage jerked to an ungainly stop. The horses swished their heads back and forth in consternation, but Clyde was smiling shyly at me.

He hopped down from the driver's perch and offered his hand, assisting me out of the coach with a brief bow. I smiled at his unexpectedly good manners. "Thank you, Clyde."

"Not at all, ma'am."

The sun blazed above, unobstructed by trees or sky-rises, and the land stretched out barren and rocky towards the horizon. I could see a few wagons ahead and behind us in the distance, kilometres away but still visible on the flat landscape. Though there was no shade, a sudden gust of wind rendered the seasonally warm air almost chilly.

Dust kicked up from under the horses' hooves as they pawed listlessly at the ground, and I threw up an arm to protect my face from the swirling earth. "I was mistaken. The kerchief is not, in fact, just an attractive fashion accessory."

He smiled apologetically. "No, ma'am. The wind blows like the devil 'round these parts. Always too hot, too cold or too windy. You never get used to it. Least Colorado's got some mountains. Real pretty, but Wyoming...Well, I don't know what a fine lady like yourself would want to be visitin' here for."

My hair whipped around my face, and I sighed. I greatly preferred even Joseph's peevishness to a face-full of dirt.

"Clyde, I hope you will not think me discourteous, but I think I would prefer to ride in the coach."

He chuckled. "Don't blame you, ma'am." He assisted me back into the wagon and hopped lithely onto his perch.

Joseph shifted when he felt my weight beside him. "Changed your mind?"

"It's tremendously dusty out there. The wind is absolutely intolerable."

I smoothed the loose tendrils of hair from my face and checked my reflection in a small compact from my valise, scrubbing furiously at a smudge of grime on my cheek with a linen kerchief.

The coach pitched suddenly into motion, and Joseph's eyes flew open. "Oh, I don't feel so well."

"Joseph?"

He turned a delicate shade of green as the coach jarred us back and forth. "I need air."

"If you can contain yourself for just a moment, I will have Clyde stop the carriage–"

He wasn't paying attention. He lurched across me gracelessly and threw open the carriage door. "Stop the coach!"

Clyde barely had time to yank the horses to another abrupt stop before Joseph leapt from the carriage. I raised my eyebrows, pursing my lips in amusement. He leaned unsteadily against the carriage wall, gasping for breath, and retched indelicately.

"You a'right there, sir?" Clyde called from the perch, grimacing, and I pressed my lips together to keep from giggling.

Joseph waved a hand behind him, and I ducked back into the carriage, peering out the opposite window. When he heaved himself into the cart, his colour had improved, but his dignity seemed to have suffered. He looked deeply discomfited.

"I see the American frontier does not agree with you," I remarked lightly.

He scowled. "You find this comical, do you?"

"Marginally."

He huffed indignantly and crossed his arms over his chest. "That is very uncharitable of you, Mrs Darby."

I handed him a canteen of fresh water. "Back to that, are we?"

He sighed and swallowed a large gulp of water, leaning back against the seat beside me. "No, we're not back to that." He turned to me, frowning. "Why aren't you sick, then, Astrid? You drank as much as I."

I smiled. "I have spent many a night idling on long journeys such as this. I find imbibing is often an agreeable way to pass the time. Nathaniel was very fond of wine. When he was alive he had a very fine cellar. I have since stopped filling it, but I have been doing an excellent job of emptying it."

He chuckled weakly, and I was pleased to see his temper was improving. "I am not entirely certain it is something I want to get used to. "

"Perhaps it's advisable to cease after the first bottle next time."

He smiled, and then he winced as the carriage moved forwards again. He looked miserable; his long legs were sprawled uncomfortably on the seat across from us, and his head lolled against his chest.

"Come here, Joseph. You look dreadful."

He looked startled. "I beg your pardon?"

The benches slid together to form a flat surface suitable for sleeping, if one is comfortable sleeping in such quarters, and I found that if we pushed our bench against the one opposite, they formed a makeshift settee. This was an infinitely more pleasant fashion in which to travel, and I sighed contentedly.

Joseph, on the other hand, seemed hardly better off. "Have a lie down, Joseph."

"Don't trouble yourself."

"Don't kick a fuss." He sighed in resignation, and I guided him to lie down, positioning a pillow in my lap to cushion his head. He stiffened for a moment, but I rolled my eyes at him. "Honestly, I'm only attempting to make you more comfortable. No need to work yourself into a state." He submitted to my urging at last and leaned against me, peering up at me doubtfully. "Don't be such a prig."

"I am not a prig!" he exclaimed, intensely piqued.

I grinned. "Dr Ramsey, I assure you, your virtue is perfectly safe with me."

He was utterly gobsmacked. "I wasn't...I didn't mean..."

I rolled my eyes at him and ignored this, sweeping his hair gently from his brow.

"Just go to sleep."

He sighed, but he closed his eyes. He lay tense and uncomfortable for a long moment, and I stroked his hair softly as I had done to soothe Xander to sleep when he'd been a small boy. Joseph relaxed by degree until eventually his breath was deep and even, and I was sure he had finally drifted to sleep.

"Foolish man," I murmured under my breath.

"Impudent woman," he replied just as quietly, and I chuckled, leaning back against the bench.

I didn't realise I had dozed until the carriage jolted to a stop. I opened my eyes, blinking in the unexpected darkness. Joseph was jarred awake when I shifted and bolted upright. I could practically feel the heat of his blush radiating from his cheeks, and I grinned.

"Sleep all right?"

He ignored my question. "What's going on?"

His enquiry was answered in moments. I heard Clyde hop down from his perch, and a soft tap on the door signalled his approach. When Joseph opened the door, it was to find Clyde standing outside with a lantern that burned so brightly, we had to shield our eyes from the sudden assault.

"Sorry about that, sir and ma'am."

"What's going on?" Joseph repeated.

"Got to stop for the night."

"Isn't there a hotel or tavern nearby to stay for the night?"

Clyde chuckled. "Sorry, sir. There's nothin' much 'tween here and Cheyenne. You'll have to bunk down in the wagon tonight."

I leaned around Joseph. "Where will you stay?"

"Got myself a lean-to. Don't fuss over me."

It seemed a dreadful way to spend a night, but I looked around the wagon and considered the available alternative. I couldn't very well spend the night in a carriage with two men who were not my husband.

I sighed and resolved again to tip him most handsomely for his trouble. "Thank you, Clyde."

"Not at all. We'll start out at first light."

"Good night, Clyde."

"'Night, sir. Ma'am."

Joseph closed the door, and I could barely discern his gaze in the darkness. "This is not exactly what I had in mind when we set out," I muttered, leaning back in the seat.

"We'll have to make do." The mirth in his voice was unmistakable. "I assure you, Mrs Darby, your virtue is perfectly safe with me."

I had to agree this was neither the time nor the place to alter the tenor of our current relationship, not with young Clyde sleeping just outside the otherwise secluded wagon. "How very heartening. What is the time?"

"I regret to inform you that I cannot see in the dark."

He did not sound regretful. He sounded cheeky. I rolled my eyes and felt around for my valise.

He suddenly gasped, and I felt him shift under my questing hand. "Mrs Darby!"

I giggled. "Sorry. I was trying to locate my valise. It contains a light."

His breathing slowed to normal, and his shadowy form moved against the wall away from me. "I find this situation rather unsettling."

"That much is quite apparent to me, Dr Ramsey." I found my valise and rummaged around inside, exclaiming softly in triumph when my fingers closed around the small, smooth silver lighter that had been a gift from my young cousin on my thirtieth birthday.

The light startled him, and Joseph threw his hand up again. "This seems to be occurring with unpleasant regularity," he complained.

"You seem to have experienced a number of unpleasant things today." I drew my pocket watch from my breast pocket. "It's nearly ten in the evening."

Joseph sighed. "I've been sleeping for hours. I don't believe I'll be able to fall back to sleep now."

"No, nor can I, I suspect." I puffed out a breath and held the lighter above my head to locate the small oil lantern we'd purchased in Denver. It was not a powerful light, but it illuminated most of the carriage. Shadows danced across the planes of Joseph's face, and for a moment he looked startlingly sinister as he peered at me from under his furrowed brow. A tiny thrill shot up my spine, but I tamped it down.

"Would you care for a novel?" This did not seem to appeal to him; he grimaced slightly. "I regret to inform you I don't have the latest edition of the mad science quarterly."

"How very amusing you are, Astrid."

I beamed at him. "I am gratified by your acknowledgement." Ignoring his disgruntled look, I settled back against the seat with one of the paperback novels and pretended to immerse myself in it. He fidgeted for a few moments, and I snuck a glance at him.

He looked distinctly uncomfortable, crossing and uncrossing his arms over his chest and staring blankly at the curtained window. His eyes darted to me and, catching me watching him, he looked quickly away again.

Colour rose in his cheeks, and I raised the book to cover my face. He cleared his throat awkwardly. I lowered my book to meet his gaze.

"Yes?" I asked, pressing my lips together to suppress a smile.

"Oh. No. Nothing, I—I think perhaps I will take one of those novels."

I smiled brilliantly at him and offered the short stack of books. He scowled at them a moment and selected one at random, opening it and slumping back in his seat.

"I didn't realise you were a fan of Miss Austen's," I remarked casually, keeping my eyes on the words in front of me.

"What?" Joseph flipped the book around, frowning at the title. "Oh, I—yes, I am."

"Really? What is your favourite tale?"

He was quiet a long moment then lowered the book to give me a baleful look. "You are enjoying my discomfort."

"Oh, are you uncomfortable? Would you care to lie back down?"

"I would not care to lie back down." He sighed deeply and settled himself against the back of the bench.

"Suit yourself." His tension was palpable, and I resisted the temptation to chuckle at his expense. Blimey, you'd think the man had never been alone with a woman before.

Just as I had begun to wonder if he, in fact, ever had, a long, piercing howl rent the silence, and Joseph and I started in alarm. "What was that?" Joseph demanded in a low voice.

"I have no idea." I groped for my valise and removed my pistol, reaching for the door handle.

"No!" Joseph caught my arm, and I paused, scowling at him.

"What?"

"You can't go out there. It's safer in here. Just stay in the coach."

"Clyde's out there."

Joseph cursed under his breath and held out his hand. "Give me the gun."

"What?" I repeated, staring at him incredulously.

"Give it to me."

"Joseph, do you have any experience at all with firearms?"

He rolled his eyes in annoyance. "Just point and fire. What's to know?"

"Are you mad?"

"Of course I'm not. Damnit, Astrid, give me the gun."

"This isn't exactly what you think it is—" He gestured impatiently, and I sighed. "Fine. Have it your way. Don't say I didn't warn you."

"Fine." He snatched the gun from my hand and alighted lithely from the carriage. I peered out the door into the night, and he spun on me. "Stay here."

"Joseph, I have far more experience with wild animals—" I frowned. "It is pitch black out here. Where's Clyde?"

"I don't know. Give me the lantern."

"This is ridiculous," I muttered, then noticed a light bobbing several metres ahead, barely piercing the darkness of the prairie night. I pointed toward the light, but before I was able to speak, a shot rang out. Joseph jumped several centimetres into the air, dropping my pistol as he did.

I rolled my eyes. "Cor, Joseph, give me back my gun."

He looked sheepish and bent to pick it up, examining it in the lantern light as he did. "Why didn't it go off?"

I gave him a haughty look. "You didn't honestly think I'd give it to you without engaging the safety, did you?"

He glared at me, but his reply was interrupted by Clyde's return. The youth was loping unconcernedly back towards the camp. "You folks all right?" he called as he neared us.

"Just a little startled, apparently," I replied, smiling sweetly at Joseph.

"Nothin' to be afraid of; just a coyote," Clyde said, tucking his own pistol back into the holster on his belt with a practised ease. Joseph eyed him crossly. "They're all over these parts. Lord, I hate Wyoming. You folks go on back to bed. I'll be all right out here. We'll leave at first light."

"Thank you, Clyde." I leaned back to allow Joseph to climb back into the carriage, grinning at him. "Well, Dr Ramsey, I do declare. Aren't you the brave gentleman, protecting your fair female companion?"

Joseph scowled petulantly and crossed his arms over his chest. "I would have if the kid hadn't gotten there first."

"I am sure you would have got on famously." I chuckled and tossed *Sense and Sensibility* into his lap. "It's just as well, sir. I do not need protecting. I get on just fine on my own."

"It's ladies with no regard for their personal safety that need protecting the most, Astrid," he muttered irritably, tossing the book aside with excessive force.

I shot him a sour look. "I'm not quite sure if you're being sweet or discourteous, Dr Ramsey."

A small smile tugged at the corners of his lips. "I can't be the only one made a fool of this evening."

"Oh, Joseph, you certainly can, right proper gentleman you are."

"You truly know how to make a man feel like a man, Mrs Darby."

"Funnily enough, Nathaniel used to say the precise same thing."

* * *

As Clyde had promised, we resumed our journey at first light, and we spent the day reading in pleasant silence or simply watching the prairie move slowly by, sharing light anecdotes about our past. We did not discuss the previous night and were relieved to learn we would not have to repeat it.

We sojourned for the night in a small, obscure town off the trail that I had first mistaken for a ghost town. It was not deserted, however, and as the stage coach rolled along the packed dirt of the main road, shopkeepers and children peered out at us from their storefronts and porches.

There were few guests at the inn, and by all appearances, the saloon on the ground floor was a popular establishment for local gentlemen, cattle wranglers and transients to seek the companionship of a lady for the evening.

I had never seen Joseph as discomfited as when approached by a thick, gaudily painted woman with a full mouth of black, rotted teeth. Hence, though this deeply amused me and Clyde seemed keen to remain in the company of a fresh-faced young lady whom had turned out to be, much to Clyde's embarrassment, the innkeeper's daughter and not a professional lady, we spent little time in the saloon before retiring for the evening.

Thus, we were awake bright and early the next morning, anxious to reach our destination before dusk. The sun had just begun its slow descent towards the horizon, and Cheyenne was alive with activity when we arrived.

Men on horseback raced through the streets or staggered in and out of the various saloons on the main thoroughfare. Women in lacy, brightly coloured dresses strolled casually up and down the lane, twirling parasols and eyeing the evening's potential clientele. Cheyenne was a dusty town, and our carriage kicked up a cloud of earth as it passed, finally drawing to a stop outside a tall, grand wooden building that bore the name Black-eyed Susan's painted in large, friendly, red letters.

"Here's your stop, sir, ma'am. Best inn in Cheyenne," Clyde announced, holding open the door to assist us onto the dirt of the road. "You want I should help you with your bags?"

"No, Clyde, thank you. We'll take it from here. Thank you ever so for your kind assistance." I gave him a smile, hefting my valise onto my shoulder, and Joseph alighted wordlessly from the coach.

"T'weren't nothin', ma'am."

We parted amicably with the youth, leaving him with enough money for the lonely return trip and the company of one of the young ladies passing along the street, were he so inclined to partake of their particular services. Joseph peered dubiously up at the saloon for a long moment.

"This looks like a bawdy house," he remarked.

I threaded my arm through his and beamed at him.

"Don't be such a pedant, Joseph. Young Clyde did say this is the best inn in town."

He sighed, but he did not resist as I tugged him inside.

The atmosphere inside Black-eyed Susan's was lively with chatter and music, despite the early hour. Beside a curtained stage, a man in a grey suit was playing a spirited two-step on a rickety wooden piano, and several of the patrons were singing drunkenly along to the familiar tune, holding up their glasses in salute and guffawing loudly at each other.

Ladies in bright dresses were wandering about, chatting up the blokes in pursuit of the finest looking or deepest pocketed. Dusty wranglers and superbly dressed gentlemen sat along a scrubbed, wooden bar, nattering affably together like old chums.

We were not the only couple inside the saloon. On the contrary, several couples dined in the quieter corners alone or in groups, enjoying the vivacious surroundings and what appeared to be uncharacteristically fine cuisine.

However, our entrance drew the attention of several patrons immediately, perhaps due to our somewhat weather-worn appearance or simply our upright, unmistakably English attitude. I felt Joseph tense beside me, but I tilted my chin and strode confidently towards the barkeep, firmly leading the reluctant doctor to follow.

The barkeep was a young, burly man with a thick, black moustache and a crisp, pristine white shirt. He raised his bushy eyebrows at us when we reached him.

"Help you?"

His voice was gruff but not unpleasant, and I smiled at him. "Indeed. My husband and I need a room for the night, if you please."

Joseph cut a sharp, askance look in my direction, but I ignored him. The barkeep glanced at him, but his ruddy face remained passive. He nodded and rummaged behind the bar for a shiny, pewter key with a small, wooden plaque reading 20 dangling from a delicate chain. He handed the key to Joseph.

"That'll be $2.50, sir."

I reached for my valise, but before I was able to extract the coins, Joseph had paid the man for the room, darting a quick look in my direction. I noticed a few wranglers had sidled up to the bar and were watching the interaction with interest. I sighed, hoping to ignore them until I had completed my business with the barkeep.

"English, are you?" the barkeep asked before I was able to proceed with my questioning.

Joseph nodded stiffly, his dark eyes darting from the barkeep to the wranglers, who were inching closer and appeared to have been at the bottle for quite a time. "Yes, we are."

"What're you doin' round here?"

I interjected, moving nearer to the bar to lean towards the barman. "Actually, I wonder if you might help us. We are looking for a man called Gideon Cross. I understand he lives around here."

"Cross?" The barkeep looked thoughtful for a moment. "Yeah, I think I know him. The English chap, lives about twenty miles outside of town. Come in here 'bout once a month for supplies and such. He usually spends the night. Never seen him with a lady, though. Think he might be a Mary. What're you lookin' for him for? You related?"

"We have some news about his father," Joseph told him rigidly.

"Bad news, then," the barkeep surmised, nodding eloquently.

"Not necessarily," I replied, smiling brightly.

"Do you know where his house is?" Joseph asked.

The barkeep was quiet for another long moment. "No, never been there myself, but you could ask old Rufus Howell across the street. Runs the general store. He's delivered some supplies there once or twice. He should be able to tell you how to get there."

I nodded happily. "Thank you very much, sir. You've been most helpful."

"Yup." The barkeep turned back to gathering the used glasses from the bar, and I cut a glance at Joseph. He was already watching the wranglers' approach.

They were a scruffy lot, weathered and grimy, and looked as if they had just returned from a long spell on the prairie. The largest of the four, a burly man in scuffed tan chaps and a mismatched black, cowhide vest with a six-shooter holstered on his belt stood slightly in front of his company, the unspoken leader of the motley gang. He wasn't wearing a hat, and his hair was over-long and wiry, matching the ill-tended beard on his chin.

"English, are ya?" he asked in a slow, roughened and deceptively polite voice. He had an ominous, dangerous air about him, as of a wild creature barely contained and poised to strike at the slightest provocation.

Joseph returned his beady stare with an admirably level gaze, though I could feel the tension in his shoulders as I leaned into to his side. "We are."

"You play poker, Englishman?"

"Ah, no. No, I don't," Joseph replied in a tone that implied he was straining not to sound too cautious, lest the looming wrangler sense his fear and press his advantage.

"You sure about that?" the wrangler asked, smiling dangerously, his teeth surprisingly large and white in a way which suggested they were the product of a dentist and not nature. He took a step closer, and I crossed my arms over my chest. Joseph remained where he was, and I found myself impressed by his constitution.

"I'm fairly sure, thank you."

"Well, you don't sound so sure." He touched the holster on his belt almost delicately, as if out of mere habit, but the threat was unmistakable. "We could play for your pretty lady there. What do you say?"

Joseph's spine stiffened. He was taller than the wrangler by several centimetres, but even in his righteous anger he was much, much slighter. "Mind your tongue, sir," he growled.

The wranglers cackled, and their leader leered at Joseph. "Just for the night, Englishman. Don't get your knickers in a twist. We'll give her back in the morning, good as new. You wouldn't be thinkin' 'bout refusin' now, would you?"

The wranglers stepped closer, surrounding us in a way that prevented escape from either side of the bar, though they seemed to be keeping their distance, advancing slowly.

The barkeep backed up, a wary look on his face, and I smiled pleasantly at him. Joseph scowled at the wranglers. "I assure you, gentlemen, we are quite uninterested in engaging in your uncouth customs, and I would thank you to apologise to my wife for making such a boorish slight on her character."

I grinned at him, and the wranglers laughed heartily, clapping each other on the backs as if they enjoyed nothing less than the indignant blather. "Is that right, Englishman?" He dropped a heavy hand on Joseph's left shoulder. "I don't see as you have much of a choice."

Having grown thoroughly weary of the confrontation, I reached into my jacket and found purchase on the grip of my pistol. Joseph seemed frozen in anticipation of an attack, and I fired the pistol unceremoniously at an empty table behind the man on my right.

The table exploded in an impressive shower of splinters, causing several ladies to shriek in alarm and the saloon to fall instantly silent. The wranglers yelped in surprise, jumping back, their eyes snapping to the weapon still raised in my hand.

"What the hell kind of gun is that?" one of them demanded in a shaky voice.

The barkeep was staring at me in utter befuddlement, his mouth hanging open, and I gave him an apologetic smile. "Gentlemen, there seems to be some sort of misunderstanding," I told the wranglers politely. "My husband does not play poker, nor am I an object for bargaining."

"No, ma'am," the leader stammered, his eyes wide and fixed on the weapon in my hand. "Just a misunderstanding. Just having a little fun. Didn't mean to offend."

"Not at all gentleman." I turned to the flummoxed barkeep. "Please forgive my discourtesy, sir." I dug in my valise and dropped a stack of banknotes on the polished bar. "For your trouble. We'd like to take dinner in our room, if you please."

"Y—yes, ma'am. I'll send one of the barmaids right up."

"Much obliged." I caught Joseph's arm and stepped away from the bar. "If you'll excuse us, gentleman. Good evening to you."

The wranglers stepped aside, watching us warily. We ignored the stares of the patrons around us, ascending the steps with unaffected dignity.

Joseph spun on me the moment we were safely inside the room. His eyes blazed, and I raised my eyebrows, startled by his ire.

"Why did you do that?" he demanded hotly, tossing his luggage on the floor next to one of the twin beds.

"I beg your pardon?"

"I was dealing with them."

"Oh, yes, you were doing a bang up job of it," I replied, frowning and crossing my arms over my chest.

"I do not need you to fight my battles for me, Astrid! I looked like a bloody fool."

"Oh, you did not." I rolled my eyes, dropping onto the bed beside him with a heavy sigh.

"In case it has escaped your notice, I am the man here."

"It has not escaped my notice, I assure you. I merely thought it expedient to put an end to the debacle before you found yourself unarmed in a shoot-out with experienced gunfighters."

Joseph scowled petulantly, but he sighed, pushing his hands through his hair and dropping beside me on the edge of the bed. "Why do you get to be the one to carry the gun, anyway? How can I protect us if I am not armed?"

I pursed my lips to keep from smiling. "I do not need protecting, Joseph. Besides, it's my gun, and it's not exactly a six-shooter."

"What sort of gun is that, anyway?"

"It is a wave gun. It was one of Nathaniel's prototypes. Actually, it's only good for one shot every few hours. It takes ages to recharge. One shot is usually well enough, however, as you saw." I eyed him in interest. "Do you even know how to use one of these?"

He straightened indignantly. "Need I remind you that I would not even be here if I had not been helping build a death ray?"

I laughed. "I thought you disliked that descriptor." When he rolled his eyes, I smiled at him. "Oh, Joseph, would you like a pistol of your own?"

"Yes, I would."

"All right, you can hold the gun from now on. Remember, it's useless after the first shot, and it vaporises just about anything you hit. Be careful with it."

"Right. I know what I'm doing, thank you very much."

"I hope my interference hasn't caused too much damage to your fragile male ego."

"I do not have a fragile ego!"

"Whatever you say, doctor."

He glared balefully at me, then sighed and looked around. The room was modest, but handsomely wood-panelled and newly painted a gentle cream. Two small twin beds covered in threadbare but freshly laundered quilts nearly filled the entire space. It did have its own loo, for which I was most grateful, having been forced to endure the indignity of a communal lavatory on numerous occasions in the past.

"Why did you tell him we are married?" Joseph asked abruptly.

I shrugged. "It seemed like a good idea at the time. I did not fancy being mistaken for a scarlet lady, though it does not seem to have done much good."

He chuckled wryly. "At least there are two beds. It's better than the stage coach."

"Why, Dr Ramsey, are you suggesting you did not enjoy our quality time in close quarters? Myself, I found it quite cosy."

"It's nothing personal, I assure you. I do not typically fancy such primitive and uncomfortable modes of travel." He was quiet a moment then met my gaze earnestly. "It is highly inappropriate for us to be travelling unaccompanied in such a fashion. I should have insisted upon a chaperone. Whatever was I thinking?"

I laughed aloud. "Is that what you're worried about? Honestly, Joseph. I think we are perfectly capable of minding ourselves."

"It's not proper. Aren't you concerned about what sort of lady you'll be taken for?"

"Joseph." I shook my head with a grin. "I have never concerned myself with what other people think about me. I have far more pressing matters to be getting on with. Besides, you don't really know what sort of lady I am, do you?"

He opened and closed his mouth in utter bemusement. "I—oh, I—well, I mean, I'm sure you're not..." He stopped talking, shooting me an incensed look. "You enjoy unsettling me, don't you?"

"I do, indeed." I grinned, hoisting my valise over my shoulder. "But you needn't concern yourself with what sort I lady I am just now. I did assure you your virtue was perfectly safe with me."

The irritated expression had vanished to be replaced by a sly look. His malachite eyes twinkled impishly. "Now, Mrs Darby, aren't you concerned for your own virtue?"

I tossed my head negligently. "Not in the least."

"You don't really know what sort of man I am."

"Are you teasing me, Dr Ramsey?"

He smiled. "Perhaps."

"I am highly affronted. Do I look like a scarlet woman to you?"

His boyish face smoothed into a serious expression. "No, Astrid, not at all."

I angled my nose into the air. "Quite right." I strode towards the loo. "I'm having a bath. Get some rest. We've another long day ahead of us tomorrow."

CHAPTER SIX

The sun was already streaming through the partially drawn curtains, casting prisms of light upon the floor. I was pleased to note the layer of dust and dirt that blanketed the frontier town had not infiltrated our room as we slept. I had half anticipated awakening under a shroud of the grime, resembling the encrusted wranglers of the previous evening's confrontation.

I turned my heard towards the other bed, only to find Joseph already awake, propped up on his elbow. The bed beneath him was tidily made, and it appeared as if he'd already washed for the day. He was watching me with a ponderous expression on his face.

"Good morning," he greeted in the muted voice of the earliest hours.

I smiled at him. "What are you doing?"

He didn't return the smile, but his lips twitched. "Wondering how I got into this mess."

"You're the one who decided to become a mad scientist."

He frowned. "I'm not mad."

"Joseph, you helped build a death ray. That's a bit mad, yeah?"

He chuckled. "I suppose." When I tossed back the coverlet, rising abruptly from the bed, he gasped and covered his eyes.

"Oh, calm down, Dr Ramsey. Haven't you ever seen a woman in her petticoats before?"

He scowled without uncovering his eyes. "Not you."

"Well, now you have. I expect it won't be such a shock in future."

As I reached the door to the lavatory, I heard his droll, mock-reproving reply. "You expect I'll see you in your petticoats again, then?"

I grinned as I pulled the door slowly closed, calling through the sliver of light, "Only if you ask very nicely, doctor."

There was a moment of silence, and I heard him clear his throat before expelling a rather breathy chuckle. As I washed for the day, I hummed indulgently to myself. Yes, the good doctor was indeed a highly amusing travel companion.

When I emerged from the bathroom it was to find he'd already disappeared downstairs. His rucksack and personal effects were gone, and he'd most considerately gathered my strewn-about sundries in a small, neat pile on the smartly made bed.

The wranglers from the previous evening's row eyed me venomously as I descended the stairs into the saloon, my valise tucked securely over my shoulder. Joseph was nonchalantly sipping a mug of coffee and looked mightily smug.

I noticed a slight bulge in the right breast of his tan jacket and assumed he'd secreted my wave pistol beneath it to discourage the cowboys' further interference. He smiled when I slid into the seat across from him.

"I trust you are prepared to depart," I remarked.

"I can most emphatically say that, yes, I am." His eyes darted surreptitiously towards the wranglers. Though they were unlikely to approach us again, they did look decidedly sinister, glowering at us from their small corner and speaking in low, rumbling tones to each other. "So what is on the schedule for today, Astrid?"

"We'll visit Mr Howell's general store across the street and hope he can tell us where to find Gideon." I looked up as last night's barkeep paused at the table. He wore an expression of forced civility, but I noticed his gaze shoot towards the splinters still littering the saloon floor. I gave him a luminous smile.

"Get you somethin'?"

"Do you have any tea? Black, preferably."

"Coffee," he grunted grumpily.

"Coffee would be lovely, thank you, sir." He shuffled away, returning moments later with a steaming, chipped mug. I suspected they received few early morning diners, and if his disposition was any indication, the barkeep was not fond of the hour. When he'd trundled sluggishly away, I returned by gaze to my companion.

"You're looking much better this morning, Joseph."

"Frontier travel does not suit me. I much prefer a nice, comfortable bed." He grinned. "And you are looking quite lovely yourself, fully adorned."

I laughed. "Why thank you."

We did not linger over breakfast as we had on preceding mornings, for the wranglers were shifting cagily in their seats and looked as if they were contemplating retribution.

Unsure of the length of our voyage or the reception we would receive when we arrived at Gideon's home, we quickly encumbered ourselves with supplies at Howell's Sundries across the street from Black-eyed Susan's saloon. The general store was small and as unsophisticated as the rest of the town appeared to be, but it was well stocked and virtually empty at such an early hour.

The gentleman at the cashier counter was ancient and wizened, but he had a shrewd look and eyed us in interest, though he did not ask questions as the other inhabitants of the barren landscape of the New World were so often wont to do.

"We hoped you might help us, sir," I said as I passed the banknotes across the counter.

"Oh?"

"Are you Mr Rufus Howell?"

"Yes, ma'am."

"We are looking for Mr Gideon Cross. The gentleman at Black-eyed Susan's suggested you might know where to find him."

"Cross..." He scratched his stubbly chin thoughtfully. "Oh. Yeah. The Mary. Deliver supplies out to his cabin every few months. He lives about twenty miles northwest of here."

I glanced at Joseph, who was examining a display of paperback novels, and turned back to Mr Howell. "I don't suppose you rent carriages here, Mr Howell?"

At this Joseph looked up sourly, and I smiled ruefully at him.

"No, can't say as I do," Howell replied, wrapping our purchases in thin, brown paper. "But ol' Tanner down the street is usually willing to rent out his old buggy for a reasonable price."

Joseph sighed grandly and dropped a few paperbacks onto the counter. Howell rang them dutifully and scribbled the directions to Cross' cabin on a scrap of paper.

"Follow the road about fifteen miles and turn onto Prairie Dawn Trail. Big stone marker. You can't miss it. Cross lives about five miles past the marker, a little off the trail. No trees 'round there. You'll see it from the road."

"Much obliged, Mr Howell," I called gaily on our way out the door. "Good day to you."

"Another carriage," Joseph lamented with exaggerated gloom.

"Now, now, Joseph, it was you who was so keen to accompany me on this expedition."

"Had I been prepared for the primitive modes of travel which I have been forced to endure, I would perhaps have taken more time to consider."

"How very fickle of you, sir. Why, just days ago, were you not insistent on finding your missing doctor? Now you face a bit of hardship, and you are prepared to scarper."

"So unkind, Mrs Darby. Don't give me up for a bad job just now. This grand adventure is only starting. There is some spirit in me yet."

"I am most faithful."

We strode quickly along the main thoroughfare as the town awakened for the day. Shops opened as we passed, and the denizens of the grimy western outpost began to emerge from hotels and flats and roll in on horses or carriages.

As Howell had suggested, Tanner's establishment was just a block further on the road. It was open, according to a small, hand-lettered wooden sign, but there were no customers so early in the day.

"Oh, you must be joking." Joseph halted abruptly, staring up at the building with distaste.

I giggled. There were several handsome wooden coffins displayed beside elaborate stone tombstones outside Tanner's Mortuary, and a gaunt, bearded man in an austere black suit and top hat stood nearly motionless outside the dark mahogany front door.

It was, decidedly, the finest building on the thoroughfare. The dark paint on the walls was fresh and shiny, and the wooden porch was well-kept and appeared recently swept. I ascended the stairs without hesitation, and the man in the suit strode forward to meet me, looking almost eager, despite his attitude of sobriety.

"May I be of assistance?" he asked in a low, drawling sort of voice.

It was exactly the quiet, grave and almost sinister voice I had always associated with undertakers and hired killers.

"Mr Tanner?" I asked, tugging gently on Joseph's arm to draw him to my side; Mr Tanner's face seemed lit from within with an eerie fervour, though the lines of his face remained perfectly still.

I suspected he was a man who greatly enjoyed his job, and if the quality of his storefront was any indication, he was quite adept.

"I am. What may I do for you today? Are you in the market for a coffin? I just received a shipment of the finest mahogany. Very reasonable."

"Thank you, sir, but we are not in mourning this morning," Joseph answered, sensing the change in my attitude. "We understand you have a carriage for rent? Mr Howell sent us."

Mr Tanner's startlingly white smile seemed to stretch across his entire face, though it was not a friendly, cheerful smile. Instead, it was almost as if he were preparing to unhinge his jaw and swallow us whole.

I turned away from him on the pretence of demurring to the men, and my eyes swept the buildings awakening around us. The post office across the street was already bustling with customers, dressed in their finest day dresses and suits, likely the citizens of the ranches and farms on their weekly excursion to town for shopping and entertainment.

I noticed the man with whom we'd shared the dining car on the train from Chicago sitting comfortably on a bench outside, reading the local newspaper. I raised my arm in salute when he felt my eyes on him and glanced up. He smiled politely at me and returned to his paper.

"Come out back," Tanner was saying, and Joseph nudged me gently, guiding me to follow them down the porch steps and around the building where the carriage was waiting. "It's been slow these days, what with the U.S. Marshals patrolling the roads and arresting all the outlaws." He appeared indecently disappointed by this, and I experienced a deeply unsettled feeling, as if there was something to which I should be paying closer attention. "Not a lot of work for a man in my profession these days and can't say as I'm pleased about it."

That much was unequivocally apparent.

"Here we are."

Joseph looked utterly appalled. I covered my mouth to stifle another giggle. The carriage was large and painted a polished black. The words Tanner's Mortuary were painted in muted yellow along both sides, and the windowless coach looked completely unsuitable for a living passenger.

It was sized to accommodate perhaps two coffins side by side. There were no benches or padded seats within, but the driver's perch was covered in delicate, grey silk brocade. It did not look completely uncomfortable, but the spindly, shining wheels presented the overall impression of a giant, misshapen insect.

Even the horse, a large, black stallion, was ominous, dancing restlessly in place and lashing its head back and forth as it peered at us with distinct dislike.

"Isn't that…"Joseph heaved an enormous sigh, shooting me a dark, askance look as if I had purposely orchestrated this situation to vex him.

"Yes, sir, finest funeral wagon this side of the Rockies, if I do say so. It hasn't seen much use of lately, though. We haven't had a shoot-out in town in a week, and it's not looking like old Jameson Finch is planning to die on us any time soon. I reckon renting it out a couple days won't hurt. Weather's nice, not too hot. Bodies will keep for a couple days. That is if there are any bodies…" He sighed heavily. "How long are you planning to keep it?"

"Just the day or two, I expect," I replied, caught between my own revulsion for the thin man in black and my amusement at the dismay on Joseph's face. "We're heading about twenty miles out of town to visit Gideon Cross."

"Ah. Yes. The Mary. What business do you have with him?"

"My husband works for his father in London," I replied easily. "We just need to speak with him."

"I reckon he doesn't get a lot of visitors all the way out there. Always buying odd things in town, too. Wire and glass and chemicals and such."

Joseph looked slightly nettled. "He's a scientist."

"Is that what he is? I always thought he was a Mary."

I smiled. "I am certain it's possible for him to be both, Mr Tanner. We really must be on our way. We are most grateful for your generous assistance." I thrust a handful of banknotes into his pale palm.

When his dark eyes widened, I was certain I had overpaid him.

"Sir. Ma'am. You have a nice day now."

"Thank you, sir," Joseph replied and offered his hand to assist me onto the perch. "I hope you know how to drive this monstrosity," he added in an undertone when he was seated beside me.

"I most certainly do." I snapped the reigns, and the horse shot forward, throwing us both backwards against the backrest. I chuckled. "Well, I have done it before. Once."

"Oh, delightful."

"Now, where's that spirit you were talking about?"

"Just don't kill us."

"Oh, Joseph. Don't be silly. If a little coach ride was enough to kill me, I would unquestionably be dead by now."

"Why does everyone in town keep calling Gideon a Mary?"

I laughed. "Joseph, most Americans think Englishmen are Marys."

"Well, that's just—that's just ridiculous."

It was mid afternoon when I guided the hearty and pleasantly obedient stallion onto Prairie Dawn Trail. As Mr Howell had advised, the small, log cabin was easily visible from the trail. Thick, black smoke puffed out of the stone chimney, and the distinct smell of sulphur hung in the air as we alighted from the wagon.

"Well, at least from the smell of it," I remarked to Joseph as we approached the front porch, "we can assume he's following in his father's footsteps. Shall we?"

Joseph nodded and lifted a hand to tap politely on the front door. He waited, standing nearly nose to nose with the wood, but no answering call issued from within, nor did the door open.

"Oh, for heaven's sake, Joseph." I rapped impatiently on the door and stepped back, frowning at it. Had the doctors noticed our approach? I wondered if, should Dr Cross see his erstwhile assistant waiting on his son's doorstep, he would be keen to grant us audience. I eyed the thick door warily. It was structured from the same steadfast, solid-looking logs out of which the rest of the cabin had been constructed. No matter. If we were unable to break it down, I was certain Nathaniel's brilliant pistol would make short work of it.

This was unnecessary. The door flew open a few moments later. A man several years older than me, dressed in a stained and scorched grey lab-coat, stood panting in the doorway. His shaggy, sandy-coloured hair was wild, and he still wore goggles over his eyes.

"Oh!" he exclaimed, pushing his goggles onto his forehead with hands swathed in thick, green rubber gloves covered in a glutinous, unnaturally electric blue substance that dribbled onto his coat and smoked slightly. I grimaced, and he started, peering at his hands. "Oh! Oh, I'm so sorry. I beg your pardon." He yanked off the gloves, tossing them hastily onto the floor beside the door. "Yes. Well. Good afternoon. What can I do for you?"

I did not bother to ask if this was, in fact, Gideon Cross. I was highly dubious that there could be more than one mad, English scientist near Cheyenne,

Wyoming.

"Hello, Dr Cross. I am Astrid Darby, and this is Dr Joseph Ramsey."

"Ramsey? My father's assistant?"

Cross looked ominously perplexed, and I was growing increasingly and uncomfortably concerned that this expedition had been in vain.

"That is correct, sir." I smiled at him.

"Well, this is unexpected." Gideon smiled widely. "How do you do?" He thrust his hand towards Joseph then seemed to think better of it when Joseph eyed it nervously and nodded instead. "Won't you come in? This is a great surprise. A great surprise. Very pleasant. Would you care to join me for a drink? I was just finishing up in my laboratory and could do with a spot of spirit. You?"

"That would be lovely, Dr Cross. Thank you." We followed him inside, and my eyes swept the cabin immediately. It was modest and rustic with furniture that seemed to have been carved by hand out of the same wood of the cabin.

I wondered if it was the younger Cross himself who had done the carving. A thick, warm, woollen quilt was folded neatly on the settee, and a large, oft-read chemistry text lay open on a small table beside it, but there were no signs anyone but Gideon had spent any evenings curled up there, reading.

I chanced a glance at Joseph's face, and he wore a similar expression of disappointment and consternation at the mounting evidence of his mentor's absence.

Gideon handed us both small port glasses of sherry, and Joseph and I sat side by side on the settee whilst he perched anxiously on the edge of a wing-backed armchair. "So what is it, then? Has something happened to my father?"

Joseph and I exchanged a forlorn look. "So he isn't here," Joseph said with a deep sigh.

"Here? Why, no. Should he be? I was under the impression he had declined my invitation."

Joseph was quiet, and I regarded Gideon a long moment, deciding he appeared altogether guileless. "In retrospect, perhaps we should have sent a telegram," I murmured. "No matter. Dr Cross, I deeply regret having to inform you that your father is missing."

"What?" Gideon's voice was soft, as if the breath had been knocked soundly from his body. "Missing?"

"Yes."

"Since when?"

"Six days ago," Joseph told him gravely. "When I arrived at work on the 21st, he was gone and all his things were missing."

Gideon was quiet a moment, and his face suddenly looked peculiarly boyish. He wrung his hands together fretfully.

"In his letters, my father mentioned he was concerned someone was trying to steal his project." He turned suddenly blazing and leery eyes towards Joseph. "He was afraid someone close to the project was involved."

"Dr Ramsey was not involved in your father's disappearance. He is as keen as you to determine what has happened to him," I told Gideon sternly. "What did your father tell you in his missives?"

Gideon frowned. "He told me a man had approached him about the—project."

"Mrs Darby has been retained by Rake & Gage to locate your father. She is aware of the specifics of the project," Joseph interjected.

For a moment, Gideon was distracted. "What is it you do, Mrs Darby?"

"I am an adventurer, sir. Your father's employers have entrusted me with the magnanimous task of discovering what has become of your father and the Eye."

He nodded, and I suspected he would perhaps have been more sceptical had he not just been delivered a significant and disquieting shock. "Father was becoming increasingly concerned for his safety. He feared the weapon he'd created was too dangerous and that someone would try to take it from him."

"He suspected Dr Phineas Cobb."

"Yes. He feared Phineas was working with someone inside Rake & Gage." He looked guilty for a moment. "In truth, I thought he was being paranoid. My father has…a history of making outlandish accusations of treachery and theft. It didn't seem to make a lot of sense. Why would someone inside Rake & Gage help Cobb steal the Eye while Father already worked for them? They stood to gain very little from doing so, as only the executives had access to the project. It is unlikely Cobb could have offered them enough money to turn on their company in such a capacity."

My mind instantly flashed to Messrs Cole and Thorne. Cole had been the one to contact me, thus I ruled him out instantly; what purpose was there enlisting me to find the Eye if he already knew where it was? The authorities were not even aware of the debacle yet. No, Cole had little to gain from such elaborate subterfuge.

Mr Thorne seemed more the type, but I doubted he would work with someone like Cobb. What could a disgraced scientist with a tarnished reputation offer a junior vice president of one of the most prominent corporations in London? I have found, however, in my line of work, that there are always elements and motivations that are not immediately apparent, and people are rarely ever what they at first appear to be.

As it was, we hardly possessed any evidence the Eye had been stolen at all. In fact, I realised with a deep sense of disquiet, we hardly had any evidence whatsoever. We had determined where Cross was not, at least, but we had come no closer to solving the mystery of his whereabouts than when I had begun six days ago.

I snapped my attention back to the two men, who were looking at me in interest.

"Pardon me," I said. "I was lost in thought a moment. Dr Cross, your father booked an airship flight to New York for the afternoon following his disappearance. He did not mention to you he was intending to come to America?"

"No," Gideon replied miserably. "I beseeched him in my last letter to take a break and come for a holiday, but he never responded, and I have not heard from him since. My father is...temperamental. I assumed he was angry with me or suspected I was not taking his concerns seriously—as I was not. In his last letter, he seemed distraught. He said he had disabled the Eye in case someone did try to take it, and he left some trick notes for Phineas to discover, should he attempt to steal the plans."

"The sabotaged notes in the lab at Rake & Gage."

"I can only presume. So Phineas didn't find them, then?"

"No. I found them when I searched the lab," I told him, frowning thoughtfully.

"I thought he sounded quite mad," Gideon whispered. "But now...Do you think Phineas does have something to do with this?"

"Yes," Joseph growled.

"I am not certain," I replied slowly. "We found the notes your father left for him, so I can safely suppose he was not in the laboratory at Rake & Gage. I was inside Dr Cobb's personal laboratory, and I saw no sign of your father or the

Eye. We have no solid reason to suspect him or anything to tie him to whatever might have happened."

"But he's appeared quite innocent in the past, as well," Joseph spat venomously. "When he was most certainly quite guilty."

"Could my father have booked the flight to New York to mislead Phineas?" Gideon put in. "He seemed quite sure it was he who was behind the mysterious man that had been stalking him."

I considered a long moment. "Perhaps. That is a worthy idea."

Gideon rose agitatedly, pacing to the small kitchen to fetch the sherry bottle. "Do you think this man might have gotten to him? Do you think something terrible could have happened to my father?"

"I...have no reason to suspect that at this time. I have been operating under the theory that he has simply taken the Eye and gone into hiding. There was no sign of struggle in the laboratory. It appears as if it was left in exactly the state your father intended others to find it. The man might have been privy to the progress of the project, but it seems as if he was not in league with anyone within Rake & Gage with access to the lab itself. If that is the case, the man's accomplice might have informed him of the doctor's absconding, thus prompting the villain to search the flat."

"His flat was searched?"

"Oh. Yes. It was ransacked. Probably in search of the Eye's designs. If they found what they were looking for, it must have taken quite a while. There was not a cranny left untouched." When I noticed the distressed look on Gideon's face, I added, "But there was no indication your father was in the flat at the time. There was no evidence of a scuffle. Just a mess."

Gideon exhaled heavily. "Yes. Yes, that makes sense. My father is extremely shrewd. Knowing him, he might have ransacked the flat himself to throw off his supposed antagonists."

Joseph and I both paused. "Would he do something like that?" Joseph asked, surprised.

"Oh, yes. He's had similar...fits of paranoia in the past." He hesitated a long moment. "After Anastasia died...Well. This would not be the first time he has concocted some conspiracy theory about factions attempting to steal his work. I am sure Dr Ramsey could attest to this."

Joseph nodded slowly. "He has always been protective of his designs and his secrets. But…do you think it's really possible all this has been some elaborate fantasy, and he's been in hiding all this time over some illusory threat?"

I pinched the bridge of my nose in utter frustration. If this had all been an intricate ruse, I vowed that the good doctor would swiftly and memorably regret having put everyone through so much tribulation.

I stood abruptly. "Well. Dr Cross, I am terribly sorry we had to alarm you. It appears there is little else to be learned here."

Joseph looked surprised, but he rose reluctantly, clearly dreading another several hours aboard the funeral wagon. Gideon also appeared startled by the unexpected departure. "Oh, I…Well, thank you for your visit, Mrs Darby. Dr Ramsey, it was a pleasure to meet you. My father has always spoken highly of you."

"Thank you, Dr Cross."

"Please, you may call me Gideon. You will contact me as soon as you discover what has happened, won't you?" he asked anxiously, and I suspected it would be long before he slept restfully. I hoped I would soon have pleasant news to depart regarding his father's safe discovery and return.

"Yes, of course. And if you hear from him, you will let us know?"

His reply was interrupted by the sound of horse hooves beating rapidly on the dirt trail outside the cabin, and we all turned our heads in the direction of the sound.

"Who else could be coming to call at this hour?" Gideon murmured. "I don't normally receive visitors."

My heart had begun to hammer in my chest, though the sound of hansom cabs had never alarmed me in the past. I thrust my hand in Joseph's direction. "Joseph, give me the gun."

"What?" He pushed his jacket aside, looking bemused by the urgent snap in my voice.

I snatched it out of his waistband, giving him a reproving look. "You're lucky you didn't lose a leg," I scolded and darted towards the door.

A thunderous cacophony rendered me motionless in shock. A shower of bullets shattered the sitting room window, and fire ignited spontaneously around us, licking at the wooden walls and furniture and the threadbare rugs on the floor.

"My lab!" Gideon screeched. "What's going on?"

"Incendiary devices!" I yelled back, vexed. The smoke was already filling the small cabin, almost completely obscuring my vision. We had been lucky to be standing nearest to the front door, opposite the assaulted window. "Joseph!"

"Here," I heard him gasp from my right and felt his hand close around my arm. "We have to get out of here before the lab catches!"

"My lab!" Gideon shouted again, and I felt Joseph drag me in the direction of the older doctor's voice.

"No!" Joseph growled at him, seizing his arm before the man could dart foolishly towards the lab and yanking us both down to the floor where the air was clearer. "If you open that door, it will explode! We have to get out now before the lab catches, or we won't make it!"

The window on the other side of the room shattered with the force of a subsequent airborne incendiary, and the resulting flames raged unimpeded through the sitting room like an abominable antagonist, consuming everything in its path to the laboratory door, which remained, for the moment, mercifully closed.

I stared at the laboratory door for a moment in dumbstruck terror, images of the impending destruction flashing unhelpfully through my head. I started from my temporary paralysis when Joseph tugged on my arm.

"Astrid, come on! The fire's spreading, and we'll asphyxiate in the smoke!" The direction of his voice changed, and I felt his body lurch as he tugged both Gideon and I towards the front door.

"No, not there!" I hissed at him, resisting his direction. "They're smoking us out. They will be waiting to shoot us down the moment we get outside! Gideon, do you have another door?"

"Kitchen," I heard him rasp, and then he collapsed on his knees in a fit of coughs. His lungs were older than Joseph's and mine, and I suspected he would not last much longer in the suffocating, black smoke.

In unspoken accord, Joseph and I hoisted Gideon to his feet, and we struggled laboriously towards the kitchen. The air was clearer there without any immediate fuel for the fire, but the wood itself could hardly withstand the blaze for long.

I was not certain there would not be one or more of our assassins awaiting us outside the back door to do us in, but I rather felt it worth risking a possible quick death by gunfire to escape a certain slow death by suffocation.

Gideon did not make it to the door. I felt him suddenly slacken, and the unexpected dead weight carried me to the floor. Joseph cursed from Gideon's other side, and he crouched beside us. He must have lifted him, for I heard a strained grunt, and the cumbersome weight was gone.

"Go!" Joseph ordered through clenched teeth, moving slowly with the burden slung precariously over his shoulder.

"I'm not leaving you, you git!" I snarled. My eyes burned, and my lungs felt fit to burst, but it was not, in fact, my first experience in the vortex of a raging fire. Surely Joseph was much worse off, and I refused to abandon him to the smoke and flame.

He didn't argue; there was precious little time or breath to spare for such futile endeavours in the present climate. The kitchen door was less than a metre away, barely visible in the dense, acrid smoke. I glanced back over my shoulder towards the laboratory door, but there was nothing to see.

Heat and smoke filled every sense, and the sweat that poured into my eyes stung. There was no way to know if the fire had begun to consume the walls of the cabin, having made quick repose of the highly flammable fabrics and furnishings that had once decorated the ravaged sitting room.

I feared that any moment the laboratory door would lose its futile battle against the flames.

Urgency gnawed at me, and I forced the images of exactly what would happen when that moment arrived from my brain. Bloody scientists with their bloody flammable houses and bloody volatile chemicals.

My hand closed over the wooden doorknob, and the heat of it seared straight through my glove. I had a split second to feel grateful it was not a metal knob, for I was quite fond of the skin on my hands and was loathe to feel it melted off.

"Get down!" Joseph shouted at me, his voice alarmingly harsh. "When that door opens, it's going to get a whole lot worse in here."

I only prayed it would not get a whole lot worse outside. I crouched and threw open the door, diving out into the fresh afternoon air. My shoulder collided painfully with hard, packed dirt. I had only a moment to register gratefully that there was not, in fact, a firing squad waiting for us behind the blazing house before I heard a deafening explosion from inside and knew nothing but darkness.

CHAPTER SEVEN

Every nerve, muscle and sinew in my body shrieked in vehement protest. I groaned and sucked in a lungful of clean air. Fits of violent coughs seized me instantly, and it was several moments before I was able to push myself gingerly to a sitting position.

"Joseph?" My voice sounded harsh, and the words scraped painfully against the tender, damaged tissue of my throat.

For the first time since we had crossed into Wyoming, I was thankful for the barren, treeless landscape and the hard, packed dirt that surrounded the smouldering ruin of Gideon's house. The conflagration had claimed the house, and the sagebrush around me was scorched and black, but the flames had found no sufficient fuel to spread further.

The fire hadn't burned itself out, not completely, and I suspected the contents of Gideon's ruined lab continued to burn under the glowing embers and ash. There was no sign of horses or wagons, and I could only assume our would-be assassins had been confident enough in their assault on the house not to concern themselves with ensuring success.

Or perhaps the attack had merely been a warning, a message, and the purpose had not necessarily been our certain death. Were that the case, I thought, frowning, this particular assignment had taken a turn for the greatly perilous, and I had absolutely no idea with whom we were dealing. I experienced a sudden, intense and ominous certainty that there were elements of this case of which I had no knowledge and which had been exerting untold influence from the very beginning.

There was no time to pause and think further about this, however. It was the time for action and reaction. Though I realised I was suddenly operating as if blind to the pertinent and necessary facts of this case, I was completely sure it was imperative we returned to England at once before any further disasters were visited upon the increasingly doomed venture.

I turned my gaze from the smoking rubble and found the crumpled figures of the doctors a few metres away, unmoving on the hard, dusty ground. The explosion, whilst rendering my body a solid bundle of aches and pains, had thrown us clear of the house and the fire and likely saved all our lives.

That was, I considered uncomfortably, if Gideon had survived the smoke inhalation and Joseph the subsequent explosion. I crawled slowly towards the men, wincing at the pain in my stiff, bruised limbs. I wanted nothing more than to lie back down on the unyielding earth, close my eyes, and sleep until it felt normal to breathe and move and speak again.

This was not to be, however. When I reached the two men, Joseph had already begun to stir. He groaned softly and opened his bleary eyes to find me leaning over him, peering anxiously at his face. "Joseph? How do you feel?"

"Dreadful." He turned his eyes to the dusky sky then to the remains of Gideon's house. "We're actually alive?"

"Yes. Can't say for Gideon, however." I moved towards the older doctor. He was in terrible shape, but aside from the bruises and a small, still bleeding cut on his left eyebrow, he appeared to be largely unharmed. He was still unconscious, and he was breathing harshly but steadily. His heartbeat was strong, if slow, and I suddenly suspected he had merely swooned in the excitement of the moment. Bloody delicate scientists, anyway.

Not all of them were delicate, I decided, turning my attention back to Joseph, who was laughing softly in relief, hysteria or both. He had been brilliant in the fire; I would not have believed he could get on so famously under such intense circumstances. I returned to his side, leaning over him again, and he rolled slightly glazed eyes back towards my face.

"Can you stand up, Joseph?"

"Can't we just—lie here a bit longer?"

"No. Gideon is not well. He needs a doctor right away. We are none the better, and we will soon lose the remaining day."

Joseph seemed to remember Gideon then and sat up abruptly, groaning and clutching his head when he did. "I must say, Mrs Darby, I have not experienced such frequent pain and discomfort in all my life before I made your acquaintance."

"You are not singular in expressing such sentiments, Dr Ramsey. There is no time to discuss my ability to bring misery and discomfort to my male acquaintances at the moment, I'm afraid." I swept my gaze over the scorched landscape. "I suppose it is too much to hope that our erstwhile assassins left Mr Tanner's funeral wagon intact and available for an easy escape."

Joseph paused and looked mournfully up at the sky. "Truly, Astrid, this expedition was foolhardy in the extreme."

102

"Whilst I am rarely one to admit my own folly, I am in accord with you on this particular point," I murmured. "Although one can hardly fault me for my lack of foresight in this instance. How was I to anticipate such an attack?"

Joseph sighed, but he nodded grimly. "Yes, that is true. Who do you think they were?"

"I honestly have no idea at this juncture, but it is deeply troubling, isn't it?"

"You have a particular knack for understatement, Astrid." He dropped his head into his hands for a long moment. "What do we do?"

"There are still a few hours of daylight left. Our only option is to begin walking back towards town and hope someone comes upon us and is willing to take pity. " I sighed deeply. "All my belongings were on the funeral wagon. This has not been the best of days, has it?"

Joseph frowned. "No." He glanced over towards Gideon. "We'll have to carry him."

"Yes, so it would appear. He is unwell, but I suspect he merely fainted in all the excitement. He does not seem unduly harmed."

I pushed laboriously to my feet and offered Joseph a hand. He waved me away gently and crawled towards Gideon. He checked his vitals, timing his heartbeat on a handsome, gold wristwatch.

"He does appear to be all right. I cannot say for the smoke inhalation. It is possible he will awaken soon." He signed heavily. "Let us hope it is very soon; we will not make it far on foot if we are forced to carry him all the way."

I nodded grimly. Our current situation was bleak indeed, but there was little time to ponder our misfortune. Hefting Gideon carefully, Joseph and I began the long, slow, impossible journey to town.

The sun was still burning in the sky, and the further we walked from the ruin of the house, the clearer the air became. Joseph and I coughed dryly, painfully. The exertion of carrying the older man would soon take its toll upon us. Had I been a woman of weaker constitution, I might have simply dropped to my knees on the well-worn trail and wept full out, tears of frustration and fear and hopelessness.

I am not a woman of weak constitution, however, and I trudged along, my mind sluggishly replaying our conversation with Gideon Cross. For a moment I had truly believed the entire affair had been an elaborate ruse concocted by the doctor himself and success could be assured if only we could discover exactly where he and his apparatus were hiding.

I had been quite confident we would find him ensconced in some lavish hotel or bawdy house in London or perhaps even a luxurious holiday hidey-hole on the Continent. I had not, at any point since I had been retained by Rake & Gage, suspected there were treacherous persons waiting in the wings to harm Joseph, Gideon or me.

There was only one thing for it, and that was to discard any preconceived theories and ideas I had contrived thus far and assume Cross was indeed either in very grave danger or his pursuers had already caught him up and were in possession of the Eye.

I ignored the irksome and mounting feeling that I was, not for the first time in my long and fruitful career, quite completely and honestly, as they say, in over my head. And I had foolishly dragged the keen but thoroughly inexperienced Dr Joseph Ramsey into the storm with me.

The walk was hard, and we were silent. I was becoming increasingly certain that Joseph was rather put out with me, but I was too distracted by the worrisome possibilities running through my mind. I wondered for the first time if Messrs Cole and Thorne had been aware of the dangers that awaited me on my assignment.

I suspected they had not, not truly, but I did suspect perhaps there had been some prior indication that the task was not quite as straightforward as they had lead me to believe.

I had little time to ponder this particular vein, for, a mere hour into our miserable journey, fortune prevailed upon us. I noticed Joseph had stopped suddenly, and I stumbled, my momentum halted by the weight of the unexpectedly immobile, unconscious doctor draped precariously over my right shoulder.

"Joseph, what--?"

"Astrid, look."

His voice held the same edge of hysterical relief with which he had laughed when he had discovered that he had, in fact, survived the fire. I followed his gaze and, myself, felt slightly hysterical.

In the manner of small miracles, Mr Tanner's funeral landau and sturdy ebony stallion were waiting several metres away.

The stallion, pawing restlessly at the ground and looking almost confused, as if he had not the faintest idea what he should be doing without a switch or reins to guide him, had likely been startled by the first burst of gunfire and fled with the carriage.

Perhaps, in the peculiar way of horses, he had sensed we would return for him and had simply waited, patiently, for further instructions. I wondered briefly if our attackers had either failed to notice the steed or had simply been confident enough that we would be too injured or too permanently incapacitated to find him.

I eventually decided I did not rightly care.

The horse did not acknowledge us as we approached, merely swished his tail and stamped his hooves anxiously, and he seemed to have already forgotten the attack.

Whilst Joseph, grunting, lifted Gideon into the landau's cab, attempting to make him comfortable in the bare, unfit quarter, I gratefully swallowed nearly half a canteen of still cold water that tasted as fresh and clean as a spring morning in Salisbury.

I poured a small dish for the stallion, who gave it a disdainful look before lowering his head and drinking contentedly. When he'd jumped down, wincing slightly, from the cab, I handed the canteen to Joseph. He sighed happily and grinned at me.

"Thank heaven for small miracles," he remarked in a ragged voice.

I smiled. "I had been thinking the precise thing. We're lucky whomever attacked us didn't make short work of it."

"We'd best get on with it. I will drive. You can take a kip, and we can trade off in a few hours." Joseph offered his hand and assisted me onto the driver's perch.

"Are you quite sure? Have you ever driven a carriage before?"

"I daresay I have not. But I am feeling particularly lucky at the moment, and I did watch you all the way here. It seems relatively easy to master. Should I have difficulty, I am sure you will notice, as you will likely be awakened by a sharp swerve or possible crash. You may then take over."

I laughed, and when he sprung lithely up beside me, I hugged him spontaneously, overcome with the same feeling of exhilaration he had described. He chuckled and returned the embrace briefly, gently returning me to my seat and taking the reins.

"I can't believe we made it," I said. "I mean—I have made it through much worse with all extremities soundly attached and merely a bump or bruise to remind me of my tribulations, but...I was sure we were in for it this time."

"Yes," Joseph replied, his own face splitting into a smile and his cheeks flushed pink. "I, too, had little hope we would come out unscathed. Well, we are somewhat scathed, aren't we? But we are still alive, and we are now assured a safe return."

"We'd best get going, then. We should have enough daylight left to make it to town." I leaned back against the cushioned rest.

Joseph snapped the reins and the stallion jolted into startled motion. Joseph was not a brilliant driver, but he was perfectly adequate. He glanced at me when the horse was plodding at a steady trot on the trail towards Cheyenne.

"I take it this isn't the first time you've been in a sticky situation," he remarked, his voice calm. I was impressed by his mettle thus far. I had at least expected an hysterical outburst or a fit of panic, but he had indulged in neither.

"No, not the first time."

"Does this happen all the time?"

I smiled. "No, not all the time. Just relatively often. How are you enjoying your taste of adventure thus far?"

"Well, not very well, now that you mention it. I suppose it takes a little time before one gets used to attempted murder and fire and such."

I considered. "Yes, I suppose it does take a bit of getting used to. You seem to be handling yourself quite well, I must say."

"Why thank you. It seems much more expedient to deal with a sticky situation as best one can, as opposed to losing my head and rendering myself ineffectual." After a moment he asked in a grimmer voice, "Do you think they're still out on the trail?"

"I don't know," I admitted. "They could be. If they are, we'll have to take our chances. I don't know how long we were out after the explosion. They might be pretty far ahead of us."

"Let's hope they are."

"Yes. And let's hope they're satisfied with their day's work. We are in no condition to outrun them or fight them off a second time."

He glanced at me. "Who do you think they were?"

I shook my head. "I have no ideas at this juncture. I don't know what the purpose of the attack was. If they meant to kill us, they did not seem particularly adept. A good assassin would have waited to be sure no one escaped and made certain our transportation had been disabled. They didn't even harm the horse. It's possible they were merely attempting to warn us away from looking for Cross." I hesitated a moment. "Although I find it highly improbable, it may be unrelated; they might have been after Gideon."

He frowned. "Do you really think so?"

"No." I sighed and closed my eyes a moment. "I am almost entirely certain it is connected to your Dr Cross and the Eye. We must return to England at once. Until we have more clues, I cannot form an adequate hypothesis. And I suspect there are no answers to be found here. I am now quite certain your doctor never left England. As to who attacked us...well, we can only assume they will try again should they discover they were unsuccessful. We'll have to keep our heads down and try to get out of the country alive. Once we're back in England, at least we'll have help."

"What help?"

"My associates. At the very least we can get you into hiding and assure your safety whilst my associates and I find out what is going on."

"I am not going into hiding," Joseph exclaimed firmly.

"Joseph, this isn't a game anymore. I don't know what's going on and who is trying to kill us. There could be more to this than we can possibly imagine. We must take every precaution."

"Be that as it may, I refuse to stand down."

"Whomever attacked us is most certainly connected to the man that approached your doctor, and they don't seem especially bothered by whom they have to kill in the course of achieving their ends. And whether it is you, Gideon or me they were after back there—likely all of us—they are dangerous. They will not simply back down."

He did not respond to this, and I suspected his mind had been made up. I conceded to end the argument there, but if it was necessary, one of my burlier associates could convince him to see reason once we returned to Britain.

"Do you think they've already killed Sebastian?" he asked quietly after a long pause.

I shook my head. "I really don't know, Joseph. We don't know why they attacked us. Perhaps someone is simply trying to keep us from getting in the way of their finding him, or perhaps someone is trying to keep us from finding out the truth. Either way, anyone connected to this project is in great danger."

He said no more, and I must have dozed after a time. When next I became aware of my surroundings, Joseph was feeding the horse from a small bag of oats. The sky had begun to darken, but there was likely at least another hour of light left before we would be unable to navigate the prairie without the aid of a lantern.

"We're nearly there," he told me when he noticed I was awake.

"Do you think we'll make it before dark?"

He paused a moment, tilting his head at me. "Usually I'm the one asking you those sorts of questions," he remarked offhandedly. "I should think so. We might have to follow the lights of town for a short time, but we should be all right. I just hope there will be a doctor on duty; Gideon still hasn't awakened. He's not looking good."

"I'll take over from here; you should get some rest."

He nodded and climbed back onto the perch with a sigh. "I always planned to visit America," he told me, his voice sleepy and unconcerned. "Sebastian used to tell me all about New York and the frontier. He always made it sound so foreign and exciting. I really don't think I care much for the New World. It did not meet my expectations."

I chuckled. "I agree; it has not been an ideal holiday location thus far. Perhaps when this is all over, you can visit again."

"I rather think I am satisfied to leave this wretched place behind never to return. Perhaps I'll take holiday in Sweden. If Sebastian is still alive, I am sure he won't begrudge me a few weeks leave after crossing the Atlantic and risking my life chasing after him."

"No, I'm certain he'll be very grateful," I replied quietly, and I glanced at him, smiling slightly when his eyes began to droop and his breathing became deep and steady.

For Joseph's sake, I hoped his doctor was still alive, and even more I hoped I would be able to return Joseph to England in the same condition.

* * *

Our luck held, and we did not encounter anyone on the road back to Cheyenne. We had not seen our attackers, and thus we would be unable to identify them should we meet them in town upon our return. Hence, we concluded it was necessary to make arrangements to leave immediately upon delivering Gideon to Mr Tanner, a handsome tip for his trouble ensuring he would see the still unconscious doctor to the local surgery for immediate treatment. I was not entirely confident that this was the best course of action, for the old undertaker seemed almost disappointed to discover the immobile but quite living body in the back of his carriage.

Our arrival in town the previous night and the subsequent disturbance at Black-Eyed Susan's had not gone unnoticed, and it was unlikely our return would be any less notable. Mr Howell's general store was just closing for the night, but our frantic pounding on the heavy wooden door roused his attention. After several minutes of begging and eventually parting with a large stack of banknotes, we were able to persuade him to sell us his small, cramped delivery carriage and an old but strong mare that had seen better days.

It was impossible to travel far by night, and we steered the carriage a little ways off the new road to Denver. We spent a worried night in uncomfortable quarters, but so exhausted were we, Joseph made no complaint about the inappropriate conditions. I woke several times in the night, despite my weariness and the aches in my body, but there was no attack upon the little wagon. If our attackers were still in Cheyenne, they had not been alerted to our return and our new means of travel.

We made it to Denver two days later, travel-worn and weary, and in desperate need of a long, hot bath. Though we had passed several other coaches on the road to Denver, none of them paid us any heed. With our supplies, I had purchased a wide-brimmed, lace-trimmed hat for myself and a red kerchief for Joseph, which served well enough to conceal our identities should anyone merely catch a glimpse of us on the road to Colorado. However, anyone intent up our untimely deaths would surely have seen through our spurious disguises should they bother to pay us any mind.

This had not happened, but upon reaching Denver, I put forth another large stack of bills to purchase proper camouflage. After making arrangements for the next train to Chicago, we visited a small clothing and general store, which served not only to outfit us in the clothing of a poor, modest farmer and his plain, unassuming wife, but also to provide us with two hot, tin bathtubs in a small, back room. We bathed side by side, separated by only a thin, white screen without even a token protestation and emerged a half of an hour later, dressed in drab, second-hand clothes and large, unseemly hats that sufficed to hide the most of both our faces.

"Well, aren't you looking lovely, Mrs Darby?" Joseph remarked in a low voice, darting a glance around in case anyone was listening or observing us.

"Don't jest, Dr Ramsey. I am fully aware of just how utterly common I appear."

He chuckled. "I say, Astrid, that is precisely the point."

"Do I look especially dreadful?" I asked mournfully, looking down at the faded brown day dress that might have belonged to the aged, Puritanical wife of a preacher.

"Certainly not. You look quite in character. And I?" He grinned and puffed out his chest, and I eyed the tattered black suit and yellowed white shirt beneath critically.

"Ridiculous," I replied, hooking an arm through his. "Positively provincial."

"Excellent."

We did not discuss the travel arrangements on this train ride, and I suspected Joseph was as keen as I to remain united on the return to Chicago. We did not explore the train or acknowledge our fellow passengers. We proceeded at once to our shared compartment and slept, side by side, until morning.

When I awoke, Joseph was still asleep, curled against the wall with his back to me. I rolled my eyes, but I sat up, peering out the curtained window at the passing landscape. There was little to see but prairie outside the window, and I suspected it would be some time yet before we ventured into the industrialised areas of the United States. I sighed and rose, keeping an eye on Joseph as I quickly dressed. I was examining the pale, yellow dress I wore with extreme distaste when he stirred and rolled over to face me, opening his eyes.

"Astrid, that dress is hideous."

I sighed heavily and flicked the skirt from my fingers with a grimace. "Yes, it is, isn't it? Well, no matter. When we've finally gotten out of this god-forsaken country, there will be silk and lace and frilly things for all."

"I think perhaps I'll pass on the lace and frilly things, but I will be quite content to enjoy the comforts of London and civilisation."

"Just so. Get dressed. I've a need for a strong cup of black coffee and some toast."

He twirled his finger in the air, and I rolled my eyes, spinning my back to him and crossing my arms over my chest, tapping a foot encased in inelegant, plain brown boots. Not even a buckle or a lace, I lamented, dropping my head and extending my foot to examine the offending footwear.

"Right," Joseph said behind me. "Let's go."

I turned back to face him and grinned. Though the tan shirt and well-worn brown trousers were not in themselves objectionable, Joseph had placed upon his head a ridiculous, wide-brimmed wrangler hat atop a tightly knotted red kerchief. He held out his arms to his sides, raising his eyebrows. "Well, at least no one will pay you any mind around here," I told him, pressing my lips tightly together to keep from giggling. "These Americans. Such silly clothing they wear."

"The same could be said of the East Enders," Joseph remarked, taking my arm and guiding me out of the compartment. In the dining car, we ordered black coffee and buttered toast with marmalade, and I closed my eyes in contentment. I barely yearned for my preferred tea, so satisfying was the first hot cup of coffee since we had left the burnt remains of Gideon's cabin.

"What will we do when we reach Chicago?" Joseph asked in a quiet voice. "Do you think someone will be watching for us?"

"It's possible. I am not sure if anyone in Cheyenne took notice of our return. If our attackers had any men stationed there to be on the watch for us, it is likely they have realised Gideon made it to the surgery, and they can rightly assume we, too, made it out with our lives. They might be anticipating that we will take a flight to New York and back to London."

Joseph considered a moment, and I frowned, my eyes drifting over his shoulder as a man strolled casually into the dining car, a brown rucksack tucked under his arm. The tall man, his blonde hair combed smartly back from his face, was instantly familiar, and I remembered his distinct Welsh accent as he had politely requested Joseph's discarded newspaper...and his brief salute outside the post office in Cheyenne as Joseph and I had transacted with Mr Tanner for the use of the garish funeral landau.

His eyes, pale and untroubled, met mine over Joseph's unsuspecting shoulder, and I froze as something suddenly clicked in my mind. He seemed to have recognised me at the same moment, and his own eyes widened.

"Oh, blimey," I muttered, and Joseph sat up straighter, seeming to recognise the urgency in my voice. The Welshman was moving quickly towards us, and I jumped to my feet, catching Joseph's arm as I did. "We have to go now!"

"What?" But he did not argue or resist as I dragged him away from the blonde man who was momentarily obstructed by the waitress that had approached him, smiling. He shoved her aside, and she shouted indignantly at him, but we were already racing through the aisles, hurrying from compartment to compartment towards the back of the train. "What exactly do you intend to do here?" Joseph growled.

"Only one thing for it." I tossed a desperate glance over my shoulder. The Welshman was one compartment behind us, but they were not particularly long compartments, and the passengers beginning to stir and move towards the dining car for the morning meal barely slowed him up. He pushed past them without a second glance or a by-your-leave, and they called insults and admonitions to his back.

As I'd anticipated, we emerged onto a small, railed-in platform upon which a keen passenger could observe the passing of the land and experience the rushing of wind and fresh air without fear of tumbling onto the tracks. Tumbling onto the tracks was not precisely what I intended, but it was close enough. I quickly unlatched a small gate and threw it open.

"What the bloody hell?!" Joseph growled, and he looked back towards the train. Our pursuer was mere steps from us, and I wondered why he did not fire upon us. I supposed an awakening passenger train was not the ideal venue for a spirited shoot-out, even in the American frontier. I did not waste precious time wondering precisely what he intended to do with us once he had caught us up.

"Jump!"

"What?"

"We have to jump! Now!"

"What? Off the train?"

"Yes!"

"But we'll—" He glanced back over his shoulder. "Can't you just shoot him?"

"I am an adventurer, not a murder! Don't forget to roll!"

I seized his arm and leapt, dragging him with me off the back of the train into the stiff prairie grass that stretched out across the barren land as far as the eye could see. I hit the flat, hard ground with a grunt and heard Joseph land beside me, cursing vehemently until the wind was knocked out of him and he lay gasping. Bullets whizzed above our heads, but the tall grass, rustling in the wind like the waves of an ocean, obscured us from the Welshman's view. I waited a few breathless moments, but he did not follow our lead and leap from the train. I began to lift my head, to ascertain the distance of the train and our erstwhile antagonist, but I felt Joseph grab my shoulder, pushing me back down.

"Stay down," he gasped. We lay for several minutes, panting, and when the sound of the train streaking across the well-oiled track had finally died away, he sat up. "It's gone. He didn't follow us. Damnit, what the hell are we supposed to do now, Astrid?"

I sighed heavily, sitting up and dropping my head into my hands. I was infinitely grateful that we had, as if in a moment of mutual, unspoken foresight, carried our luggage with us to the dining car. I had experienced a number of adventures in which I had lost everything I'd carried, and it was inconvenient at best. This adventure was, however, shaping up to be as inconvenient as any other, valise in hand or not.

"I have no idea," I replied, looking dismally around at the endless plains.

"We are in the middle of nowhere," Joseph complained.

"Would you prefer we'd stayed on the train?"

"No. How did you know he was one of them?"

"I remembered him from the train to Denver. I saw him again at the post office whilst we were speaking to Mr Tanner." I shook my head. "He seemed such a nice gentleman."

"Yes, well, don't murderers often seem perfectly nice before they slit your throats?"

"The good ones do." I pushed to my feet. "Are you all right?"

"No, not really, but I'm still alive. Nothing broken. Just bruised."

"Start walking, then."

"What?"

"What else can we do? Perhaps another train will pass by and we can jump on. We'll stick close to the track."

"Are you mad?"

"Joseph, you just jumped off a train. Do you suspect jumping on will be any more dangerous? Transients and hijackers do it all the time."

"I am beginning to seriously regret becoming involved with you."

I smiled at him askance. "Are you?"

He sighed deeply. "No. This is the most excitement I've had in my entire life."

113

We walked, weary and aching, for what seemed like hours, travelling abreast of the track towards Chicago. The wind was light, and the weather was pleasant, warm, breezy and comfortable. No trains passed us, however, and we trudged silently, side by side. Afternoon ascended, and, as if as one, Joseph and I looked at each other.

"Perhaps we need a break," I murmured unhappily, dropping onto the ground to dig through my valise for a hunk of dry bread and a canteen of water.

"How long do you think it will take to get to Chicago on foot?" Joseph asked in a low, hopeless voice as he joined me in the grass for an afternoon snack.

I shook my head. "I don't know."

He met my gaze. "We probably won't make it."

"Don't be silly. We only need to make it to the nearest town. If there's no train station we can hire a hansom cab. We'll probably find something soon."

"We have no idea where we are."

"No...we don't. But this is America. I mean, it's the new frontier, isn't it? People are setting up farms and camps from the Atlantic to the Pacific these days. We can't be that far from civilisation." I reached towards him and grasped his hand. "We'll be fine, Joseph."

"As long as our food and water doesn't run out," he muttered darkly.

"Don't be such a pessimist. We've plenty of provisions to last us a couple days if we are sparing."

He didn't reply to this, but he did not complain further as we resumed our desolate, unpromising journey. It was nearing dusk, and the sun had begun to descend at our backs, casting red, orange, pink and purple hues across the sky.

"It is rather pretty, isn't it?" Joseph asked quietly, and we paused to watch the slow movement of the sun, sighing softly at the unexpected beauty piercing the misery of our predicament.

The sunset, in all its fiery, blazing beauty, was not the only thing emblazoned on the horizon when we turned towards the west. Out of the flames of the early evening sky, a large, white, covered wagon appeared over a small rise, moving steadily towards us. I felt Joseph clutch my hand; in shock, hope or fear, I knew not, but I returned the pressure on his hand, waiting breathlessly for the carriage to near us.

The driver was a slim, middle-aged man in a faded, tan suit that looked as if it had been of high quality when it had first been purchased but had since seen better days. He wore a dark green bowler hat and round spectacles, and he squinted at us as he came closer, as if startled to see us standing there, holding hands and watching him approach with awe and desperation on our faces.

He slowed his horses to a stop as he drew up beside us, and a woman with a plain, lined face that looked both curious and kind, her hair tucked under a wide, strikingly white bonnet, poked her head out of the canvas flap behind the driver's perch. "Gregory?" she asked, and her eyes lighted upon us. "Oh, hello."

"What are you folks doing walking out here in the middle of nowhere?" the man called Gregory asked in an interested voice, leaning towards us and squinting, as if this might help him understand.

"It's not by choice, I assure you," Joseph told him wearily. "We were unavoidably obliged to leap from a train several kilometres back."

"Leap from a train?" Gregory repeated, aghast.

"We are adventurers, you see, sir, and we came upon some trouble," I told him, smiling broadly.

"Where are you headed?" the woman asked, her eyebrows raised.

"The nearest airship port," Joseph replied. "We need to return to London at once."

"London? That's quite far, isn't it?"

"Yes, indeed quite."

"We're heading to Des Moines ourselves," Gregory told us, smiling kindly.

"Can we trouble you for passage?" I asked, keeping my voice appropriately demure and desperate. "We haven't seen another person for miles, and we're not sure we can make it to the next town like this."

"No," Gregory mused. "I can't expect as you can. It's about ten miles, give or take, to the nearest settlement."

"We can pay you most handsomely, and we won't be a burden; we have our own provisions," I told him earnestly.

Gregory and the woman in the bonnet shared a glance, and the woman nodded. "You seem like decent folks," Gregory said, smiling. "All right, hop on in. My name's Gregory Bloom, and this is my wife Tessie. We're travelling to visit our daughter in Des Moines. She's just married a wealthy farmer, you see."

"I'm Joseph Ramsey," Joseph told him, assisting me up into the back of the canvas-covered wagon. "And this is...my wife, Astrid."

Tessie was eyeing us expectantly, and thus I added, "We came to America looking for an acquaintance of ours. He left town unexpectedly a few days ago, and he has family in Cheyenne."

"Did you find him?" Tessie asked. Her face, though not especially pretty, was pleasant, and she had a distinctly gentle, motherly attitude that was both trusting and honest.

"I am afraid we did not."

"We're pleased to meet you both," Gregory called through the opened flap from the driver's perch. "I'd like to hear how you two ended up jumping a train and being stranded on foot in the middle of the prairie, but you look like death. You should take a sleep. There's a bit of time left before we lose the light, and we should be in the next town before nightfall."

"Thank you so much," I murmured, already feeling the weariness in my bones and muscles as Tessie laid out a makeshift bed of thick quilts and goose down pillows for Joseph and me. We settled upon them without delay and were asleep, exhausted and aching, before our heads hit the pillows.

CHAPTER EIGHT

"Here we are," Gregory announced jovially, and I stirred as the carriage hitched to a stop. "Nebraska City, Nebraska."

"Nebraska?" Joseph murmured sleepily beside me and sat up.

"Yes, sir. We'll bunk down for the night then set off for Iowa first thing in the morning," Gregory replied happily. "Will you folks be joining us?"

I sat up to find Tessie still napping peacefully, curled up against the canvas wall of the wagon. I felt instantly guilty; with Joseph and I stretched out across the floor, the poor woman had had no room herself to settle comfortably.

"Is there a train station in Nebraska City?" I asked, glancing at Joseph.

"Sure is. You might still be able to catch one tonight, if that's what you'll be wanting."

"Yes, that will be most convenient. We truly appreciate you taking us this far."

"Go on and shake Tessie," Gregory said in lieu of reply. "She sleeps like the dead, I tell you. She'll be up all night at this rate."

Joseph looked appalled, and I chuckled, reaching over to gently shake the older woman's shoulder. "Tessie?"

She snorted and jerked in her sleep, opening her eyes and staring at me in silent shock for a moment. I smiled at her, and she relaxed, blinking bleary eyes. "Are we there already?" she asked in a thick voice.

"Time to get up, Tessie," Gregory confirmed. "We'll be saying farewell to our young passengers. They'll be catching a train to Chicago, I reckon."

Joseph and I exchanged another look, but we nodded and climbed out of the wagon, stretching painfully and assisting Tessie out. Joseph helped Gregory unload their night time luggage, and Gregory directed us to the train station, a mere ten minute walk along the main thoroughfare. We shook hands with Gregory, and Tessie hugged us both in a matronly fashion. They refused to accept payment for the ride, despite my insistence, and we parted with fond farewells and well wishes.

When they had disappeared inside the loud, boisterous saloon in which they would spend their night, I turned to Joseph. "Let's head to the train station. Perhaps we'll be able to catch the last train."

"Are we heading to Chicago?" he asked sceptically, but he fell into step beside me.

I considered. "They will expect us to head there, whoever they are. It was on the train from Chicago when we first met our mysterious assassin."

"So what do you plan to do?"

"I'm not yet sure."

He sighed, but he didn't question me further, and when we reached the train station, it was to find it unusually crowded for such a late hour. I guided him to the ticket counter where a young, tired-looking man in a brown uniform slouched forward in his seat, clearly ready to see an end to this particular day. I was in whole-hearted accord.

"Pardon me, sir," I said politely, and he started, sitting straight up as if he'd been gently dozing.

"Ma'am?"

"Where is the nearest airship port, if you please?"

"Chicago."

"The nearest airship port that is not Chicago."

The young man considered a moment, frowning and peering at something on the wall behind him. "Got one in...Springfield."

"And do you have a train that leaves for Springfield this evening?"

"Uhh, yep, but you better hurry. It leaves in ten minutes. That's it there." He extended a long finger towards the train behind us where a man in a conductor's uniform was shouting a final boarding call into his cupped hands. "Hold the train, Ernie!" the young man shouted back to him, drawing his attention. "We've got two more for you."

Ernie looked momentarily sour, but he nodded, and I passed the young man a stack of bank notes. "Thank you kindly, sir."

I caught Joseph's hand, and we moved as quickly towards the train as our lately much-abused limbs could carry us. As before, we had opted to share a compartment, and we closed ourselves inside without hesitation. Joseph peered out the small window at the passing landscape as the train began to pick up speed, whistling shrilly as it pulled out of the station and into the night.

"Well," Joseph remarked wryly. "At least if we have to jump off this train we probably won't be stuck in the middle of nowhere"

"Lucky the Blooms came upon us," I agreed, dropping onto the thin mattress.

"What exactly is your plan here?"

"We'll get off in Springfield and take the next airship to Philadelphia. They can't have figured out where we've gone; we'll probably be able to lose anyone who is after us with the misdirection."

He sighed and turned to face me. "I could use a drink."

I chuckled. "Are you sure? You remember what happened the last time."

"Indeed, but I intend to drink myself into such a state as to completely forget the events of the last few days, however temporarily, and sleep until I am both cured of any ill effects of the over-indulgence and we have made it safely to our next stop."

I laughed, and he smiled weakly. "Dr Ramsey, that sounds like a brilliant idea. I am in absolute accord."

* * *

The train ride to Springfield was mercifully quiet and uneventful. Joseph and I took our meals in our compartment as often as we were able to coerce the nice, young Irish waitress to deliver them. No one paid any particular attention to Joseph and me, and our disguises seemed to render us unworthy of scrutiny or second thought. We were perfectly content to accept this otherwise nettling circumstance, and we undertook the ride in general ease.

Joseph seemed more subdued on this ride than any of the last, and I suspected that he would need a bit of time to cope with the events of the last several days, now that he had the opportunity to sit and ponder them. I did not attempt to persuade him to talk about what was happening in his mind; if he felt the need to discuss his feelings or thoughts, he would do so. I was not particularly adept at consolation and sensitivity, besides, and I was perfectly satisfied to remain solemn and silent as he.

We reached Springfield in only a couple days and immediately boarded an airship to Philadelphia. Though we had been careful to conceal our identities and did not tarry in town, pausing only to gather enough provisions to last the remaining hours in the air, this was unnecessary. As I had predicted, there was no one awaiting us in Springfield. We were of no more concern than a common farmer or tradesman and his plain, unremarkable wife.

Seated in the corner of the zeppelin, facing a clear, blue sky, Joseph spoke for the first time in several hours. "I think perhaps something dreadful has happened to Sebastian and someone doesn't want us finding out what that is."

I nodded, leaning back against the padded bench. I had come to this conclusion almost immediately upon leaving Gideon's ruined home, but I did not mention this. "I think you are very probably right."

"Furthermore, I don't think Phineas has anything to do with it," he said slowly, as if hesitant to speak the words.

This surprised me, and I turned my head towards him, raising my eyebrows. "No? You were certain he was involved somehow."

"He is a thief and a fraud, but he doesn't have the resources to execute this level of subterfuge. If he is involved somehow, I do not believe him responsible for what happened at Gideon's cabin." He sighed heavily. "I find that deeply troubling. If not Phineas, then who? Who is so intent to cover up whatever they have done that they are willing to kill three innocent people?"

"I do not know, Joseph, and I, too, am deeply troubled. I do hope Xander's all right," I murmured softly, voicing the dread that had been darkening my thoughts since we'd left Wyoming. "I left him alone to keep an eye on Phineas. He is dead clever, though. He'll survive."

Joseph smiled and slid an arm around my shoulders, drawing me against his side. I sighed and leaned my head upon his shoulder. "So will we," he promised in a low voice. "We're rather clever ourselves, and we have made it this far." He was quiet a long moment, and I closed my eyes wearily, enjoying the steady warmth and comfort of him. At length he asked, "What will we do when we get back to England?"

I opened my eyes and frowned slightly, disappointed the contented moment had passed so quickly. "I have at friend at the Ministry of Defence. Agent Key. I gave my word I would not alert the authorities to what has transpired, but I think attempted murder voids the confidentiality agreement."

We took it in turns to sleep, keeping watch with Nathaniel's pistol in case of any attacks. Surely Joseph realised, as did I, that such measures were superfluous, as it was unlikely anyone wishing us harm would strike on an airborne vessel. Just the same, I was awake and alert, eyeing anyone who moved or neared us with a suspicious eye, when we landed in Philadelphia. I shook Joseph gently awake, and he sat upright, resettling his glasses and meeting my gaze.

"We're here," I told him unnecessarily. We peered at each other a moment then disembarked, our eyes darting in all directions for anyone who would pay us any particular attention. There were none, and I was fairly certain our Welsh antagonist and his comrades had not anticipated our redirection.

We boarded a flight to Bath, certain someone would be waiting for us the moment we alighted in London. If they were resourceful, I noted uncomfortably, and I could safely assume that they were, they would likely have agents waiting at every airship port from England to Northern Ireland. In Bath, however, I was confident I possessed the upper hand. The zeppelin was already crammed with passengers when we boarded, but no one paid us the slightest heed, and we sat quietly in a congested corner, blending into the crowd and relying upon the teeming numbers to conceal us from notice.

We could not freely discuss our plan further in these close quarters, but we were at least protected by the strength of numbers; if our assassins had managed to locate us, it was unlikely they would open fire on a crowded airship several thousand kilometres over the Atlantic Ocean. Joseph did not sleep on this last leg of our journey. Instead, he sat close by my side, reading the scientific journal he had purchased at an airship port newsstand whilst we'd waited to depart for Britain.

I stared, unseeing, out the window, pondering the situation and revisiting our plan. I was no closer to determining the identity of our assailants or who had sent them, and extreme exhaustion and a much-abused body were of no help sharpening my mind at this crucial juncture. I clutched reflexively at Joseph's hand on the bench beside me, Xander's handsome, youthful face swimming into my mind and, with it, a shiver of dread and fear.

I felt Joseph respond, clenching his fingers around mine. His presence beside me was soothing and solid and steady, and I was grateful for him. He seemed more on edge than me, having no experience in the area of outrunning murderous strangers, but he was remarkably well-matched to it and held his composure admirably.

Finally, giving into the exhaustion and the fears obscuring my rational thoughts and preventing me from coming closer to solving this mystery, I leaned into Joseph's side. I rested my head on his shoulder, drawing comfort from the arm he draped over my shoulders and the soft, chaste kiss he laid on the top of my head, and fell into an uneasy sleep.

* * *

Joseph roused me just as the airship was descending. His green eyes were alert and determined, and though he said nothing, I knew he was anticipating having to run the moment we'd landed. I sat straight up, checking my valise for the gun. Joseph nudged me gently and lifted his right arm so I could see the grip under his jacket. I nodded, a small smile on my lips. In this instance, I voiced no protestation or insistence upon my ability to mind myself.

"Where will we go, Astrid?" he whispered under the din of our fellow passengers, who'd begun to stir when they had felt the shift in altitude. "We can't go to our homes; they'll be waiting for us."

"I know. I need to contact Xander, make sure he is all right and find out what he has uncovered, if anything."

"How?"

"We can't telegram; it will be too dangerous. It could be intercepted, and he probably isn't even at home to receive it." I turned earnest eyes on him. "I have a plan. You will need to get to the Ministry of Defence and explain what has happened. They will place you under their protection. Ask for Agent Asher Key. He will help."

"Absolutely not," he hissed. "There is no way I am leaving you to do this alone."

"I will not be alone. As I said, I have a plan. We are still being followed, and this is my chosen occupation, not yours. You are safer in the hands of the Ministry."

"I don't care. I am not leaving your side until we are both safe. Besides, how do you propose I make it to the Ministry of Defence on my own with any number of assassins chasing me?"

I sighed. "A fair point. All right, you will have to accompany me."

"What exactly is this plan?"

"I have a friend. He can help us. He lives in Bath."

"Anything you're leaving out?"

"I don't want to talk about it here; it might not be safe. Just trust me."

He sighed, but he did not argue. The zeppelin landed softly, and the crowd around us began to move as one towards the exit. Joseph stood, assisting me to my feet and keeping tight hold of my hand.

"Where is this friend?" Joseph asked softly.

"Close." I took a deep breath, and we disembarked, remaining in the centre of the throng, hoping the crowd would provide us a bit of time. "They'll be waiting for us."

"I know."

"We'll have to run."

"I think I'm growing quite accustomed to running in your presence, Mrs Darby."

When we stepped off the ship, we instantly spotted the four men in ill-fitting suits pacing almost idly outside the platform. They looked as if they were waiting for someone they suspected might never appear and were growing increasingly frustrated with the unrewarding task.

"There," I said softly, catching Joseph's hand.

"I see them."

They spotted us in nearly the same instant, looking startled only for a moment before they were in motion, shouting instructions to each other and reaching into their jackets. "Not exactly a clandestine operation, is it? Run!"

"Where?"

I caught his hand, and together we raced through the teeming crowd, shoving aside the disgruntled travellers as we attempted to reach the street. "Just follow me!"

Our pursuers did not fire upon the crowd, but nor did the masses hide us for long. We emerged onto the street, and I heard the mysterious foot soldiers shout as I yanked on Joseph's hand, directing him to take a sharp, left turn. The men's heavy footsteps pounded behind us, but they were still jostled by the angry crowd. We ducked into an alley before they had reached the street. Joseph threw a look over his shoulder. "They are almost upon us, Astrid!"

A bullet whizzed past us, striking the stone wall of the alley behind us, and Joseph cursed. "Don't fret, Joseph, I have a plan."

I swerved abruptly, darting into a narrow opening in the alley beside the entrance to a seedy, dimly lit tavern already bustling with professional ladies and their clientele. This alley wound sharply right, then left through a labyrinth of dilapidated flats and tenement buildings. I led Joseph up the rickety, winding stairs of an oft-used fire escape. I could hear the pounding footfalls of the men behind us, though they had yet to wind their way through the confusion of the afternoon mothers shouting orders to their children and the washer women hanging their linens to dry in the sun.

I stopped several stories up the crumbling tenement and threw my shoulder against a rotting wooden door. We burst into a dim, smoky flat. It smelled of old pipe tobacco and peppermints, and I slammed the door breathlessly behind us.

A stocky, middle-aged man emerged from the tiny kitchen in alarm. He held a still burning pipe, and a tendril of smoke drifted gently into the air, slightly obscuring his rough-hewn face and scruffy, over-long, sandy blonde hair.

"Astrid!" Morgan Reinhart, my frequent associate and long-time friend exclaimed. "What are you doing here?"

"We're being followed, Morgan," I told him calmly, though my pounding heart belied my urgency.

"And what have you done this time?" Morgan grinned broadly, tamping out his pipe hastily and beckoning us to follow him. "Who is your friend? Where's the kid?" he continued cavalierly as he led us quickly out of the flat and down a long, winding flight of stairs.

"This is Dr Joseph Ramsey. There's no time to explain now. We have to get to the meeting place," I scolded.

"Right." Morgan shouldered open a heavy, steel door and led us into a dank, dripping, unfinished basement. He gestured expansively and yanked open another similar door on the opposite side of the room. It opened into a long, dark, steel tunnel resembling the one leading to the laboratories in Rake & Gage. I clutched desperately at Joseph's hand, ignoring the tightening in my chest and the sudden discomfort; I was grateful for the escape route, despite my instinctive reaction.

"What is this place?" Joseph asked in awe, looking around at the patched steel walls and ceiling.

"Shh." Morgan hissed, scooping up a small lantern from the floor and securing the door behind us. "We're not far from the surface. If they are still running about, they might hear us down here."

The tunnel opened into what appeared to have once been a sewer, and a distinctly sour scent hung in the air, though the passageways had long since been disused in their original capacity. Joseph wrinkled his nose in distaste, but I took a deep, grateful, albeit unpleasant breath.

"This way, doctor," Morgan said brightly, sweeping his arm towards a grimy metal ladder leading back onto the street.

Joseph glanced at me, but he did not argue with Reinhart. He climbed the ladder quickly, and we followed, emerging into a small, dark and slightly musty room. Morgan brushed past us, opening another door. The light was almost blinding compared to the dark of the tunnels, and we blinked a moment before realising we had entered a small, freshly polished kitchen. I sucked in a deep lungful of the clean air, and Joseph peered at me in concern.

"Are you quite all right, Astrid?"

"Fine, thanks."

"Doesn't like the dark, closed spaces, does she?" Reinhart remarked casually, already moving towards another door.

I glared at my associate; I had not realised Mr Reinhart was aware of that particular quirk. I waved a hand at Joseph impatiently.

"Where are we?" Joseph asked, delicately changing the subject.

"The Penny Gaff," Reinhart replied.

"What? A brothel?"

I raised my eyebrows at him. "You are familiar with this particular establishment?"

He scowled at me. "Sebastian was familiar with most establishments of this nature. He was especially fond of this one. What exactly are we doing here?"

"Don't worry, doctor," Reinhart put in. "This is a safe place."

"We seem to have found ourselves in an unusual number of brothels since we began this excursion, Mrs Darby," Joseph said dryly.

"It happens a lot more often than you'd think," I replied blithely, and we followed Reinhart through a long, narrow corridor panelled in elegant mahogany.

"May I ask why, exactly, you have an escape route through the sewers into a bawdy house?" Joseph asked in such a mild tone of voice, I glanced at him, concerned he had finally reached his breaking point and descended into the throes of complete apathy.

As I met his malachite gaze, however, I noticed he looked amused rather than mentally weary, and I raised my chin. "Well, I don't have an escape route into a bawdy house, do I? It belongs to Mr Reinhart."

Joseph turned to Reinhart, his brows raised. "Mr Reinhart?"

"Well, useful, isn't it?" Reinhart grunted, pausing before a closed door at the end of the corridor. He knocked, perhaps more loudly than strictly necessary, and a soft, feminine voice bid us enter.

"Morgan's dead paranoid," I added in an undertone, and Reinhart shot me an ominous glance, though he did not attempt to argue.

The office was elegantly appointed, decorated tastefully in rich scarlet brocades and polished mahogany, and it was sweetly scented, delicately feminine. The Penny Gaff had once been the home of a wealthy earl, long since passed. The Abbess, possessing a cunning avarice in the area of business and an even greater talent in anticipating the desires and needs of the discerning gentleman, had acquired the property in a marvellously executed coup involving the city property clerk, a clergyman and several solicitors, who, as last I'd heard, remained steadfast and well-favoured customers.

The Abbess, a tall, slender woman with dark auburn hair, dressed in a deep blue day dress, stood as we entered the office, a smile on her crimson, bow-shaped mouth. Her large, pale blue eyes sparkled merrily; she was still quite beautiful, despite her advancing age, and I nudged Joseph gently as he paused beside me with a slightly dazed expression.

"Ah. Astrid. Morgan. What a pleasant surprise." She gestured grandly towards the velvet cushioned, wing-backed chairs spread about the office. We did not sit, however. She moved around the desk so gracefully, she might have been floating, her long, sapphire blue skirts swirling gently around her. "Might I presume you are in a spot of trouble?"

Reinhart turned to me expectantly, long since accustomed to the Abbess' charms, and I grinned. "Just a bit. No more than usual, I assure you."

"I see. And who is trying to kill you this time?"

"Well, we're not sure, actually," I replied, but in this room, with my associate and long-time friend by my side, this lack of knowledge seemed less worrisome, less urgent. Perhaps it was the warmth of the room or the gentleness in the Abbess' smile, but I suddenly felt calmer, more in control of the desperate situation.

"Ah." She turned her gaze to Joseph. "And who is your handsome friend, Astrid?"

Joseph flushed slightly. "Dr Joseph Ramsey, this is Delphia Simms, proprietress of the Penny Gaff."

"How—how do you do?" Joseph said in a husky voice, clearing his throat

126

nervously. I rolled my eyes at him.

"Oh, very well, thank you," Delphia purred, placing her hand in his and bending in the sort of charming, elegant courtesy I was quite certain I could never execute without utterly abandoning my dignity. "But you, my dear, look very much the worse for wear. How did our Astrid entangle you in one of her messes?"

"He insisted, I assure you. It was entirely out of my control," I replied indignantly. "He entangled himself most effectively without my assistance."

"Is that so?" Delphia turned sparkling eyes on Joseph.

"I am beginning to believe I have made a grievous error in judgment," Joseph added, though a small smile played across his face. I shot him a good-natured glare all the same.

"Beginning?" Delphia laughed gaily and moved past us, beckoning us towards the door. "Come this way. I assume you will require the usual accommodations?"

I nodded, following without awaiting the men. "Indeed. We need a place to lay low until we can determine the whereabouts of my wayward cousin."

"Is he missing?"

"Not as such," I replied uncomfortably.

Delphia did not press me for further information. She led us down the corridor to a small, private room with which I was most contentedly familiar. The draperies were drawn tight over the windows, assuring our complete privacy, and a round, polished wood table dominated the greater part of the small space.

There were no beds or settees, as one would normally expect to find in an establishment of this nature; the Penny Gaff did not exclusively cater to the discerning gentleman. It was also considered, amongst the more select businessmen and surreptitious consortiums of the city, an attractive venue for meetings or discussions of a confidential nature without the threat of discovery or eavesdroppers.

"Someone will be with you shortly." Delphia gestured expansively towards the table. Morgan and I appropriated our preferred seats; we had spent many hours ensconced behind the draperies of the Penny Gaff under a variety of desperate circumstances and were quite at our ease. Joseph, on the other hand, remained standing politely, as if waiting for Delphia to take her own place at the table. Delphia smiled brilliantly at him and swept from the room, pulling the door closed behind her without another word.

"Sit down, Ramsey," Reinhart ordered in a gruff voice.

"Kindly return your eyes to their sockets, doctor," I added mildly, rolling my eyes at him. "We have more pressing concerns to be getting on with."

"Oh, I—right," Joseph stammered, sitting hastily in the nearest seat.

I turned to Reinhart, and the urgency that had been simmering quietly in my belly whilst in Delphia's soothing presence returned full force. "Morgan, I need you to find Xander and bring him here."

Reinhart sighed deeply, shaking his head dolefully. "I had expected as much. The demands upon my superior intelligence today. When did I become a glorified errand boy, Astrid?"

"Please, Morgan," I said in a quiet, pleading voice.

His expression grew sombre, and he nodded. "Where can I find him?"

"I…" I paused, glancing at Joseph grimly. "He has been watching the home of Phineas Cobb."

"The scientist?"

"Yes."

Reinhart raised his eyebrows. "When I return with the boy, I expect an explanation as to what precisely is going on here, Astrid."

"And you shall receive it. Now, however, we have little time. We must find Xander and assure his safety at once."

"I understand." Reinhart stood. "You can rely on me, Astrid. I'll find him." He spun, nodding shortly to Joseph and striding from the room.

Though I was confident Reinhart was more than suited to the task, I sighed worriedly. Joseph reached across the table, squeezing my hand in his. "Do not fret, Astrid. I am certain your Mr Reinhart will return your cousin safely."

Before I was able to respond, the door swung open almost silently. Joseph sat up straighter, as if anticipating Delphia's return, but to his credit, he did not stumble as he rose from his seat. It was not Delphia, however. It was a young, timid-looking girl in a plain, black maid's uniform. Her pale, blonde hair was tucked into a demure bonnet. She bowed deferentially, carrying a tray of refreshments, which she placed on the table, keeping her head down and avoiding our eyes.

"From the Abbess, sir, madam," she said.

"Thank you," Joseph said gently, passing her a handful of coins, but there was an odd glint in his eyes that I had not yet seen on our journey together. The young woman seemed startled, and her eyes widened as they met his.

"Th-thank you kindly, sir," she squeaked and rushed from the room as if he had snapped at her.

I turned to him curiously. "What is the matter, Joseph?"

He scowled. "That girl can't have been more than fifteen."

"Yes." I did not understand his sudden ire. "What troubles you?"

"She is only a child. This is no place for her." His eyes remained on the door, as if he intended to follow the young woman.

I smiled. "Ah. Fear not, doctor. Delphia may be an Abbess, but she is a philanthropist at heart. She often takes in strays from the street. Do not misunderstand," I added when his chest swelled indignantly. "She gives them shelter and employs them as servant girls."

He seemed taken aback by this information, but he relaxed, and I experienced a fleeting sense of jealously. Delphia Simms was, by all accounts, a woman of beauty, poise, elegance and compassion. I did not dwell on this, however, as Joseph swiftly changed the subject.

"Now, if you would kindly explain what exactly is going on, Mrs Darby? Who is Mr Reinhart? How do you know Madam Simms? Why are we hiding out in a brothel, of all places?"

"Well, that's obvious. Who would think to look for a lady of refinement and sophistication in an institution of this nature? Delphia is most kind to offer us sanctuary here when we are in need of a safe place to take refuge for a time." I reached towards the tray the young servant had provided and smiled. "Ah, Delphia has provided well, as always. Brandy?"

Joseph shook his head. "I believe mental incapacitation is ill-advised in light of our present circumstances."

"Suit yourself." I poured a small measure of sweet, dessert sherry and sipped it appreciatively. My nerves seemed immediately soothed, and I sighed contentedly.

"Please do not assume I am ungrateful, but why does your friend, Mr Reinhart, possess a secret passage to a brothel beneath his flat?" Joseph asked, pouring himself a cup of tea.

"Ah." I smiled over the rim of my goblet. "As he stated, it is useful, is it not? Mr Reinhart is a mechanic and an engineer. He is also one of my most valuable associates. We are, after all, adventurers. As you have seen, we often find ourselves in situations requiring a hasty and daring escape. Morgan and my late husband discovered the tunnels several years ago whilst being chased by Spanish thieves from whom they had recovered a legendary cursed locket. They escaped them, only just, by climbing into the sewers. The possibility of such a convenient escape route was simply too great for their inventive minds to let pass. They spent many years constructing the passage. It is quite genius, is it not?"

"I suppose so."

"It has saved our skin more than once. Fleeing from murderous pursuers is not a fresh experience, I'm afraid."

"But why does it open to a brothel?"

"Truly, Joseph, I marvel at the insignificance of the details upon which you focus that brilliant mind of yours. Delphia was one of Nathaniel's dearest childhood friends. We can trust her not to alert anyone to our presence. Moreover, no one thinks twice about a man entering a place like this. I often meet with my associates here." I sighed deeply, my gaze sliding away to peer unseeingly at the lovely, intricate tapestries on the walls. "I do hope my young cousin is all right. We know nothing about our pursuers but that they have a certain keenness to dispose of us in an entirely conspicuous fashion. If Xander is recognised..."

Joseph squeezed my hand gently across the table. "I am certain he is fine. He is an adventurer and taught by the very best. I am sure he, as you, possesses an uncanny ability to stay alive."

I smiled weakly. "I do hope you are not mistaken."

CHAPTER NINE

Joseph and I had grown accustomed to wiling away long periods of time in each other's company over the several days which we had spent on our ill-fated journey, and we passed the following two hours in nearly silent contemplation. The young servant girl had delivered more sherry, tea and a light dinner, which I devoured almost indecently and Joseph pushed around his plate without eating. He appeared weary and listless, as if the waiting was driving him to heights of anxiety even I had yet to achieve. I suspected he felt as I did. The wait proved nigh unbearable as I anticipated my cousin's safe return and the results of his investigation. I could not abandon my fears, and an air of bleakness shrouded our idle repose. It was not the first time I had felt thus, but I loathed the uneasy sensation of helplessness.

I sighed deeply, and Joseph turned his unfocussed gazed towards me, opening his mouth to deliver a comforting murmur. Before he was able to speak, however, the door burst open impolitely, and we turned towards Reinhart, who gestured with a flourish towards a dishevelled Xander as he entered the room.

"Xander!" I exclaimed and rose to embrace him tightly in sheer relief.

Xander seemed startled by my sudden lapse in propriety, but he patting my back gently, smiling awkwardly at the older men. "It's all right, Astrid. I am in perfect health."

I grinned up at him, smoothing my skirt as if to regain my poise. "So you are. And I am most delighted to find you thus. Come, sit. We have much to discuss."

Joseph rose and offered his hand to Xander. "Young Mr Knightly," he greeted warmly. "I have heard much about you. I am pleased to meet you at last and find you wholly unharmed. I am Dr Joseph Ramsey."

Xander appeared slightly awed by Joseph, which startled me slightly until I remembered that Joseph was, in fact, the lone assistant to a man whom Xander deeply admired. "It is an honour to meet you, Dr Ramsey. I am a great enthusiast of your master's work."

"So Mrs Darby has said." Joseph smiled morosely. "Let us pray we find him, as well, in as robust health as Mr Reinhart has found you."

I waved my hand impatiently, eager to learn what had happened whilst Joseph and I were away. "Sit, gentleman," I ordered. "There is brandy and tea for all.

Please, there is little time to waste. Much has happened since we last met."

The men joined me at the table, settling in for what was surely to be a long, dramatic tale in my customary style. I was especially keen to hear Xander's part, however, and I did not linger over the details of our grand adventure or embellish expansively as I would ordinarily have done. Xander's and Reinhart's eyes widened in all the appropriate places, just the same, but I saw a light in Xander's eyes that I recognised instantly. It was the brightness of relished knowledge.

Xander knew something I did not, and I was too impatient to learn precisely what that was to be more than briefly irked by it. I turned my eyes to him, narrowing them suspiciously. "I can see by the twinkle in your mischievous eyes, my dear young cousin, that you have something of great consequence to share. What has happened to you since I left for America?"

Xander sat upright in his seat, taking a deep breath and a sip of tea before he spoke. He paused, as if determining that he possessed our full and undivided attention, and I was gratified by his show of hereditary finesse. "I have been watching Cobb's house, as you instructed. To my great surprise, I found there was a security detail patrolling his house day and night. I had intended to install rudimentary listening devices in his lab and sitting rooms, but it was all I could do to remain hidden. He never left the house, and I was unable to find a way to sneak inside without being discovered."

"Did you notice anything unusual?" Joseph put in.

"Aside from the security detail?"

"Right. I suppose that is a bit out of the ordinary, even for Phineas."

"Your social call must have shaken him more than we realised," Xander added. "I can only assume he did not have such stringent security measures in place when you approached him."

"Indeed he did not. Please continue, Xander. What did you discover?"

"Nothing at first. He never left his home or received any visitors. Unfortunately, I had no way to determine what was afoot inside. However, two days ago he received a most familiar caller."

When he paused, I raised my eyebrows, gesturing him impatiently to continue. "Who?" I demanded eagerly.

"Mr Edgar Thorne."

"What? Thorne?" I repeated. Beside me, Joseph looked as stunned as I felt.

Xander nodded gravely. "Indeed."

"So Cobb and Thorne are in collusion?" I mused.

"They must be. Sebastian was right," Joseph put in darkly. "Someone inside Rake & Gage was working with Cobb."

"But why didn't they take the sabotaged notes?" I murmured, almost to myself. "It doesn't make any sense."

"Do you think Thorne let Cobb into the lab?" Joseph said, peering at me with a confused expression.

"It is impossible to say," I replied. "Perhaps your doctor arrived at the laboratory to discover the apparatus was missing and fled, realising his suspicions were correct and fearing for his life."

"Or perhaps he came upon Cobb and Thorne in the act of the theft," Reinhart mused.

Joseph's eyes snapped to him in alarm. "We mustn't think so just now, Morgan," I interjected quickly. "We lack certain vital information." I returned my attention to my young cousin, dismissing the question presently for more pressing topics. "Did Thorne recognise you, Xander?"

"He must have done. Yesterday a man approached me while I was sitting in the park across from Cobb's house. He showed me a badge and ordered me to accompany him. Well, I knew the badge was counterfeit straight away. It was the same as the sort we got on Fleet Street when we were infiltrating the German embassy. You remember?"

I nodded shortly. "What did you do?"

"I went with him; I didn't see as I had much of a choice but to appear acquiescent. When he turned his back, I fled."

"Where did you go?"

"Murdock's, of course," Reinhart put in for him. "Where I found him."

"Ah. Yes, of course. Very clever."

"I have been waiting for you to fetch me ever since," Xander finished.

"Good boy," Reinhart added, clapping Xander on the back appreciatively. "The barmy old codger has more security than Parliament."

"So, we know Thorne and Cobb are in concert. We just don't know exactly how," Joseph said, turning to look expectantly at me. "What do you intend to do now, Astrid?"

I considered a long moment, spinning my long since empty goblet between my fingers, then looked up resolutely. "Xander, go to the Ministry of Defence and find Asher. Tell him what's happened. I am going to visit Cobb again."

"What? Are you mad?" Reinhart demanded. "They knew who you are, and they are looking for you. All of you."

"They will never expect us to call on Cobb again since Xander's escape. Anyway, Del is a master of disguise. She will be able to get us out of here undetected."

"You don't truly believe he will speak to you?" Reinhart added.

"I am quite certain we are still missing most of the pieces of this convoluted puzzle, and I believe Cobb possesses several. I am most adept at persuading even the most stubborn of witnesses to speak when desperation calls upon me to do so. I am confident I will find a way to win him over."

Xander sighed deeply, but he knew better than to argue with me.

"What do you want me to do?" Reinhart asked wearily.

"Stay here." When he opened his mouth to protest, I held up my hand, cutting him off gently. "It might not be safe to return to your flat just yet; surely, whoever our pursuers were, they are still in your neighbourhood. We will need your services yet." He sighed as Xander had, but neither did he raise a complaint. "Send one of Delphia's couriers to contact Murdock—"

"Oh, he's already here," Xander put in.

"You didn't really believe the old busybody would let us come without him, did you?" Reinhart added in a cantankerous voice, but his lips twitched in amusement.

"Right. Jolly good. He'll be most useful. Ask him to find Swan and bring him here, as well."

"Swan?" Xander and Reinhart said together in surprise.

"Are you sure you want to involve Swan in this?" Xander continued. "You remember what happened the last time we brought him along on an adventure. We had to replace half of the library's Astronomy section."

I waved my hand dismissively. "Trifles. My dear cousin, we have already outrun mystery assassins and most likely murderous security guards. I believe we need the muscle."

Xander sighed, but he nodded. "Right."

I stood. "Joseph, you will come with me."

He started as if he had forgotten he was in the room with us. "Really?"

"Of course. Unless you would prefer to stay here? I am sure Delphia can find something to occupy your time."

Joseph blushed and hastily jumped to his feet. "No! No. I am coming with you."

"Ace. Step lively, then."

* * *

Delphia stepped away from me, her blue eyes twinkling in mirth. I narrowed my eyes as she suppressed a giggle. "What, madam, do you find so amusing?" I demanded suspiciously.

My ginger antagonist grinned innocently. "Now, Astrid, you asked me to disguise you. I believe I have accomplished this task most admirably."

"What have you done to me?" I spun towards the mirror in the small, dim dressing room and gasped in repulsion. "Delphia Simms!"

She cackled merrily. "Well, you can be quite certain no one will recognise you."

"I had hoped you would select something a little less conspicuous, Del," I scolded. Reluctantly, I conceded that she was probably quite spot on; I would never be caught dead in such a ghastly ensemble. It was dubious anyone would presume I was a lady of urbanity and panache beneath the red rouge, crimson lipstick and thick, dark eye powder that almost entirely disfigured my features. The dress in which she had squeezed my callipygian figure was garishly green and so tight in the bodice I could scarcely speak without gasping. My unkempt hair was braided tightly and tucked under a long, curly chestnut wig that tumbled across my shoulders and the indecent décolletage of the bodice.

I shuddered dramatically. "I am thoroughly appalled."

"I am sure you are, in fact, most grateful, so I will ignore your discourtesy, Mrs Darby." Delphia smiled amiably and beckoned me towards the door. "I am certain your young, handsome doctor is equally unrecognisable by now. Shall we have a look?"

"I tremble to think what your ladies have done to him," I muttered darkly, but I allowed her to lead me towards another dressing room. From inside I could hear delighted laughter, and I pressed my lips together disapprovingly. "Honestly. What is going on therein to inspire such indecorous glee?"

What, precisely, was causing Joseph Ramsey such indecorous glee, I learned moments later when the door swung open and a portly old gentleman in a pin-stripe suit emerged. His walrus moustache was handsome, large and grey, and he grinned, twirling it lazily around his finger.

I blinked, my mouth dropping open in shock. "Joseph?"

He bowed with exaggerated gallantry. "My dear Mrs Darby, it is indeed I beneath this fetching moustache and wig." The wig to which he referred resembled mine, though it was steely grey, and atop the ridiculous tangle of curls was a tall, black top hat tilted at a jaunty, roguish angle. I grimaced.

"You look absurd, Joseph."

"Oh, don't tell me you do not like it, Mrs Darby. I think I look quite smart. Do you not appreciate the hilarity of our present circumstances?" He spun in a circle and tipped his hat to me. The enormous belly bobbed ludicrously up and down, and I snorted indelicately, conceding a reluctant smile.

"You, Dr Ramsey, resemble a stuffed walrus in a second-rate suit."

Joseph laughed exuberantly and twirled me in a circle that caused me to totter dangerously in Delphia's impractically high-heeled boots. "And you, Mrs Darby, are looking positively scandalous."

Delphia's eyes gleamed. "My dear man, if I excel at anything, it is scandal."

"I do not doubt that for a moment, madam," Joseph replied. "I am beginning to appreciate a little bit of scandal now and again."

"Why, Joseph, it's as if you are a new man under that outrageous getup," I told him petulantly.

"I am exploring my disreputable side, Astrid, and I have you to thank." He grinned, looking thoroughly pleased with himself, and I huffed indignantly.

"Well, if you are quite finished indulging your iniquity, may we please get on with it? We have a tube to catch."

* * *

Joseph's light mood sobered considerably as we rode the Underground towards Cobb's London home. "What exactly is our plan here, Astrid? How do you intend to get inside to talk to him?" he said in a low voice as we disembarked at our destination, glancing around at our fellow travellers.

136

This was an unnecessary precaution; despite my initial doubt regarding the ridiculous costumes in which Delphia and her ladies had clad Joseph and me, they were decidedly successful. While we received several disapproving stares from the city's more sanctimonious residents as we passed, no one seemed overly attentive towards us. A mature gentleman wandering the streets by night with an unsavoury lady friend was as uncommon as a London fog.

I smiled brightly, meeting his gaze. "Not to worry, Joseph. I am sure we will come up with something."

"That does not sound like a very well-contrived plan," he hissed, taking my arm as we emerged onto the twilit streets of London. "What if the security detail is still patrolling the house?"

"Then we shall simply find a means past them. Do not fret; I am highly skilled at subtle subterfuge. We will find a way."

My smile was slightly wan; I was not as confident as I would have Joseph believe. I had yet to devise a suitable method to deceive the guards and ensure our audience with the scientist. However, my instincts were very much insistent that Phineas Cobb possessed the answers we so desperately required, and I was reluctant to give up the plan to seek them.

"I fear I lack your buoyancy, Astrid."

"Do you have a better idea?" I asked in a low tone as a throng of young university students passed, likely on their way home from a night of spirit and debauchery, whistling and shouting uncouth asides which set Joseph's teeth to clench.

He sighed. "No. I can see no other alternative. I am simply concerned that we are once again strolling foolishly into the clutches of unforeseen danger."

I laughed. "That is practically a requisite for any worthy adventure."

We needn't have troubled ourselves with the quandary of Cobb's security detail, however. The street outside Cobb's house was eerily quiet, as if it had been recently unceremoniously abandoned. Joseph and I glanced at each other warily, peering up at the dark, noiseless house. No lamps blazed in the sitting rooms or corridors, and the curtains were drawn tight over the windows, as if the occupants had jealously sealed the house from intruders or passers-by and were hiding out in the dark, breathless and silent.

"Perhaps he is in his laboratory," I suggested dubiously.

"Perhaps. But why has his security left?" Joseph whispered.

I frowned. "Something is deeply amiss." I started determinedly towards the door, but Joseph tugged on my arm, holding me back.

"What are you doing?" he demanded.

I turned to him in exasperation. "I am going to ring the bell, of course."

"You can't just walk up to the front door."

"Why ever not? I see nothing stopping us; do you? Would you prefer we break in through the back? We can do it, you know; I have had some experience."

Joseph exhaled in a low, incensed growl then shrugged in resignation. I did not ring the bell when we reached the scarlet front door. This seemed wholly unnecessary, as it was already slightly ajar, as if someone had lately entered and merely forgotten to latch it behind them. Joseph and I exchanged another grim look, and I bent down to examine the jamb. It was not damaged, as I had expected. In fact, it appeared as if Cobb himself had opened it from the inside to allow his mysterious visitor entry.

"This is most disturbing, Mrs Darby," Joseph whispered.

"Yes, I am in accord, Dr Ramsey. Nothing else for it. Step lively." I glanced at him, and he sighed heavily. Finally, he nodded wearily.

We had not come unprepared for the ambush; Joseph removed Nathaniel's pistol from under his jacket and held it as if readying himself to charge down a cavalry. I smiled appreciatively and slowly pushed open the door.

The elegant vestibule was as we had last seen it, immaculate and handsome in its luxury, but it was dark as a tomb and echoed dismally with our cautious steps. We paused in the enormous parlour, but this, too, was unnecessary. If anyone heard our entry, they were unconcerned with the intrusion. We crept softly through the main floor rooms, checking for signs of life, but our stealth was in vain; no one greeted us. In fact, we heard nary a sound from any corner of the massive home save for the gentle clicking of our shoes.

"The lab?" Joseph murmured, glancing doubtfully at me.

"This way." We moved towards the closed door through which Dr Cobb had led me on our first visit. Though I had been in the house before and was certainly not unaccustomed to sneaking around, my nerves were raw and my heart fluttered in trepidation. "Ready?"

Joseph exhaled heavily, as if he had been holding his breath. "Do I have a choice?"

"Not really." I clenched my fingers around his and whispered, "I really don't want to go down there on my own."

He turned a small, crooked smile on me, and I moved closer, taking a deep breath before approaching the door. The knob turned easily. My disquiet intensified. It was extremely unlikely the treacherous scientist would be labouring in his laboratory without troubling to secure either the front or the laboratory door.

"I am most emphatically uneasy, Astrid," Joseph murmured. I decided I felt quite the same towards the uncanny stillness.

I grunted softly and nudge the door open. It creaked slightly. We froze, breathless. I was not surprised when no admonishment sounded from above or below. "Something's wrong."

"Again, I admire your flair for understatement, but now is truly not the time." His voice was strained, and he blocked my descent, steadying the pistol and preceding me down the stairs. I appreciated his gallantry, but his sudden sharp intake of breath startled me. I shoved past him to see what had elicited his alarm.

Quite contrary to the state in which I had found it during my previous visit, Cobb's lab lay in utter devastation. The shelves and tables were no longer well organised and pristinely polished. Broken glass, unrecognisable rubbish and twisted, melted metal littered the floor, and the distinct scent of burnt chemicals hung in the air. I grimaced.

"This looks somewhat familiar," Joseph muttered grimly.

"Indeed it does." I moved forwards, gingerly picking my way through the detritus. When I reached the centre of the laboratory, I stopped in utter astonishment, calling Joseph's name in a strangled whisper. He was beside me instantly.

"Bloody hell," he swore weakly.

An angry sunburst blackened the concrete floor, and the source of the wreckage was immediately apparent. Joseph squinted at the ground, his green eyes scanning the silt for the remnants of the explosive. My own gaze swept the destroyed room, hoping to discover a clue as to what had occurred. Beyond the scorch mark laid the twisted, charred remains of the scientist's prize invention. The sleek, shining skeleton of the flying machine now resembled the discarded carcass of a large, slow animal picked clean by a faster, deadlier predator.

I cocked my head to the side and felt an odd swooping sensation in my belly. It was terribly tragic, terribly inane and meaningless somehow. I felt strangely hollow, as if I was looking at an appalling joke, the punch line of which I failed to comprehend. I turned away from the heartbreaking sight and gasped, pointing silently towards the wall on our left.

Phineas Cobb sprawled in a crumpled heap against the stark concrete wall. Crimson blood was smeared along the wall above his head, as if his body had been thrown forcefully against it with all the consideration of a petulant child discarding a displeasing toy and had slid to the floor from which it had not moved. I approached the disconcertingly still body tentatively, but Joseph gently brushed me aside, crouching beside his erstwhile nemesis. He glanced up at me, shaking his head morosely, and stood, backing away from the corpse.

The proud, strong scientist that I had met days ago was like a sad, abandoned rag doll in death, broken and diminutive and futile. I turned away from him, and my breath hitched. I felt Joseph's hands on my shoulders. For a moment I leaned back against him, closing my eyes. There was no time for comfort now, however.

I straightened and spun to face him. His face was ashen and dismayed, but there was a new determination in his eyes. "We have to get out of here," he said so calmly, I felt a thrill of admiration. "This has gone too far. I draw the line at assassination attempts and murder."

I nodded and laced my fingers with his. Our ascent was much hastier than our slow, careful descent, but it was not sprightly enough. Having once already failed, I, possessing a shrewd wit and not inconsiderable cleverness, would perhaps have employed an alternative method of attack. Our tenacious foes, however, seemed thoroughly disinclined towards ingenuity.

A sudden, explosive din rent the silence of the house, seeming to shake the ground beneath our feet. We froze in our tracks, meeting each other's wide-eyed gazes in horror.

"No!" Joseph cried, hauling me towards the laboratory door. He, as well as I, was utterly, dreadfully familiar with the sound. We had heard it once before, from within the tiny, wooden cabin belonging to Gideon Cross. It was a sound neither of us was likely to forget. It was the terrifying cacophony of dozens of windows shattering from the outside. "Astrid, hurry!"

If our assassins had not been intent upon our certain death when they had attacked Gideon's modest home, they certainly seemed so now. Thick, noxious, black smoke assaulted us as we burst through the laboratory door into the parlour. My eyes stung horribly, and Joseph dropped to his knees beside me, his momentum dragging me to the floor with him. We crawled towards the direction in which we hoped to find the door, blinded by the stinging, choking smoke.

Heat singed our skin and clothes. I distinctly recognised the scent of burning hair.

If we expected to encounter the front door and an escape from the deadly inferno, we were dreadfully disappointed. We skidded to a halt before a wall of blue, orange and red flame. "Joseph, get up. We have to run. We have to find the back door." But my voice was weak and tired, and my limbs felt sluggish. My head throbbed horrifically, as if one of the incendiary projectiles had struck me. I heard a loud pop and crash at our backs, and I feared the structure splintering and falling around us. My mind churned, flailing desperately for a plan, but I could not think, could not feel anything but the heat and the pain and fear.

For a moment, I thought I heard someone shouting my name, calling urgently to me, but I realised this was fantasy; I heard nothing but the crackle and spitting of the flames as they consumed the handsome, luxurious furniture, walls, draperies and paintings that had once belonged to a sad, broken dead man in the ruined laboratory below. My hand, slick with sweat and soot, slid from Joseph's weakening grip, and I turned towards him. He wasn't moving, wasn't speaking or looking at me. He had collapsed, overwhelmed by the pungent smoke and searing heat.

"No!" I tried to shout, but the word tore at my throat, and no sound escaped my cracked lips. I shook him feebly, but I knew the effort was wasted. Tears streamed from my eyes. I choked out a soft, desolate sob. "Joseph."

His name was a silent, anguished plea, and grief pierced through me. My eyes stung and fluttered. I knew death was not, as I had heard tell, cold and numb and peaceful. It was heart-rending and excruciating and so scorching, the tears evaporated as quickly on my stained cheeks as they fell. With a final racking, shuddering breath, I pitched forward across Joseph's chest and abandoned the battle with the darkness.

CHAPTER TEN

My first impression upon waking was deep, dark red. I whinged piteously, certain I was still peering at the blazing conflagration that had vanquished Joseph. But in the brief, mindless terror of the moment, I realised there was no heat, no pain, and the smoke that had suffocated and torn at my lungs was merely a terrible memory.

The red I perceived was soft, gentle light filtering through my eyelids. I sighed, overwhelmed with relief, but there were no tears. My eyes felt glued shut, and the effort to unseal them terrified my disoriented mind. I tried to raise my hands to touch my face in alarm, suddenly afraid the fire had melted my eyelids shut and permanently blinded me. My hands would not move, and I squirmed desperately, whimpering like a small, frightened animal.

"Ah, awake are we, Astrid?"

I froze. The voice was horribly, startlingly familiar, and my teeth clenched. In the same moment, I understood that my wrists were restrained. I was lying on my back in a soft, warm bed, and I was quite immobilised. I drew a deep breath to calm myself, willing my tense muscles to relax, but my ire was such that every nerve in my body hummed in impotent fury.

"Don't try to move. You've had a rough time of it, but you'll be all right. As usual, I arrived just in the nick of time to save your skin."

This only served to intensify my indignation. I bared my teeth, struggling to open my eyes. I felt fingertips dance gently across my face and tossed my head as if attempting to shake an irksome insect.

"Stop behaving like a child, Astrid. I am just trying to help. Be a good girl now and stay still. I'm going to give you something for the pain."

I felt the sharp, biting tip of a needle against the crook of my arm and finally found my voice. "Don't you dare stick me with that thing, Asher Key!" I rasped and immediately felt him draw back the needle.

He clucked patiently, as if dealing with a young, ill-tempered child. "Now, Astrid, you've just been through a very difficult ordeal. You need to rest."

"Untie me right now, Asher," I ordered in a low, dangerous voice.

"I think not. We can't have you rushing foolishly onto the next adventure before you have a chance to heal." His voice was even and calm and unendurably patronising. I snarled at him, straining against my bonds. "Besides, it isn't every day I have you at a disadvantage, is it? I would hate to yield my position at this so early a juncture in our much anticipated reunion."

"You are an insufferable cad, Asher Key. Free me at once. You'll have to do eventually, and the sooner you do, the less likely you are to be introduced to hitherto un-explored avenues of unbearable pain and suffering."

He laughed delightedly. "You are quite plucky for someone in such a compromising predicament. In case you have forgotten, and I suppose it has been quite some time since last we met—'

"And who is to blame for that?" I snapped.

He continued as if I had not spoken. "I am a highly respected affiliate of the great and powerful Ministry of Defence. I am sure no one will question my keeping a mad, raving woman under lock and key for the protection of society as a whole."

I was in no mood to banter with the intolerable man. "Asher," I whispered, and even I was stunned by the pathetic sound. I winced, disgusted by the pleading note in my voice. I am a woman of strong will and stronger pride. I certainly do not beg colossal arses like Asher Key for mercy. "I am in no fit state to deliver upon your vile person the damage to which I would normally aspire, but if you do not release me this moment, I will use the convening time in which I remain imprisoned to, not only return to my usual robust and vigorous health, but concoct methods of such innovation and creativity with which to torture you, Tartarus itself will be shocked and revolted by the atrocities you will endure."

He was silent for a moment. I felt him vibrate slightly beside me and realised he was shaking with soundless laughter. "Truly, Astrid, I have missed your drollery."

"Pray I am in jest. I believe you deserve a sound thrashing for the manner in which you treated me when last we met."

"I fear I have absolutely no idea to what you might be referring. Perhaps you could refresh my failing memory?"

"You know perfectly well to what I am referring, you prat."

"I daresay I am at an utter loss. What has happened to have hardened you so, Astrid? I suppose a woman in your line of work becomes embittered over time. Perhaps you should take a nice extended holiday."

"I despise you with every fibre of my being," I spat petulantly.

"Now you're being ridiculous. Do you speak thus to the gentleman whom we pulled out of that burning house with you?" His voice had changed. I almost imagined he sounded hurt. Sheer folly, I decided. It had been long since I possessed the capability to wound the intractable Agent Asher Key.

At his words, I instinctively shot upwards. The leather straps binding my wrists and ankles ensured I could do little more than arch awkwardly from the waist. I dropped back down with an outraged growl, but I did not dwell on my quandary. "Is he all right? Is Joseph alive?"

Asher was silent. My heart plummeted. "He's alive," he replied finally. I moaned in relief, and the playful tone in his voice vanished as if I had imagined it. "He's infirm, as well, a few doors down."

"I want to see him."

"Don't be absurd. You can't even open your eyes." He sounded almost cold now. I sighed.

"Am I—am I blind?"

At this, Asher chuckled again. "Of course you aren't." I felt his touch on my cheeks again, and I tensed. "Don't be a fool, Astrid. I have something for your eyes. Stop acting like a squalling infant."

"I do not appreciate your cavalier affronts, Agent Key."

"I do not appreciate your malice, Mrs Darby."

I sighed, but I did not attempt to elude his touch again. His fingers were light as a moth's wing. I felt them pass over my eyelids, as a mourner tenderly brushes the eyes of a lost loved one. Whatever he had applied was cool, like menthol. When he blew softly in my face, it was as if he had spread ice across my lids.

I twitched angrily. "Please avoid doing that again," I growled.

"There is no need to be so shirty. Just a few moments now, and you will once again be granted the considerable pleasure of looking upon my glorious face, at which time you may properly thank me for my daring and timely rescue."

"At which time my aim will improve, though I suspect your head is so outrageously inflated, I could merely aim towards the broad vicinity of the sound of your voice and land a sufficient blow."

His voice sounded disapproving. "These sorts of remarks are not improving your chances of an expedient release from bondage."

I sighed; he did present a valid argument. "All right. Let us propose a truce."

"What sort of truce?"

"If you release me, I will not attempt to cause you unreasonably grievous bodily harm."

He chuckled. "Hardly a mutually beneficial arrangement. As if you possess the necessary faculties to cause me anything more than reasonably grievous bodily harm." He paused a moment, and I envisioned him stroking his roguishly unshaven chin in mock consideration. "No, I believe there is more to be gained in this covenant."

I gritted my teeth. "I am beginning to regret my rash proposition."

"It is much too late to leave off now, my dear." He snapped his fingers centimetres from my face, and I flinched. "I've sussed it. I will release you without further harassment, remark or unadulterated recreation if you agree to offer the gratitude to which I have undisputed right, considering I did save you from certain fiery death." I grunted in displeasure, but I did not make any argument. "And you will tell me why you are so cross with me."

"I will do no such thing! I would prefer to convalesce in silent oppression to the end of my days than engage in such a conversation with you, Asher Key."

He sighed. "It was worth a try, I say. All right. You will tell me exactly what you were doing at Phineas Cobb's house and what in the bleeding hell is going on before I have you, Xander, your motley and disturbing associates and your mysterious partner in crime imprisoned for treason."

"As if you'd dare. And his name is Dr Joseph Ramsey."

"Ramsey? Well, that's dead convenient. We've been looking for him."

"I beg your pardon?"

"First things first, as they say." He leaned over me. I felt his breath stir the fine, loose hairs on my forehead. In moments, my left wrist was free. I tried to rise, twisting to unclasp the right, but I collided with Asher, who still hovered over me.

He chuckled low in his throat, but he leaned back. I waited, seething, for him to release my other hand. When they were both, at gratuitous length, liberated, I raised my hands to my face, gingerly dabbing at the glutinous salve on my lids. "You can open your eyes now."

His voice was soft, almost tender, and a shiver raced down my spine. I loathed that tone; it had been my undoing enough times in our tumultuous past that I had come to regard it as the first indication I would shortly be indulging severe errors in my better judgment.

Despite the overwhelming compulsion to remain as contrary as it was feasible to do, I slowly opened my eyes. They burned horribly in the light, but as I blinked, the salve cooled the dry, stinging orbs, soothing the tenderness until it was scarcely a painful reminiscence. I sighed in relief and turned my head towards him.

"Better?" he asked, smirking.

My vision unclouded presently. I could at last see him clearly. I did not fail to notice with ever increasing temper that he was as dashing as I'd ever found him. I savagely reminded myself this was merely the relief in finding Joseph and me alive and relatively unharmed and not, in fact, a renewed attraction, which was entirely out of the question.

It had been at least two years since last I had seen him, and the separation had been gallingly kind to him. He appeared as youthful, fit and flash as ever he did. In fact, he looked quite unabashedly pleased with himself.

"Quite the contrary," I replied through gritted teeth. "Whilst the pain has momentarily abated, I find myself in almost equally unpleasant company."

"I can't say as I'm especially impressed by your new mien, either, Astrid, darling. I daresay I prefer you a bit more demure. Less...well." He cleared his throat.

I shot him a malignant glare. He grinned smugly, flicking fine, sandy blonde fringe from his eyes with a toss of his head. His face was fuller than I remembered, as if he'd put on a bit of weight. It suited him agreeably. His previously thin, rangy features seemed softer, almost younger. His bronzed skin indicated he had spent recent time in a warm climate.

I wondered briefly if it had been business or pleasure that had led him to such a destination before I remembered I did not rightly care.

"It's propitious, then, that I am no longer adorned for your pleasure," I retorted scathingly.

Asher shook his head mournfully. "Now, Astrid, I understood we had achieved concord. I have honoured my vow."

I clenched my teeth. "Thank you, Asher," I said stiffly.

"That was quite difficult for you."

146

"There is no need to belabour the point. I have now, as well, honoured my vow. Now, why has the Ministry been seeking Joseph?"

"I believe there is still the not entirely inconsequential matter of what has led us to this, the joyful and festive occasion of our reunion." The sanguine expression vanished. I was almost startled to be once again faced with the ruthless, capable agent that had ensnared my attention so many years previous. "Young Knightly has apprised me of what you have been up to. Is there any specific reason you chose not to tell me until someone was trying to kill you?"

"Yes."

"And that would be, aside from your palpable and unrestrained distaste for me, what exactly?"

I tightened my lips. "I was paid not to involve you."

He snorted. "Naturally. Honestly, Astrid, you are cleverer than that. Not that I should expect anything less. You always had more pride than sense." He sounded genuinely angry now. I hissed in outrage.

"In case you have forgotten, or it is simply outside your capabilities to perceive, seeing as nature seems to have passed you over in the bequeathing of this particular quality, but I do possess integrity," I snarled, incensed. "I entered into a binding agreement with my employers that specifically forbade the interference of your organisation, and I intended to honour the agreement unerringly until such as time as it became quite unfeasible to continue to do so. I assure you, it is my most vehement disinclination that I even come to be in your company, but I simply saw no viable alternative."

Asher stared at me a long, contemplative moment. Finally, he seemed to conclude the row was experiencing a decline and was best left to a more auspicious moment.

"Let us, for a moment, disregard our clearly differing perceptions of our prior parting and instead focus on the situation at hand, as I am quite confident we, as professional and mature adults, are both fully capable."

I bristled at this admonishment. I was certain it was the precise reaction he had endeavoured to achieve. There was absolutely no possible way I could allow Asher Key to best Astrid Darby in a battle of wit, poise and aplomb.

"You are quite right, of course," I replied loftily, straightening my shoulders and affecting the steadfast and competent aspect for which I was so widely esteemed. He blinked, nonplussed by the sudden shift in the ambiance of our reunion. Triumph thrilled through me.

Asher was not caught out for long. "Would you then care to explain exactly what you were doing breaking into Phineas Cobb's home?"

"As I am sure young Xander has clarified, we have been traversing the New World in search of Dr Sebastian Cross, who has been missing for several days," I told him serenely.

"I am acquainted with the circumstances leading up to your burglary of Cobb's home. It is the objective of this particular exploit which I fail to comprehend. What, exactly, did you hope to achieve?"

"Does it matter at this stage?" I inquired. "It was, of course, in vain."

"Let us not disregard foolish in the extreme."

I gritted my teeth, but I did not challenge this. "I hoped to speak to him regarding Edgar Thorne."

Asher rolled his eyes. "And this disgraceful attire would be...?"

"A disguise. Leave off." I glowered at him. "We thought it prudent to conceal our identities lest our lately foes recognise us and attempt further attacks."

"I find it compulsory at this stage to point out the error in this logic."

"My logic was sound, indeed! It was not until we had entered the house and discovered the departed doctor in his laboratory that our presence in the house drew the attention of our assassins. Up to that moment, we remained quite covert." I tossed my head airily. "And we were not 'breaking in' as you so indelicately allege. The door was, in fact, open when we arrived."

"And you considered it appropriate to enter unannounced and uninvited?"

"Well, not unannounced, as such. We did intend to ring the bell. It was simply rendered moot, as we discovered the house amenable to our entry."

"So you intended to speak to Cobb regarding his liaison with Edgar Thorne," Asher prompted.

I inclined my head. "It became quite clear upon hearing Xander's tale that I had been thoroughly deceived by the treacherous doctor when first we met. I intended to take him to task for his ruse and demand to be enlightened on the circumstances of his involvement with the unctuous turncoat."

"I see. What did you find when you entered the house?"

"It appeared recently abandoned. The laboratory was in absolute ruins. It appeared as if an explosion of some magnitude had occurred." I expressed the image of the doctor and his tragically devastated invention in clipped tones, but I did not describe the sensation I had experienced, the sense that a terribly cruel cosmic joke had gone horribly afoul. "I am sure whatever evidence existed to substantiate this event has been lost to the inferno."

Asher now inclined his head. "The house and any evidence contained therein are unsalvageable. We have only your account to confirm the doctor's fate."

I sighed. "Have you and your agents any idea who attacked us and murdered Cobb? Surely Thorne cannot be acting alone; sedition of this enormity seems thoroughly beyond his capability."

"I am in accord, but we are unable to determine the extent of the conspiracy at this juncture; we have not yet located your Mr Thorne."

"He's not my Mr Thorne."

He ignored this. "According to his employer, he has been unreachable for two days."

"Since he discovered Xander to be lurking outside the residence of his collaborator, I shouldn't wonder."

"It is reasonable to suppose. As to Cobb's death, it is not impossible it was merely a terrible accident. You know the dangers of chemical experimentation. It is not rare for this sort of thing to occur in his line of work. He may have been exclusively responsible for his own ill fortune."

"Perhaps, but it seems an incredulous coincidence, do you not think?"

"I am willing to entertain the possibility that foul play was to blame. However, I am confident we will be better informed of the circumstances of his death as well as the nature and scale of the plot against Sebastian Cross when my agents locate Thorne and bring him to me." He hesitated an ephemeral instant. "And when once I have spoken to your friend, Dr Ramsey."

I narrowed my eyes at him. "Why have you been looking for him?"

"The Ministry has, not for the first time, I might be so bold as to venture, succeeded where you have failed. Not long after you and the rogue Ramsey departed for America, we found Dr Sebastian Cross."

"What?" I sputtered, astonished. "You found him? Where? Why were my associates not privy to this development?"

"We thought it sensible not to publicise such a potentially alarming situation. The weapon, I am afraid, has not been found."

"But where is he?" A sense of dread gnawed at my belly. My voice was almost hushed.

"I am afraid he is dead, Astrid. He was murdered."

I exhaled deeply. "That is alarming indeed. But where did you discover him?"

Asher peered at me a moment in silent contemplation. A dark look flickered briefly in his cobalt eyes. I was instantly reluctant to receive his response. "Cross' body was discovered in Dr Ramsey's home when his housekeeper arrived to perform her weekly duties."

I opened my mouth as if to reply, but I could fashion no suitable response. "Blimey," I breathed finally.

"While you have been traipsing around the new world on a grand, impetuous adventure with your new friend, we have been scouring the countryside for him." He did not seem smug now, however. I almost believed there was kindness in his gaze.

"But Joseph has not been out of my sight since we met. He can't have been responsible for Cross' death."

Asher shook his head grimly. "The medical examiner is quite clear that Cross has been dead since before you made Ramsey's acquaintance. It is believed the murder occurred the very day he disappeared."

"But that is impossible. I have been alone with him for several days. If he is truly responsible for the treachery, he has had abundant time in which to dispose of me. Our assassins have been quite expressive in their inclination towards this; why would he have spared me, were he involved?"

Asher's eyes were narrow and intent. I flushed slightly, uncomfortable under such scrutiny. "You fancy this bloke, don't you?"

I averted my gaze, but I did not respond to this. "I am simply unable to accept it. It cannot make sense of it. At the very least, it is categorically impossible for him to have been in any way involved in Cobb's death; this alone should exonerate him, should it not?"

Even I was aware the logic was feeble at best. Asher's eyes were sympathetic, as if he understood my desperation to trust this reasoning. "While it is indisputable that Ramsey had no direct hand in Cobb's death, there is quite evidently more than one player in this game, Astrid."

"Perhaps Cross had gone to call upon Joseph when whoever murdered him caught him up. Joseph did state he had been looking for Cross the entirety of

150

the day on which he disappeared." I met his eyes grimly, and understanding passed between us; this seemed highly improbable, but I was unwilling to accept this shattering revelation. I adhered frantically to this questionable explanation. "How...how did he die?"

Asher angled his head, grimacing slightly as if reluctant to reveal the details, lest I lose the tenuous battle with my composure. "He was bludgeoned."

I winced. "With what? Did it happen in Joseph's house? Could the body have been relocated to misdirect the investigation?"

"I am sorry, Astrid. It is impossible. We are absolutely certain the misdeed occurred in the doctor's home. All the evidence needed to condemn him remained at the scene. The weapon was a steel pipe from your Joseph's lab; the same lab in which Cross' body was found. There was blood everywhere. He could not have been moved post mortem. He died directly where he lay."

He reached a hand towards me as if to offer comfort but seemed to reconsider, dropping his arm ineffectually at his side. His looked at his feet in a rare, inadequate silence.

I leaned back against the pillows and closed my eyes, momentarily allowing anguish to overwhelm me. I steeled my resolve, however, and straightened, though my voice was a soft, plaintive murmur when I spoke. "But...it could have occurred whilst Joseph was out of his home searching for him."

Asher's brow knitted. There was compassion in his gaze, but I understood at once my objections had not swayed his conclusion in the least.

"It's...not within the realm of absolute fantasy, but if he is unable to present a sound explanation for his whereabouts that day and how it is possible he failed to notice a murdered corpse in his own home, we will have no choice but to bring him to justice. I am sorry, Astrid."

I pressed the heels of my hands to my eyes, pausing a moment to collect my troubled thoughts and suck in a deep, shuddering breath.

"It still lacks credibility. If he is involved in this artifice, why would his own co-conspirators attempt to harm him? It is not as if they acted with any measure of restraint; it is quite apparent they intended our demise."

"There is much of this case we do not yet understand. The depth and dynamic of the conspiracy still eludes us. It is possible the people with whom he was in league betrayed him." He paused a moment. "Or he betrayed them, and it was retribution they sought."

My eyes snapped to his. I fixed him with a defiant glare. "Or perhaps someone is attempting to frame him."

"I will concede to consider that, but as I have stated, the evidence is severely damning. Until we are able to speak to Edgar Thorne and uncover the remaining elements of the mystery, it is merely speculation; we have no alternative but to consider the facts to which we are privy."

I stiffened, but I was not unsympathetic to his position. "What is your working hypothesis then, Asher? I cannot be convinced you lack one."

He hesitated a long moment. He had never hesitated to expound, candidly and without demure, any theory or thought that flitted through his mind in all the time in which we had been acquainted. I could see him struggle with indecision now, however. I suddenly realised, quite uncomfortably and not without a modicum of hurt, that he did not trust me, not now and not with this.

"Astrid..."

"Asher, don't. We are effectively working in concert now, and I am still a professional, emotional investment besides."

Asher raised his eyebrows archly. "In concert? Might I remind you, Mrs Darby, that this matter has now fallen under the jurisdiction of the Ministry of Defence. You should consider yourself fortunate you aren't under arrest for obstruction of justice and excessive foolishness."

"Asher, don't be preposterous. If excessive foolishness were criminal, your entire Ministry would have been sent to the gallows ages ago."

His lips twitched almost imperceptibly.

"My working theory is that Ramsey, Cobb and Thorne have colluded to deprive the doctor of his apparatus and sell it to the highest bidder. There are innumerable hostile factions who might have an interest in acquiring an instrument of such incalculable destruction."

I considered this. "That is conceivable. However, by what impetus do you suppose Joseph accompanied me on my journey to America? Surely if he were involved in this grand plot, he would prefer to remain close to the project rather than abet the investigation into his mentor's whereabouts."

"If he had committed the murder, he would be confident of your inevitable failure, in addition to possessing a very compelling motive to flee the country."

"Yes, that is true, but it seems unnecessarily complicated. If he were guilty of the murder and subsequent theft, why not simply abscond with the apparatus and seek sanctuary in some remote hidey-hole until such a time as the item was conveyed to the purchaser? Then they would all be free to pursue the life of wealthy fugitives in relative peace. There was no need to fabricate such an elaborate diversion."

"Their complicity would be instantly apparent were they all three to disappear. Cole engaged you, against Thorne's protests; you were an unexpected impediment. It would be prudent to remain close by your side and ensconced in a wild goose chase rather than risk allowing you to cotton on to their scheme. If Ramsey led you to America, you would be out of the way and under control."

I bridled at the implication of my credulity. "On the contrary, it was not Joseph who led me to America, but my own..." My voice faded. I met his eyes in disquieting realisation.

He seemed to understand. "He is the one who presented to you the idea that Cross might have fled to America."

"He facilitated the discovery of Gideon's letter," I whispered, experiencing a queasy sensation in the pit of my stomach.

"He might also have booked Cross' reservation on the flight to New York following his crime. With you securely under his direct and constant supervision, the other two and any number of as yet unidentified accomplices might operate without the threat of your interference or risk of detection."

"But they did not succeed; Xander was shadowing Cobb."

"Indeed. And when he was discovered, he was forced into hiding. He learned little more than that there was an association between Cobb and Thorne."

"Which was quite a lot, I think. My young cousin is fortunate he escaped with his life." I sighed, regretting once more my precipitate directive. "So, then, you speculate it was Cobb and or Thorne who dispatched the assassins to Joseph and me?"

"It is my suspicion that, once Ramsey fulfilled his utility, which he would have done once the Eye had fallen into his collaborators' possession, they concluded it would be more expedient to eliminate him."

I shook my head thoughtfully. "What I still cannot fathom is why. What could possibly be the motivation for such an elaborate ruse? Cobb's intentions can be easily surmised, but I simply cannot ascertain what Thorne or Joseph could gain from conspiring with him."

Asher shrugged as if this was presently of only trifling interest. "I have already offered my theory. Money, power, fame; whatever you prefer. Whoever possesses that apparatus can likely acquire as much of any of these as he wished."

It remained perplexing, however. I believed I possessed the measure of Joseph. I was quite convinced these incentives would do little to persuade him to betray his beloved tutor.

No, there was something more afoot than the terse and lacklustre explanation Asher presented, of that I was certain.

"Joseph and Thorne were already legitimately attached to the project and so were already reasonably assured all those things. Again, the only participant who stood to gain was Cobb."

"Only based upon the evidence as we currently understand it. We require more information to reveal the connections and motivations behind this conspiracy." He exhaled heavily, but his voice was strong when next he spoke. "I am most convinced your doctor friend holds many of the missing pieces we need to complete the puzzle."

I pondered this a long moment, staring at my hands. I was momentarily distracted by the angry red tone of my hairless skin and, for the first time since I had awakened in the Ministry of Defence, I perceived the raw tenderness of my flesh. I grimaced, but I did not dwell upon it for long. I glanced up into Asher's gentle gaze, my jaw set.

"I cannot be convinced. There is simply not enough evidence to support your theory. I agree the discovery of Cross' body is damning; however, there is but circumstance and conjecture to support your assertion. There is as much confirmation to reinforce my own, and I possess the advantage of having spent a number of days in the close company of the man; I believe I have the measure of him better than you."

Asher frowned. "How close has this company been?"

I glared malignantly at him. "That is absolutely none of your concern, Asher, but I am not a woman to bestow my affections indiscriminately." I narrowed my eyes coldly. "Though I have, historically, been known to blunder."

Now he scowled, his dark blue eyes flashing in fury. "This is the Ministry of Defence, madam," he said with a sneer. "We do not base our investigations upon the fickle whims of a woman's affection. The man is guilty. There is no evidence to the contrary."

"And only incidental evidence to condemn him."

"I should think the discovery of a murdered corpse in his own home is a somewhat more unyielding confirmation of my theory than the protestations of a capricious woman with a passing fancy for a man she has quite clearly grossly miscalculated," he growled.

I sighed deeply and closed my eyes, leaning back against the pillows. My temper faded as quickly as it had flared; I was not up to the task of the scorching row in the wake of the devastating revelations.

"Asher, I grant that it might seem thus, but have you ever known my judgment to err so catastrophically?"

The anger flooded from his face. He, too, sighed, slouching dejectedly in his chair. "I admit I have not," he replied quietly. I nodded, thankful for the reassurance. "But I am forced to consider the evidence as it appears before me at this time."

I inclined my head tiredly. "You must examine every angle. I understand, Asher, but Joseph is not a killer. He is innocent in this. I am most confident. I trust him."

"I admire your confidence, Astrid, but we must agree to diverge on this point at this time. Quarrelling will only impede our progress."

I nodded resignedly. "You are, of course, spot on again. I am certain it will sort itself out once we have secured an audience with Edgar Thorne."

Asher raised a dubious eyebrow. "Once we have secured an audience?"

"You do not expect me to languish idly whilst you conduct the interview, surely?"

"Astrid, you know that is counter to policy. And you are not exactly to be found in the Ministry's good books, so to speak. You are still considered a somewhat hostile entity."

"Am I? I should have thought your people would have forgiven and forgotten the incident in Prague by now."

"The Ministry does not forgive and forget. You should consider yourself lucky you have not already been given the Boat."

"Oh, curb your disapproval. I am certain your people appreciated my services, as they were. You did, as they say, get your man."

"But not without extraordinary and expensive damage to several military vehicles, our dignity and an only circumspect harmony with the Czechs."

I waved my hand dismissively. "Trifles. I demand to participate, Asher."

He sighed, squeezing his eyes shut as if in prayer and pinching the bridge of his nose. Finally, he met my burning gaze. "All right, Astrid. You may attend the interview. But I will be in command. This is still my agency."

I conceded grudgingly. "Yes, all right. I will conduct myself in a thoroughly deferent fashion."

Asher snorted. "I will believe a statement of such obviously dubious veracity when I have myself experienced it."

I smiled brightly. "Brilliant. Now, I would request an audience with Joseph."

This seemed to catch him out again. "Out of the question."

"Asher, I demand to see him. He has yet to be charged with the crime for which you have so cavalierly denounced him. An audience will have trifling impact upon your investigation."

"He is officially in Ministry custody until such a time as charges are rendered unjustifiable. I cannot allow it."

"Ash, please."

The querulous tone of my voice seemed to soften him. He sighed forlornly. "You do fancy him."

I hesitated, but I saw no alternative to candour. "It is increasingly incontrovertible."

He surged to his feet abruptly and spun towards the door. I blinked at his back, nonplussed, fearing he intended to leave me alone without gratification or explanation. He paused in the doorway, half turning his head so I glimpsed only the line of his profile.

"I cannot see a reason it would damage the investigation at this juncture. You may see him briefly."

This time, my gratitude required neither solicitation nor insincerity. "Thank you, Ash."

CHAPTER ELEVEN

Asher led me tacitly through the clinically sterile corridor of the Ministry's sanatorium. Doctors and nurses in clean, white livery bustled past us as if there was something infinitely pressing to attend, and they paid no heed to my bedraggled aspect or Asher's taut bearing. I deduced it was not an altogether uncommon spectacle.

Asher remained a step to the fore, and I found myself ogling, unwillingly to be sure, the sleek, tense line of his back. I scowled, silently rebuking the inspection.

He halted tersely before a door several metres from my own and motioned curtly towards it. "You have half an hour, Astrid," he said dispassionately, avoiding my gaze, and spun on his heel, striding away without further banter.

I blinked, peering after him in preoccupation until I remembered my objective. When I entered, Joseph tilted his head slowly, as if expecting another nurse or doctor and hardly aflame with enthusiasm.

When, after a confused moment, he recognised me, his face illuminated. He sat up groggily. "Astrid," he murmured in the sort of sluggish, slurred voice of one who has recently awoken or has been administered a potent dosage of medication.

"Joseph." I lowered myself gingerly into the seat beside him, suddenly keenly aware of the ache and tenderness of my limbs proceeding my brief commute. I reflected that, if I looked as abused and unkempt as he, I was in a sorry state, indeed.

I did not permit the sudden return of my vanity to distract me, however. I touched his hand delicately. He squeezed my fingers weakly with his own.

"You all right?" His voice sounded harsh, as if it were scraping against gravel or small, sharp rocks.

"Yes, Joseph, I am quite well." I hesitated, grimacing in discomfort, but resolved a direct approach was most expedient under the current circumstances. "Joseph, something dreadful has occurred."

His brow furrowed. His gaze, suddenly wary, snapped to mine. "What is it? What has happened?"

"The Ministry has found Dr Cross."

He was quiet a moment. His mouth tightened. "By the bleakness of your tone I can only assume he has not been discovered in vigorous health and high spirits."

"I am afraid not, Joseph."

He nodded wearily, as if he had been anticipating the unfortunate news. I searched his face for any indication of deception. He appeared to me to be quite genuinely bereaved. Nevertheless, if Asher's conjecture was correct, Joseph Ramsey was exceptionally adept at subterfuge.

"Is he dead?" he murmured disconsolately.

"I am sorry, Joseph."

The staggered, crestfallen expression on his face was utterly convincing. My heart lurched. I discarded any further misgivings towards his fidelity. Asher's theories seemed remote and fantastic against the pain evident in Joseph's green eyes.

"Joseph," I continued cautiously when it appeared he had no immediate response to the news, and my tone must have alerted him to the severity of the circumstances. He narrowed his eyes charily. "Your housekeeper...she discovered his body. In your lab."

"In my...what? In my lab? Are you in earnest?"

"I rarely jest in situations of such acute gravity."

The grief had faded instantly from his face to be replaced by a look of such dumbfounded bafflement, I was certain even Asher would have been convinced.

And then, as if the information were simply too great to be borne, he asked in an utterly calm, detached voice, "Where are we?"

I blinked, but I did not tarry over the abruptness of his transformation. "The Ministry of Defence."

"Oh. Yes. Naturally."

"You are...well, the Ministry has decreed you are in official custody until such a time as it is determined you bear no culpability in the matter of Cross' death."

"What? Why—what?" He sat up sharply and winced, pressing his hand to his forehead. "They believe I am responsible for his death?"

"Joseph..." I sighed deeply. "His death has been declared a homicide. He was murdered in your laboratory with your weapon. It is most damning. Until we can determine what truly occurred, the Ministry intends to place the burden upon you."

"Astrid, I am blameless in his murder! You must tell them I am not responsible. I have been with you for several days." He clutched my hand. I cringed.

"Joseph, I have told them. I was most passionate in your defence. However, Cross died prior to our fateful encounter. They have established his time of death within the very day he disappeared."

My voice was soft and gentle, but I detected a slight note of condemnation in my tone. I realised I was still ever slightly persuaded by Asher's conviction. I resolved not to dwell upon Asher; he had offered ample grounds for mistrust. Joseph, however, had been steadfast and honourable from our earliest meeting.

"But how can that be?" Joseph's voice was unusually shrill. I did not blame him for the undignified reaction under the circumstances. "In my lab? In my home? Surely they are mistaken."

"I am afraid they are not. The Ministry, whilst not exactly a crack team of astonishingly gifted investigators, are quite successful when faced with the task of determining wherein they stand." He did not appear impressed at the drollery, and I subsided sheepishly.

"But I was home the whole night following his disappearance. I think I would have noticed the body of the very man for whom I had been searching all day!"

I smiled apologetically. "Yes, Joseph, they are in accord. Hence their suspicion of your involvement."

He leaned back against the pillows and squeezed his eyes shut for several long moments, as if struggling to remember the events of the day in question. "I arrived home, and I...did not enter my laboratory."

"Are you quite certain?"

"Yes! I can't have done, can I, or I would have noticed the recently murdered body of my mentor lying on the floor, wouldn't I!" He took a deep, calming breath through his nose and peered at me entreatingly. "He was there the entire time?"

I nodded grimly. "Until your housekeeper discovered him."

He paused, as if suddenly distracted by a tangential concern. "Why was no one aware of this development? Surely a murder and subsequent search for the perpetrator must have reached the ears of the public by now."

I shook my head. "Well, Joseph, the Eye is as yet unaccounted for," I answered reluctantly.

"What? The Eye was not in his possession?"

"I am afraid not."

"Then whoever killed him has it! This is a catastrophe!"

"Of monumental proportions, I shouldn't wonder. Hence the Ministry's failure to report the events to the general public. The outcry and resulting panic would be of even greater detriment to the state of the realm."

Joseph blinked. I could almost envision the whirlwind of disturbing deliberation in his mind. "I spent an entire evening in my home with Sebastian's dead body in my laboratory? How does one fail to notice something like that?"

"Well, I should wonder the same myself, but as you clearly have done, we must simply accept that it is indeed possible and move on to more pressing areas of concern. You must tell me precisely what you did and where you were to the exactest moment the day Sebastian disappeared. It is of utmost import you leave nothing out. Even the slightest of errors will lead the Ministry to pursue the matter of your guilt. When did you arrive at Rake & Gage, and what did you do when you discovered Sebastian was not in attendance as expected?" I leaned towards him attentively. "Did you return to your home, or did you embark on your quest immediately?"

Joseph shook his head, his brow furrowed in concentration. "No. I did not return to my home; I immediately commenced my search. I left my flat on the morning in question and caught the six-thirty tube to Rake & Gage. I arrived at the offices at seven. Upon entering the lab, I realised Sebastian was missing right away. I was gone by seven thirty."

"Where did you go then?"

"I stopped at the bakery near the offices on the way back to the tube and purchased scones and a cup of tea. I caught a tube back to Kensington around eight, intending to call upon Sebastian's home. I assumed he had over-indulged the previous night and was having a lie in. I planned to entice him with the scones and rouse him. I arrived at his house around nine. He was not home, of course. The house was undisturbed, thus I was neither uneasy nor concerned for his safety."

"No, nor would I have been at the time. Was there a precedent for this sort of behaviour?"

Joseph nodded reluctantly. "Only once. One morning I arrived at the laboratory to discover him missing and found him cataleptic on the floor of his flat, dressed in little but a dilapidated dressing gown and still clutching a bottle of scotch." I stifled a giggle, for Joseph did not appear amused by the vision. "He was a brilliant scientist, but he was prey to his vices, I am afraid. It was something of which we did not speak."

"I can surmise how your opinion of him might have suffered."

Joseph scowled, meeting my gaze chillingly. "He possessed an exceptional mind and gift for invention the like of which the world has rarely seen since the days of da Vinci himself. If he occasionally indulged in the transgressions of spirits and women, I did not begrudge him his escapes. My opinion of him never faltered."

"I am regretful, Joseph. I misspoke."

He sighed, gently squeezing my fingers. "No, Astrid, I am regretful. It is troubling to be obliged to account for my whereabouts to save my own skin when my mentor lies dead. He is owed a more respectful mourning. Alas, now is not the time to wallow in grief, for I am compelled to explain myself. I should not project my misery upon you."

"No, Joseph, you are not to blame. You have become the victim of a terrible tragedy. I do not resent your attitude. Please, continue and I shall endeavour not to interrupt."

He smiled weakly. "Do you not believe I am responsible? We have only just met, Astrid. Do you have no doubt as to my innocence? Surely the Ministry presents a compelling argument of the evidence."

I cocked my head and studied him a moment. "No, Joseph, I have no doubt. Their argument is compelling indeed, and I must confess I did experience a moment of great misgiving. However, I must rely upon my greater instinct, as I have done on innumerable occasions in the past and with quite successful results. There is but one recourse available, and that is simply to trust that my impression of your faithfulness and integrity is spot on. I am incredulous of your capability to commit the acts for which the Ministry has impugned you."

Joseph nodded, and his tremulous smile was almost good-humoured. "I am relieved I still remain in your good graces, Mrs Darby. I shouldn't wish to incur your ill favour at this juncture in our relationship."

"Then, by all means, continue your exposition. I should very much like to hear what transpired in the remainder of the day. I suspect the truth will out soon enough."

"Your devotion is most gratifying. In short order, I attended the locations he was inclined to sojourn in his leisure time. The museum, the university, Hyde Park, being unaware, of course, of his encounter with the treacherous gentleman that had rendered him too frightened to resume his daily visits."

"Did you come upon anyone who might be in a position to confirm this?"

He did not pause to consider. "Yes. My former professor, Andrew Dawne."

I leapt keenly upon the small glimmer of hope. "How long were you in his company?"

"A few hours, I am certain. I left prior to his afternoon lecture, which I recall was scheduled for four o'clock. I explained that I was in search of Sebastian."

"You informed someone you had discovered him missing?"

Joseph nodded. "Well, yes. He was unconnected to our employers and the project; I saw no harm in discussing the details. I was assured of his confidence."

"Why did you not mention this before now?" I demanded, frowning thoughtfully.

He shrugged. "It did not seem important in light of the circumstances. We never had occasion to discuss the details of my day prior to our meeting. Do you believe it is important?"

"We must consider every detail of the day of great importance at this stage. Did you discuss the minutiae of the project with the professor?"

"Not the particulars. We discussed the overlying theories, and I detailed Sebastian's recent unusual behaviour. I was under contract not to discuss the Eye itself, and Professor Dawne did not press me for further information. He was concerned, as was I, for Sebastian. I was uncertain what next I should do, as the search had yielded thus far inadequate results. He suggested I return home, read a book and wait for word from Sebastian. I was discontented with the inaction, but I saw no alternative. It was my intent to wait the night, and if I failed to receive word by morning, I would attempt once again to reach him at home. If this bore nothing, I had planned to inform Mr Cole straight away. I feared for my position and Sebastian's reputation, but I was quite at a loss."

"I came upon you before you were able to see these plans to completion."

"Just so, and thus our perilous and foolhardy adventure began."

I smiled. "What precise time did you arrive home?"

He pondered this. "Approximately eight in the evening, I believe."

"Eight? But you stated you left the university around four, did you not? It could have taken but an hour to arrive home by tube." I frowned at him sceptically. "What became of the missing three hours?"

"I, oh, well...I paused for a meal."

My brow furrowed, and I peered at him dubiously. "Joseph, you dined alone for three hours?" I demanded disdainfully.

He sighed. "No..." He avoided my gaze, and I raised my eyebrows in expectation. "Exhausting my search in all the savoury locations Sebastian frequented, I at last conceded I might be better served to attempt to locate him in one of the...more vulgar."

"I see. And where exactly might that have been?"

"A brothel on Fleet Street," he admitted, and the flush on his cheeks deepened his already reddened skin to garish scarlet. "The Gilded Cage. Sebastian visited often when he was feeling tense or under-appreciated. I understood they were quite accommodating to even his most irreverent requests. I had, of course, never had occasion to visit, myself," he added quickly. "It is most discreet. Thus I experienced some difficulty locating it."

I rolled my eyes and gestured impatiently. "And what transpired upon your eventual arrival?"

He heaved a deep sigh. "I approached the Abbess, most reluctantly I assure you, and inquired as to his status. She was disinclined to assist me at the first, but when I introduced myself, she seemed to recognise my name. I can only presume Sebastian had spoken of me on occasion. She professed she had not seen him since the previous week." He paused, glancing warily into my sceptical expression.

"Right. I suspect you have rather more to impart, taking into consideration your sudden reticence. I require full disclosure. Please declare yourself, lest your credibility experience a decline."

Joseph nodded penitently. "I was persuaded to enter and availed myself of the well appointed bar," he admitted.

"Did you attend any of the ladies?" My voice was even, but his eyes snapped to mine in astonishment.

"Of course not!" he gasped. "I merely enjoyed a drink."

"A drink?"

He sighed. "All right, I enjoyed a few drinks. The Abbess recognised my anxiety and insisted I indulge myself. I was presently joined by one of the young ladies, and I was inclined to buy her a drink, as is only courteous."

I wearied of his vacillation. "There is no need to be coy, Joseph. I am unconcerned with your transgressions prior to our acquaintance. I would much prefer to presume you frequent bawdy houses and lusheries than that you have committed murder and criminal collaboration. Please continue forthrightly."

His expression remained ashamed. "She suggested we advance our familiarity and continue the conversation upstairs, but I declined. As you might have surmised, I am distinctly uncomfortable in the company of professional ladies."

"Yes, that is becoming increasingly apparent."

"She was persistent in her seduction, thus I was obliged to depart quickly lest my judgment become impaired with spirit and my resolve waver. I then caught the tube back to Kensington. I called upon Sebastian's home a final time, in case he had returned, before determining I would have no luck locating him that day."

"Did you enter his home?"

"No. I merely rang the bell. I received no answer, thus saw no sense in persistence. I had already entered uninvited once and was familiar with the outcome. I was feeling quite drowsy, in thanks to the Abbess' excellent offerings, and I was content to wait until morning to pursue the search. I arrived home, as I earlier stated, around eight in the evening."

I inclined my head. "That wasn't so arduous, now was it?"

He scowled. "I hesitate to offer further reason to mistrust my decency."

"That is the least of our concerns at this time. You stated that when you arrived at your home, you did not enter your lab."

"Yes. Well, I had imbibed spirits, as I said, and we are both familiar with my capacity for such indulgence." I merely smirked and tilted my head. "The liqueur had sufficed to sooth my apprehension over my mentor's absence, and I was calm, if not entirely sanguine. I still believed Sebastian to be on some sort of bender or unannounced holiday. That something dreadful had happened had yet to occur to me. I spent the evening reading. I must have dozed in my chair, for I awoke around two in the morning and retired to my bed. It was not until I returned to Sebastian's home and discovered the state of it that I became deeply troubled."

I exhaled heavily. "That is the entirety of your account?"

"Yes," he replied firmly. "There is nothing else."

I leaned forward to rest my elbows on my knees. "That is not a very well-constructed alibi."

He growled in frustration. "Had I known I might require one, I would have endeavoured to conduct myself in a more conspicuous manner! I am at the mercy of circumstance."

I held up a bracing hand. "Joseph, I understand. I accept your story. Please do not fret. We will disentangle this misunderstanding with the Ministry. They are, as we speak, pursuing Thorne. He likely scarpered when he realised he was exposed, but Agent Key excels in uncovering deserters and renegades. I am confident he will be located promptly."

Joseph frowned, cradling his head in his hands. "But what will we do until then? The Eye is still missing; we cannot sit idly by awaiting word. We should be attempting to do something."

I shook my head grimly. "I agree the possibilities of such an apparatus in the hands of unknown hostiles is disquieting, but this has fallen under the Ministry's jurisdiction. We are rendered inconsequential."

"Surely you do not accept this indifferently?"

"Of course not. I am quite cross, indeed, but I am powerless to object. I rather suspect we are, at least for the moment, quite captive. However, I have faith in Agent Key. He is stalwart and clever. We must share your tale with him and convince him of your blamelessness. He will see reason."

I was not entirely certain of this, however. Asher was a reasonable man, but he was dead stubborn. He rarely faltered in his resolve, and, once convinced of his own righteousness, was unlikely to relent. I did not dwell on this, for there were graver concerns with which to be getting on.

Joseph frowned broodingly. "Sebastian must have intended to impart his suspicions to me on the day he died."

"His faith in you had not wavered, on balance."

"While that is heartening, I am forced to wonder if, had I been home to receive him, his fate might have altered."

"You mustn't dwell upon that, Joseph. It is more likely you would simply have shared his misfortune."

"Perhaps. But why did I not? Why would his killer have neglected to eliminate me, as well?"

I shrugged. "It makes little difference. Perhaps they intended to implicate you as the responsible party."

"They certainly did that," he muttered darkly. "And thus I find myself in this compromising position."

"I am sure it will sort itself out."

"We truly have learned nothing from our journey, have we, Astrid?"

I considered this. "While I agree we seem to have elicited more confusion and uncertainty than clarification, I remain confident the answers we seek are soon to be revealed. We have, though not in the manner in which we anticipated, located your mentor."

"Due to the condition in which we found him, I count that as a failure rather than a success, Astrid. And the Eye is still missing, to potentially devastating consequences."

"Yes, this is true. I have yet to achieve success in my obligation. However, we are closer to the crux of the matter than ever we might have been without the Ministry's assistance." This was somewhat galling to admit, but I conceded that there had been little else to be done. "We will soon realise gratification."

"Perhaps. I am still troubled. I find it difficult to understand by what motivation Thorne became involved in this scheme with Phineas. I can see clearly what possible gain Phineas might hope to achieve, but I am still unable to determine what could compel Thorne to commit such treachery. Phineas is quite wealthy, but I find it unlikely he could have offered Thorne more than his job was worth to steal the Eye and murder Sebastian."

"Agent Key suspects they intend to sell it on the black market."

"That would be cataclysmic."

"Oh, indeed it would. What perplexes me is why Phineas was killed," I mused absently.

"Perhaps so Phineas could not implicate Thorne in the scandal?"

I shook my head doubtfully. "No, I think not. We have already discovered they were connected. He would be certain we will have deduced that their association relates to the Eye. Thorne may be a cretin, but I do not think him a fool. Cobb's murder would not have exonerated him in any way. It makes little sense."

"If the impetus is money, perhaps he became greedy and wished not to share it."

"That is a possibility, but I am of the increasing opinion that the available facts are but confusing the heart of the matter. There is surely something else afoot, something we have yet to even consider. I believe it is not as Asher says; this is not simply a plot to steal the Eye and sell it. The matter is of far greater consequence."

"We are already aware there is at least one more conspirator," Joseph offered. "The man whom approached Sebastian."

"Yes. And so then the true question is who wanted the Eye and who was merely assisting the buyer."

"You do not believe it was Phineas alone who wanted the Eye?"

"It simply does not ring true. He could not have presented it as his own; only Thorne was in collusion. Both Cole and yourself would have been available to dispute his claim. As Sebastian's killer did not lie in wait to dispose of you, as well, I am led to believe that was not the intent. As Cobb was murdered, it is reasonable to assume his role was not as great as it might appear. He was expendable, clearly, and thus unlikely the principal party."

Joseph considered, pushing a hand through his wildly mussed hair. I wondered fleetingly what had become of his hideous wig. Perhaps it had been lost in the conflagration and mercifully destroyed. "Why do you suppose the unidentified man approached Sebastian?"

"To obtain the plans, as Sebastian stated in his journal."

"Yes, but, if Thorne and Phineas intended to steal the apparatus all along, what was the purpose of approaching Sebastian and attempting to obtain them legitimately? Well—marginally legitimately. He did offer to buy them."

I blinked. I had not contemplated this before; I had simply assumed the man was related to the plot and had not given him further consideration. "Yes...that is odd indeed. Based on the evidence, it is possible covert measures were taken only when this approach failed." I sighed mournfully. "There is little else to be learned in speculation. I am quite at a loss for the moment."

Joseph deflated in dejection. "As am I, and I am in a spot of trouble, aren't I? I suppose I should offer my statement to your Agent Key."

"He isn't *my* Agent Key," I growled, and as if in response, the door flew open with a startling clatter.

Asher burst into the room, his cobalt eyes alight with excitement. I leapt to my feet immediately; I had grown to associate that expression with action and thus was instantly alert. "Astrid! We have located Edgar Thorne!" he exclaimed keenly.

"What?" I said in astonishment.

"That did not take as long as I would have expected," Joseph muttered, quite forgotten in the exhilarated moment.

"He is in transportation now. We discovered him in Brighton hiding away in a squalid hotel. All and all, not the most challenging of quarries."

"He is unlikely accustomed to the nuances of a fugitive existence," I opined. "Ah, a stroke of most convenient fortune!" I spun towards Joseph. "We shall have our answers in a trice. Do not fret, Joseph. I shall sort this out."

His smile was wan, but he squeezed my fingers in assurance. "I trust you, Astrid."

When I spun back towards Asher, it was to discover he awaited me in the hallway several paces from the door, peering balefully at the floor. I reached towards him and lightly touched his shoulder. He started and spun to face me with a cross expression. The rigid lines of his visage softened as he met my delighted mien, however, and he smiled fractionally.

"Did you learn anything constructive?" he asked in a tone of voice which suggested he had already concluded anything I might have learned was unlikely to be of anything more than trifling interest.

I was in no mood for vilification. "Nothing of which I was not already convinced," I replied, tilting my chin. "Joseph was not at home when the murder occurred."

Asher's eyebrows knitted dubiously. "And he merely failed to notice the body in his laboratory?"

"He did indeed. As he did not enter the laboratory that evening, he had no occasion to discover it," I replied resolutely.

Asher was thoroughly unconvinced. "That is not the most persuasive of arguments, Astrid."

I nodded curtly. "No, I concede it is not. However, I am satisfied. He is in earnest." I nudged his shoulder gently. "I am quite confident all will become clear when once we have spoke to the traitor Thorne."

He did not argue with this, for which I was grateful, but his eyes scrutinized me sternly.

"You had better clean yourself up. I expect he'll be arriving any moment, and I daresay, I cannot allow you into an official interrogation looking like that."

He caught my shoulders and propelled me towards my room. I scowled indignantly. "I thought we had established a truce," I muttered, offended.

He smirked and thrust me unceremoniously inside the room, closing the door behind him.

Piqued, I spun towards the mirror in the lavatory and gasped in abject horror.

CHAPTER TWELVE

Edgar Thorne's appearance had deteriorated since last I had made his acquaintance. Sweat beaded on his forehead, and lank wisps of greasy, greying hair stuck out in all directions, as if he'd lately been tugging in agitation at the grubby locks. His suit was filthy, and I suspected his accommodations had been disreputable and fetid indeed. His eyes were watery and wild in his pallid face, like a trapped animal that had just discovered its inability to outrun its infinitely faster and deadlier predator and had run out of places to hide.

Though I had despised the despicable man from the very moment of our meeting, I experienced a brief moment of contemptuous pity.

He was alone in the small, stark interrogation chamber, and his trepidation was tangible even through the thick glass separating us. Asher glanced at me when I joined him outside the door. His eyes were so bright, so alive, I felt as if I were peering into two tiny, flashing lightning bolts; he lived for this. His mouth turned up smugly. "I trust you are sufficiently prepared, Astrid," he said teasingly.

I nodded tersely. Having overcome the initial dismay of discovering the ghastly state of my appearance, I had managed to tidy myself up and was reasonably satisfied that I appeared at least respectable, if not as smart as I would conventionally require for such events.

"I am looking very much forward to this conference. Shall we?"

He grinned, and his features softened appealingly. "We shall. Like past times, is it not?"

I chuckled wryly. "Although I suspect our past methods might not be as acceptable in the offices of the Ministry of Defence as in the streets of Bangkok."

"We will attempt to control our baser impulses, then." The mischievous expression faded as suddenly as it had appeared, and he nodded to me.

The cold, determined expression he adopted in times of battle returned, and I sucked in a breath, steeling my own nerves as he threw open the door, allowing it to bang against the empty, white wall.

The unexpected noise startled Edgar Thorne, He jerked violently in his chair, nearly toppling backwards onto the floor. He looked afraid for a brief moment, but then his eyes found me, and fury overcame his podgy features.

"You!" He shot to his feet, his ashen face suddenly darkening to an alarming shade of purple. "What are you doing here?"

I cut my eyes to Asher, who had remained stoic, though I recognised the slight twitch of his mouth as suppressed hilarity. I crossed my arms across my bosom, leaning casually against the door, facing him.

"Mrs Darby has agreed to attend our interview as an interested party, Mr Thorne," Asher informed him, drawing his eyes. "I am Agent Key of the Ministry of Defence." He lowered himself stiffly into the chair across from the prisoner.

Though I remained standing at his back, I imagined the tight set of his jaw and his intent, glacial pool eyes.

Thorne's expression was distinctly wary. His eyes darted beadily from Asher to me. "What—" He paused, flicking his tongue fretfully across his lips. "Ah— what is it you want?" he asked with unconvincing nonchalance. "What am I doing here?"

"Come now, Mr Thorne," Asher replied genially. "I think you know perfectly well what you are doing here."

Thorne's eyes darted agitatedly between us. He gulped almost audibly. "We know that you conspired with Phineas Cobb to steal the Eye of Ra from Dr Sebastian Cross, right under the very nose of your employer," I said. "Why? What did you stand to gain?"

He glared at me. Asher interrupted my question. "Mr Thorne, where is the Eye of Ra now?" he demanded dispassionately.

Thorne balked, tugging uncomfortably at his collar. "I'm not saying anything else without my solicitor present," he said finally, irascibly.

Asher's mouth twisted in cold amusement. "This is the Ministry of Defence, Mr Thorne, not a common tribunal. If you do not reveal the location of the Eye and what part you played in its disappearance, things could become extremely uncomfortable for you. I am certain Mrs Darby, in particular, would be most eager to dream up several ways in which this can be accomplished. We can make you disappear, Mr Thorne. We can convince the world you never existed. I suggest you begin your explanation presently, lest you experience first-hand precisely what I am capable of."

Thorne stared at him, wide-eyed, as if he had suddenly realised his impotence; casual corporate browbeating would do little to daunt the inflexible Agent Key. "It wasn't...it wasn't supposed to happen like this," he said disconsolately. "It wasn't supposed to be this way."

I circled the table to stand behind Thorne, meeting Asher's gaze for a fleeting instant before he asked, "And what way was it supposed to be, Mr Thorne?"

Thorne grimaced. He was positively green, his shoulder's slumping in utter resignation. He was a cowardly man, but I was suddenly, incontrovertibly certain that this man was not a killer; he simply did not possess the constitution.

"I suggest you declare yourself, Mr Thorne," I added coldly. "What was Dr Joseph Ramsey's part in your scheme?"

Asher's expression didn't change, but the sudden tension in his jaw communicated his irritation at my interruption. Nevertheless, proof of Joseph's innocence was foremost in my mind at present. I held my breath for Thorne's response.

For a moment, it almost appeared as if he would burst into laughter. "Ramsey? Cross' little lapdog? Blimey. The man has no ambition. He's nothing. An upstart."

I attempted to catch Asher's eye, but he was staring contemplatively at the prisoner. "Did you kill Sebastian Cross?" he demanded abruptly.

"No! I didn't know he...I didn't kill anyone," Thorne squealed, recoiling as if Asher had struck him. "He's dead?"

"He's dead."

"I don't...I didn't..."

"Tell us what happened, Mr Thorne, and perhaps we will consider leniency. If you continue to vacillate, I am prepared to charge you with the murders of both Drs Cross and Cobb."

Thorne's eyes snapped to Asher in horror. "Cobb? I didn't have anything to do with Cobb! He was already dead when I found him!"

Asher's eyes narrowed. "So you were in his home after the explosion?"

Thorne lapsed into grim silence again. "Mr Knightly saw you visit Phineas Cobb, Mr Thorne," I reminded him. "We know you were involved in Cross' and his apparatus' disappearance. The evidence against you is irrefutable."

"It wasn't me! It wasn't my idea!" Thorne burst out in a rapid series of denials. "I was coerced! I didn't know what to do! I was in fear for my life!"

"What happened, Mr Thorne?" Asher demanded, cutting him off.

Thorne sighed heavily, twisting to glance at me then back to Asher. "I was approached a few weeks ago by a—a man."

"What man?" Asher asked harshly.

Thorne hesitated, and I understood that he was quite terrified. I also understood, in the same moment, that the man who had approached him was the same man who had accosted Cross in Hyde Park.

I rounded the table to sit beside Asher, leaning forward keenly to hear the traitor's response. "Bengel. Luther Bengel," he squeaked, his eyes darting around the room as if the mysterious man was waiting in the shadows to attack the moment his name had passed the craven man's lips.

I glanced sidelong at Asher. He blinked. For a moment I fancied he looked startled. He was suddenly rigid, and I frowned slightly, returning my gaze to Thorne. Asher's voice was even and undaunted when he spoke, however. "And what did Bengel want from you?"

Thorne looked ill. "He knew Cross was building a weapon for Rake & Gage. He offered me a very large sum of money to keep record of Cross' progress and inform him when it was nearing completion."

"And you did," I interjected with a sneer.

"I didn't have a choice! He threatened me...I was frightened."

"He threatened you? What did he say?"

"At first...at first I refused. I am not a defector, despite what you might think. The money was not enough to give up my standing with Rake & Gage. It wasn't easy, you know, becoming a junior VP. I worked hard. I...he was frightening. Dangerous. He told me if I did not agree to work with him, life would become perilous for my family and me. I thought he would kill me and my wife, my children."

I was momentarily caught out by this, never having considered him a man upon whom a family relied. I did not pause to contemplate this sudden alteration in my perception of the man, however.

Asher was speaking again in the sympathetic, honeyed tones I had heard so often and to which I had so often fallen prey. "I understand how that might have been a frightening situation, Mr Thorne. Luther Bengel is...a very dangerous man."

I snapped my eyes to him. His voice was taut. I understood instantly that he was in possession of significant information I presently lacked.

I exhaled heavily, anxiously anticipating the conclusion of this disappointingly effortless interview. "So what did you do, Mr Thorne?" I asked, returning my attention to the prisoner.

"I kept him apprised of the progress of the project, as he instructed. I had no alternative," he added vehemently.

"Did you send someone to approach Cross a month past to receive information about the Eye?" I continued. At this, Asher's eyes darted to me, an eyebrow raised interestedly; perhaps Xander had not been entirely candid with him, after all.

"What?" Thorne's surprise seemed utterly genuine. "No. Why would I have done? I saw him nearly every day and received regular reports."

Asher waited silently, watching me. "Dr Cross was approached by a bald man with a scar on his cheek," I explained. "He requested to purchase the designs for the weapon."

"That's him!" Thorne exclaimed breathlessly. "That's Bengel!" Asher and I exchanged a glance as the traitor's face grew purple with rage until it very nearly resembled a ripe plum. "That...that treacherous son of a bitch! He was attempting to acquire the designs from Cross himself, right under my nose!"

I raised a smug eyebrow. "It appears you were merely a backup plan, Mr Thorne. Just another pawn in this complicated game. Bengel probably intended to dispose of you the moment he achieved his end."

Thorne glared malignantly at me. I returned the gaze with a pleasant smile.

"Did you alert Bengel when the Eye was complete?" Asher asked, sensing the decline in Thorne's control.

To his credit, Thorne no longer appeared afraid; on the contrary, his eyes blazed with fury, and his voice gained confidence as he spoke. "No. I didn't know it was complete. Bengel called upon my home, demanding to know if it had been finished. I attempted to evade him; it was not my fault the project was incomplete. I could hardly control the doctors' schedule. The morning of Cross' disappearance, I was at the office early, watching him and hoping to learn something of his progress, as I had done on several previous mornings. I saw him arrive, enter the lab and leave almost immediately with a large bundle under his arm. I suspected it to be the Eye.

"I sent Bengel a telegram at once. I considered my part in this concluded from there and demanded to be paid for my services." He scowled. "I have yet to receive my earnings."

174

I shot him a distasteful look. "And when Cross disappeared, you said nothing."

"Of course I said nothing! I had nothing to do with his disappearance, did I?"

"Right. Nothing at all. You do not believe your report to Bengel lead to his subsequent death? You do not consider you are to blame for the proceeding events?" My voice was arctic, and I sneered in disgust at him.

Under the table, I felt Asher's hand touch my knee. I subsided reluctantly.

"I didn't kill him! I only related what I saw!"

Asher's voice was soothing and utterly calm, despite the magnitude of the revelations thus revealed. "Mr Thorne, what happened next? How did you become involved with Dr Phineas Cobb? Was he also in league with Bengel?"

Thorne looked uncomfortable for a moment, his eyes darting cagily about the room. "That night...after our audience with Mrs Darby, Bengel approached me on the tube as I was travelling home. He was furious. The Eye did not work as stated."

I nodded. "Cross sabotaged it. He mentioned this in his journal. He suspected your treachery, Mr Thorne."

Thorne ignored this and spoke directly to Asher. "I was in a panic. I went to Cobb, whom I had heard possessed a reputation for dishonesty. I trusted he could be easily persuaded to remain silent. I offered to pay him handsomely and allow him to keep the original designs if he rendered it operable. I was quite desperate. I saw no alternative."

"He agreed?" Asher asked, leaning forward.

"Of course he did," I put in disapprovingly. "He's been attempting to salvage his reputation for ages and possessing the designs would assure his return to grace." I paused for a moment, narrowing my eyes thoughtfully at Thorne. "Why did you not take the notes I found in the laboratory?"

Thorne glanced at me, his face twisting in misery. "I couldn't. I tried to enter the lab, but only Maxwell and the doctors themselves were able to enter. I was unable to obtain the key, and I couldn't very well steal them in front of my boss."

"They would have afforded little success, anyway," I told him. "Cross suspected the man who had approached him had been sent by Cobb, and he sabotaged the notes, as well. He believed someone within Rake & Gage was working with them."

Thorne shrugged, as if this was of little consequence. "He must have gotten the right ones from somewhere. He had them when I visited him a few days later."

"The day Xander caught you paying him a visit and you discovered him." When he looked away, I switched tactics, attempting to control my temper. "Did you ransack Cross' home?"

"No. It must have been Cobb as he searched for the designs."

Asher and I exchanged another glance. I knew he, as I, suspected Thorne was correct in this supposition.

"You were not aware Bengel killed Cross?" Asher demanded, his voice cold now, losing patience with the sweet, cajoling tone with which he had opened.

"What? No, I...I had no idea. I mean, I...I thought...well, I thought he probably had. And when Ramsey disappeared, I thought...well, I thought he had probably gotten them both. So much the better," he muttered bitterly. My temper sparked.

"Until you discovered he was with me and sent someone to kill us both?" I growled.

Thorne glared at me defiantly, but he offered no concession or denial. Asher seemed to prefer to visit the topic of our attempted assassinations at a more auspicious moment. "Why did you visit Cobb the second time? When you discovered his body?"

"To find out if he had completed the project, of course," Thorne replied sullenly. "I wanted it to be over. I wanted Bengel out of my life."

"Yes, you were merely a victim in all this, surely," I put in contemptuously.

He ignored this. Asher glanced sidelong at me, as if to silent me. "What did you do when you discovered the body?"

Thorne sighed. "I didn't know what to do. I ran. I went into hiding."

"In Brighton."

"Yes."

"Is that all?" Asher demanded coldly.

"Yes. That's everything I know."

Asher looked sceptical. His voice was measured, as if he were barely concealing his impatience. "Are you quite certain? Where is Bengel now?"

"I don't know. I was hiding from him when you found me...I feared now that he surely possesses the Eye, he would finish me as he did Cobb. I am of no use to him anymore."

His dismay and the knowledge of his own insignificance were etched pitifully into every line of his face. I could not muster the empathy to feel sorry for him, however, not knowing he had been instrumental in Xander's, Joseph's and my attempted assassinations.

Asher's jaw, however, was tightly set, and the line of his mouth was grim. I frowned slightly. "Did Bengel tell you for whom he was working?"

My eyes turned to him again. I felt a distinct sense of foreboding. His voice was still even, but the slight edge set my nerves to singing.

"For whom he was working?" Thorne looked confused. "No, I...I assumed he was working alone. He was the only one I spoke to."

"To what purpose did he intend to put the weapon?" I demanded, scowling.

Thorne shook his head again, almost violently. His words came out in a plaintive, desperate rush. "I didn't know. I didn't ask...I didn't want to know. I was scared. This isn't my fault! I didn't have a choice. Everything I did...I didn't have a choice!"

Asher's expression was glacial now, dangerous. Thorne snapped his mouth shut with a tiny peep.

"You did have a choice, Mr Thorne. You could have alerted someone. You could have come to the Ministry, and we would have protected you and Cross. Instead, two men are dead because of your cowardice and greed. And how many more will die with the Eye in Bengel's possession? Do you have any idea what you have done, what you have caused?" I laid a hand gently on his arm, and he subsided, taking a deep, calming breath. "Mr Thorne, you will be charged with treason."

"Treason!" he exclaimed, stunned. "But I...I was under duress! I would have been killed! I am innocent!"

"Innocent," I scoffed, my lip curling coldly.

Asher shot abruptly to his feet, hooking my elbow and yanking me up with him. He didn't speak, but he guided me, a bit more forcibly than strictly necessary, towards the door. He gestured with his hand. Two young agents entered the room, moving purposefully towards Thorne, who squeaked in surprise.

"Wait!" Thorne protested. "Wait!"

Asher spun. His body was unusually tense, his expression cold and stiff. His cobalt eyes were burning. I sucked in a deep breath, taken aback by the intense rage in his gaze.

When he spoke, his voice was a low, tremulous growl. "You have no idea what you have set in motion, Mr Thorne."

When the door slammed on Thorne's stricken face, I yanked my arm from Asher's grasp, whirling on him.

"The little worm," I snarled then caught sight of Asher's pallid face. "Ash?" He glanced up, into my eyes. The anxious expression I saw worried me. "What is troubling you, Ash? You know who Luther Bengel is. I saw your expression when Thorne said his name."

"Yes," Asher said, his voice low. "I have heard of him."

"Who is he?"

Asher caught my arm again, hauling me further into the hall, away from the small interrogation room. His voice was low and tense, and I listened intently, dread gnawing at my belly. "Luther Bengel is a mercenary. He's originally from Austria. He was military trained but was eventually discharged and exiled from the country for horrific war crimes. He's been hiring out to various nationalist and terrorist organisations ever since."

He turned suddenly, striding purposefully through the corridor. I jumped to attention, hurrying to catch him up. "Most recently he's been linked to a French terrorist group called Colère De Dieu. The Wrath of God."

"The Wrath of God?"

Ash seemed to have forgotten me for the moment. I was alarmed by the sudden agitation in his manner. "We have no time to lose," he said almost absently. "We have to evacuate the Ministry at once."

"What? Why?"

My questions fell upon deaf ears. I struggled to keep up with his frenzied pace as he proceeded towards a large office at the end of the hall. The word Director was lettered in careful, elegant script upon the door. When Asher burst into the room, the tall, thickly-muscled man behind the desk started, dropping a quill and splattering droplets of ink across a stack of papers.

"Agent Key," he growled. "What have I told you about knocking before you enter?"

Asher ignored the admonition. "Sir, the situation with the Eye of Ra is far more ominous than we originally surmised."

A small, black nameplate identified the dark, formidable-looking man as Charles Norton. Uneasiness simmered in my belly; this man was, I realised, Asher's superior, and, unless something had changed in the twenty minutes in which we had been occupied by the interview with Edgar Thorne, he was not a particular admirer of mine.

His cool, dark-eyed gaze slid past Asher to glare at me as I hovered uncomfortably in his doorway. "Might I assume I am finally in the presence of the famous Astrid Darby?" he asked wryly.

I raised my chin with dignity. "You would be correct in that assumption, Agent Norton. I am pleased to make your acquaintance."

"That's Director Norton, Mrs Darby, and I can hardly say the same." The expression on his deeply lined and deeply tanned face was disgruntled. He flicked his eyes to Asher. "What is the meaning of this, Key?"

Asher seemed almost to be vibrating with impatience. "Sir, Luther Bengel is in possession of the Eye of Ra."

"Luther Bengel?" Norton said with sudden clarity. "Good god, man. We must evacuate the premises at once."

"Just so, sir."

Norton moved as quickly from the room as Asher had entered, scarcely sparing me a glance. I spun towards Asher to demand a further explanation, but he was already hurrying back into the corridor. "Asher!" I scolded, practically jogging to keep up with his long strides. "What is happening?"

My voice was drowned by a sudden, maddening wail that rent the relative quiet of the building. I clapped my hands to my ears, glaring at Asher's back.

"That's the emergency alert!" he called over his shoulder. "Step lively, Astrid!"

"Where are we going?"

"A safe house. It's standard procedure in the event of a threat to the Ministry."

"A threat to the Ministry?"

"And every other government facility from here to France," he replied grimly.

He ducked abruptly into an empty office, cursing vehemently as he shuffled papers around a desk that appeared as thoroughly ransacked as had Cross' home upon my arrival.

His voice was terse and clipped as he explained, not bothering to glance at me as he did. "The Wrath of God are anarchists. Their purpose is to dissolve all systems of organised government; they believe the people should answer to no one but God."

I snorted. "Yes, I am sure they will be welcomed into Heaven with open arms."

Asher paused and peered up at me for a moment, as if I had said something utterly frivolous. "Yes, well, we and the French Ministere de la Defense have received a series of threats from their leader, Gerard Vaurien, over the last fortnight."

"What sort of threats?" I asked tensely.

"They intend to destroy every major government post in Britain and France. This one, Parliament, the Palais Bourbon, amongst others," Asher replied. "So far, these threats have not come to any fruition, but Vaurien is a very serious and very dangerous man. If he's enlisted Bengel..."

"And Bengel has the Eye," I murmured uncomfortably.

Asher was sombre. "Just so."

"So, you think they intend to use the Eye to carry through with these threats?"

"It is extremely likely."

"This is very dire indeed. Bengel has had the Eye for at least two days."

"Yes, and thus we have no time to lose."

He seemed to locate the papers for which he had been searching and swept them up with a flourish. "Are those the threatening letters?" I demanded, attempting to peer at them over his shoulder.

"Yes." He caught my arm again as he surged past me. I was caught out by the almost wild expression on his face. He was worried, and my pulse leapt. Asher was always calm, always collected. If he was alarmed, the situation must be more desperate than I ever could have anticipated.

"If we're too late stopping him discharging the weapon," he continued, steering me into the corridor as if there had been no interruption, "at least we can try to save some lives."

180

The halls teamed with confused agents and employees, murmuring in varying tones of interest and apprehension as they moved as one towards the exits. I searched the crowd for my associates and saw none of them, but I was confident they would be clever enough to await me outside for further instruction. When we emerged onto the street, I was startled by the glaring sun. I wondered for the first time since I had awakened in Ash's company how long we had been inside the Ministry. It felt like ages since I had lingered in the fresh air, enjoying the warmth of the sun.

Now was not the time to do so, however. I had lost Asher in the confusion and the thickening crowd outside the building. I searched anxiously for a brief instant before discovering him speaking in low, imperative tones to a small group of competent-looking men in suits. When he turned from them, I was directly at his back. He reared backwards to avoid colliding with me. "Astrid," he scolded in a distracted growl, his eyes darting about with an almost manic alertness.

"Ash," I said sweetly. He did not respond. I knew he was oblivious to me; I had seen him thus on rare occasions. I knew better than to disturb his concentration. Matters, however, seemed pressing enough to necessitate my intrusion. "Ash!"

He started, returning his gaze to me. "What?" he demanded, his eyes blazing.

"I want in on this."

"What?" He scowled at me, appearing confused as to why I still remained in his company.

"What about Joseph?"

"Joseph?"

"Dr Ramsey! Can we now assume he is blameless in the matter of Dr Cross' death?"

Asher paused. "Oh. Yes, of course. Ramsey." He spoke the name through clenched teeth, but he pivoted and called over his shoulder to a passing agent, "Collins, Ramsey is free to go. In fact, he may be expelled from our custody with haste."

"Ramsey, sir?"

"Ramsey! Dr Ramsey. In the infirm. He is no longer under suspicion for treason and murder. Please locate him and inform him he is free to go. I expect he will not be difficult to locate amongst the crowd; he will likely be the one looking bedraggled and confused."

"Yes, sir."

Asher shot me a glare. "Satisfied, Astrid?"

Without awaiting a response, he resumed his stride, delivering hasty instructions to the gathering agents in a commanding voice. I sighed in aggravation, leaping forward to catch his arm. "Asher!"

"What, Astrid?" he growled. "Can you not see my position is somewhat urgent at the moment?"

"Yes, I can see that. As is mine! I want in on this!"

He blinked as if finally understanding my words. "You want in? As I mentioned before, you are lucky you're not being held for failing to bring this disaster to my attention from the offset! It's sheer luck they haven't already attacked!"

I smiled unrepentantly. "You would never do such a thing to me. We can help."

He glared at me. "No, Astrid, this is the Ministry's operation now."

"Asher, I was hired to return the Eye to its rightful owners; I will not accept failure at this juncture."

"Astrid, you have nearly been killed several times already in the course of this assignment. I suggest you cut your losses."

"Never!"

"It is out of the question."

"I think we both know that only compels me to persist." I beamed despite Asher's disapproving expression. "Come now, Asher. We work very well together. Surely you haven't forgotten."

He narrowed his eyes at me. "That's stooping rather low, Astrid, considering your attitude towards me since you awakened." He sighed, peering at me silently for a long moment. I continued to smile brilliantly at him. "All right, we could use your team. But you are under my command! You don't make a move unless I say so. I assume that won't be too difficult for you?"

"Of course not. I am at your service, Agent Key. I will gather my entourage." I spun on my heel, striding several quick paces away then paused and turned back to him. "Where exactly is the safe house?"

Asher snorted and rolled his eyes. "I'll wait here."

"Ace."

Ash sighed. "Yes. Brilliant. And step lively! I won't wait all day for you!"

* * *

The Ministry's safe house was, despite its hopeful designation, merely a large, underground shelter a scant city block from the main building. Murdock and Xander eyed the slapdash accommodation with a professional sort of disdain, but they remained quiet, apparently hesitant to incite Asher's further ire. I suspected they preferred it remain, for the time being, directed exclusively towards myself. As it was, his tight expression suggested he was distinctly put out, but he had voiced no further protestations regarding mine and my associate's involvement in the operation. In fact, he had voiced little more than a short, impatient grunt upon my return to his side with Xander, Reinhart, Murdock and Swan.

This uncustomary lack of complaint could be, I considered, the effect of the appearance of Julian Swan, whom Asher had met only once before. If my memory was steadfast, their previous encounter had involved a very grave cultural miscalculation and Asher's timely rescue from a tribe of angry head hunters by the slightly daft but terribly loyal Mr Swan.

I suspected Ash was remembering the capability of the disturbingly oversized man and was, despite the Ministry's standard operating procedure, quite grateful for his attendance. Swan's methods were questionable, at best, but if one is facing a murderous mercenary with a death ray, one is often willing to overlook a few trifling explosions and accidental broken bones.

The temporary briefing room to which Asher led us was crammed with eager and excited agents sitting against the dirty stone walls or pacing anxiously when we arrived. Our entrance drew the slightly disgruntled gaze of every occupant, and silence fell upon the room. Asher strode purposefully to the front of the assembly.

I was momentarily impressed by his confident gait. I suspected I was not the only one affected by his commanding presence; the congregation's attention turned instantly to him, anticipation practically crackling in the air around us.

I noticed Director Norton waiting for him at the front of the room. The older man shot him a hard gaze, tilting his head towards my associates and me. Asher glanced back at me wearily. I smiled cheerfully, perching primly on the edge of a rickety wooden chair while my associates stood behind me, forming a motley court.

Asher spoke in inaudible tones to his superior, who exhaled in a long-suffering sigh but nodded tersely and sat, gesturing as if to yield the floor to the younger man.

"For those of you who are not acquainted with our guests, this is Astrid Darby and her team," he announced in a voice that brokered no argument. "They will be assisting us with this operation. As you should all now be aware, we have received a series of communications from the terrorist group, Wrath of God, in which they have made threats upon various government posts, including the Ministry. We believe the purpose of these attacks will be to weaken the operational capacity of the British government. Thus far, they have failed to follow through on these threats. However, we have recently uncovered new information which suggests they now possess the necessary means to successfully carry out their plans."

An uneasy murmur passed through the assembled crowd. I glanced up at my fellows who were watching Asher warily. Despite our considerable experience in adventuring, it was, I realised, the first time any of us had participated in such an operation.

More specifically, it was the first time any of us had been in a room with so many esteemed members of the British government and not been the focus of suspicion either due to a grave misunderstanding or a poorly judged scheme involving petty larceny, fraud or property damage. My associates were, understandably, quite apprehensive in the present company. However, we had been charged with a prodigious duty. I was unwilling to yield my forecasted victory at this stage.

The tension in Asher's voice as he continued was palpable, and my attention snapped back to him. "Our target is Luther Bengel." He held, to my surprise, a sharp artist's rendering of the Austrian mercenary, which he passed around to the assembled team. "Learn his face, and do not forget it."

I stood, craning my neck to see the sketch, but the men around me were too tall, too broad, and they seemed just as keen to glimpse the face of the man who had stirred such concern in Agent Asher Key as I. Julian Swan unceremoniously plucked the sketch from the hands of a young, muscular agent with very short, cropped hair and handed it to me.

The agent spun, menace in his eyes, but Swan stared at him with such a bland, unrepentant expression that the smaller man merely turned away, shrugging at the agents around him.

Well, harmonious rapport between my team and the Ministry was hardly a reasonable expectation, I decided. Mending fences would be a focus for a later day.

"Thank you, Mr Swan," I said brightly, settling comfortably back into my seat to examine the rendering.

Bengel looked younger than I had expected and certainly less dangerous, though it might merely have been the lack of expression and detail in the sketch that suggested so. His features were even and strong, and the long, jagged scar criss-crossing his left cheek made him appear almost dashing, like the charming rogue in a penny dreadful.

His eyes were pale and large, the nose prominent and aristocratic, if not slightly crooked where he appeared to have broken it a number of times. The man in the sketch appeared hardly capable of great malice, but I was not to be fooled by poor attention to detail. When I was certain I would know the man, I ignored the expectant agents around me, handing the sketch to Xander, who snapped it up eagerly.

I turned my eyes my eyes back to Asher. Whilst I had been memorising the deceptively blank features of our villain, he had tacked a map of Westminster on the wall behind him. The map was marked with garish red ink and indicated, I presumed, the centres the Wrath of God intended to target.

Asher seemed impatient. He cleared his throat, drawing the attention of the room back to himself. "Bengel has come into possession of a very dangerous directed energy weapon. We suspect he will attempt to discharge the weapon upon one of these locations. We have called for a complete evacuation of the pertinent facilities and the surrounding areas; the evacuation is taking place as we speak. The French Ministry has been apprised of the situation and is presumably doing the same.

"It's unlikely Bengel has found his way out of the country, but we cannot be certain which location he will target. We have to assume, in the interest of caution, he intends to attack soon.

"We believe the Wrath of God's most likely target will be Parliament Square. However, we will have teams stationed at Downing Street, Paddington Green and the Admiralty, in addition to the House and Treasury. Scotland Yard has been notified of the situation and can presumably mind themselves," Asher continued. "Please see Director Norton for your assignment. We will leave at once."

He nodded to the assembly, who wasted no time queuing up to receive their instructions from the director, and strode towards us. I rose to meet him, keenly eager to receive my own designation. I was, much to my surprise, quite content to follow Asher Key's directives in these particular circumstances. The situation was, I admitted quite reluctantly, completely outside my expertise.

"Agent Key," I said, inclining my head as if to defer to his command. "We await your instructions."

He seemed momentarily startled by this attitude, having been, I expected, prepared for a less compliant countenance. "Mrs Darby, you will be with my team in Parliament Square. Young Knightly, you will accompany Agent Morris at Paddington Green. Messrs Reinhart and Murdock will be with Seymour at Downing Street. Mr Swan...erm...well, you will accompany Agent Shivington on the Bridge. They will be your commanders from here, so follow their instructions to the letter." He turned warning eyes towards me. "That goes for you, as well, Astrid."

I smiled brilliantly. "Naturally, Agent Key. I should expect no less." I turned to my entourage, who were eyeing their assigned teams with expressions of varying determination and excitement. "Our objective is to recover the weapon," I told them, aiming a warning finger at Mr Swan, who appeared rather keen on the prospect of tangling with a nefarious terrorist. "There is no need to act rashly or act the hero. We now have the Ministry for that."

Reinhart snorted, and Murdock rolled his eyes dubiously, but Xander nodded keenly. "Yes, Astrid. Oh, this is most exciting, isn't it?"

"Don't get used to it," I warned quietly, my eyes finding Asher, who was speaking earnestly to his team leaders. "I have every intention of remaining as far from the Ministry of Defence as is physically possible whilst still occupying the same countryside as immediately as this debacle has concluded."

"Astrid," Asher said. I nodded shortly to my team, striding towards him.

He did not speak when I reached him, but he motioned to his force, striding purposefully towards the door. He was practically vibrating with worry and excitement. I was suddenly and forcefully reminded of the powerful, determined agent that had attracted me so long ago.

"Astrid, I mean it," he said in an undertone, glancing sidelong at me. "Do not do anything foolish."

"Foolish? Me? Agent Key, I am astonished at your implication. I am hardly a woman of whimsy."

Asher snorted, but he suddenly halted dead in his tracks as we emerged into the dank, muddy vestibule that would lead us back to the surface and into the merciful light of day.

Dr Joseph Ramsey was striding towards us through the Ministry's underground tunnel with a determined step. The young Agent Collins walked beside him. His expression grew increasingly uncertain as he glimpsed Asher's suddenly livid countenance.

I paused beside Asher, resisting the urge to embrace Joseph, so delighted was I to see him up and looking so much better.

"Collins?" Asher demanded, his jaw set so tightly, I wondered how he moved his lips at all. "What is the meaning of this?"

"He insisted I bring him straight to you, sir," Collins replied in a quavering tone. "He said he has information you require. He said you would insist on seeing him straight away."

"Did he. I see. Thank you, Collins. Please check with the director for your assignment; we have little time to waste."

Collins seemed to understand that he had made a grievous error in judgment. I suspected he would receive a severe tongue lashing once the current trouble had been sorted out.

I pitied him; Asher was, I knew from considerable experience, quite adept at stern tellings off. Collins hurried past us into the briefing room, looking miserable. I beamed at Joseph, who returned my smile with a small wink.

Asher turned a glacial glare on the doctor. Joseph still looked ragged and tired, but I suspected Asher would find a most formidable adversary should he attempt to refuse him whatever he was intending to request. I was in no doubt of precisely what that might be.

"Dr Ramsey," Asher said stiffly. "I see you've made it out of bed all right."

"I have."

Asher opened his mouth to retort, but I interrupted cheerfully. "It's nice to see you up, Joseph. Doing all right, then?"

"Discharged with a clean bill of health and no criminal record, I am happy to report." His eyes flitted coldly to Asher, as if in remonstration. Asher, however, merely lifted his chin and looked unrepentant.

"Might I assume your claim to possessing information for which I am in immediate need was, in fact, merely a ruse to hoodwink the obviously slow-witted Collins into bringing you to us despite my orders?" Asher asked almost tiredly.

"You might assume that," Joseph replied unabashedly.

I grinned. "I am thoroughly impressed by your clever subterfuge, doctor."

He straightened his shoulders, his mouth twisting in a wry smile. "Yes, I suppose it was quite brilliant, wasn't it? So what are we doing then?"

"We are currently on official Ministry business," Asher growled. "You are returning home a free man, despite my inclination towards your continuing incarceration for your part in creating the disaster we presently face."

"Joseph, our interview with Thorne not only exonerated you in the matter of Cross' murder but uncovered the identity of our true villain," I interrupted brightly.

"Astrid, might I remind you we are in a bit of a hurry?" Asher demanded through clenched teeth, clutching my arm rather more tightly than necessary.

"Ah, yes, of course." I threaded my other arm through Joseph's, leading him along the corridor with us as I continued speaking. "The man who approached your doctor is named Luther Bengel. He is a mercenary working for a French terrorist organisation known as the Wrath of God. It was he with whom Thorne conspired to steal the Eye of Ra. Cobb, you see, was merely a navvy."

"And this mercenary is in possession of the Eye?" Joseph asked, aghast.

"He is indeed. Or he has passed it along to his employers by now. They have sent a number of missives over the past several months threatening the destruction of any number of government holdings in Britain and France. Their intentions are to dissolve the government, you see."

Joseph's face was pallid with dismay. "Astrid, this is most catastrophic."

"Agent Key is placing surveillance teams outside all the pertinent locations in hopes we can thwart Bengel and his people before he is able to discharge the weapon. We are going to Parliament Square."

"What? You're placing yourself in the direct path of the Eye?"

"Well, we do not intend to place ourselves between Bengel and his target. That would be absurd."

"I will accompany you."

"I beg your pardon?" Asher finally interrupted. "No. Absolutely not."

I scrutinised Joseph interestedly, deciding he could be very useful, indeed.

"Oh, come now, Asher. He's with me."

"You must be jesting. This is the Ministry of Defence, madam, not a pleasure jaunt."

"This is a dark, dirty underground tunnel beneath the Ministry, not the Ministry. Moreover, you agreed to allow my entourage to assist with this operation. Joseph is a member of my entourage."

"This is completely ridiculous."

"Asher, Joseph is the only living person who has worked on the Eye. He can assist us in understanding and disabling it, should we be successful in obtaining possession of it."

Asher sighed deeply, eyeing Joseph reluctantly. "All right. You've already practically commandeered command of this operation as it is. What's one more civilian? Your doctor may as well accompany us."

I threaded my arm through his and beamed. "Step lively then, gentlemen. We've a terrorist to catch."

CHAPTER THIRTEEN

I had never seen Parliament Square so utterly deserted, even in the stillness of the late evening. We assembled on a battlement overlooking the Palace of Westminster from the Abbey's Lady Chapel across the square, and from our position I could see perfectly the empty, abandoned grounds. The buzz of human habitation I had come to associate with most areas of the city was jarringly absent.

Even the pigeons, which descended each day upon the square as if compelled by some incomprehensible biological imperative to gather upon the church turrets and launch kamikaze attacks upon the passing pedestrians, seemed to understand that tonight something was amiss. Or, I considered, perhaps it was merely the absence of overfed politicians strolling below from whom the feathered vermin might scavenge a crumb or crust.

"It's rather eerie, isn't it?" Joseph commented, as if he had read my mind. "I've never seen it so quiet." He glanced sceptically at me. "I find it unlikely anyone intent upon attacking the Palace won't realise it's been evacuated."

"I don't know that it matters overmuch to them," I mused. "Their goals don't necessarily involve murder. I believe the place itself and what it represents is the target, not the inhabitants."

"Still, surely they'll suspect we're here. We're not exactly inconspicuous, are we? I can see the other teams' spyglasses from here. The least they could have done was cover them up. At this rate, they'll spot us long before we ever spot them."

"It cannot be helped," Asher growled, appearing beside us. "You prefer to risk the lives of all those innocent people to remain undetected?"

"No, of course not," Joseph replied coolly.

"Leave the Ministry to the planning, doctor. You just keep an eye out for the weapon of mass destruction you created. We'll call if we require a scholar."

"Asher," I scolded quietly, but he strode away, a hitch in his shoulders.

"Is there any particular reason Agent Key is so averse to me?" Joseph asked conversationally. "Or does he merely take issue with doctors?"

I patted his shoulder. "I think Agent Key is merely bad-tempered this evening.

No need to trouble yourself."

Joseph frowned at me. "I almost think you are enjoying this, Astrid."

I smiled brilliantly. "I most certainly am. I am exceedingly fond of a proper stake-out."

Joseph's expression was sour. "That is not what I meant."

The long, tedious hours atop the Abbey's battlement did nothing to improve the temper of the men. Joseph paced restlessly in front of me, glancing out over the Square now and again with a deep, angry sigh, as if it were a great burden. I suspected, however, he was merely highly put out by the cold and perfunctory way in which he had been dismissed by Agent Asher Key. As full night fell, the team slept in short shifts or talked in the soft, hoarse voices of the earliest hours.

Though I drifted in and out of a doze, Asher seemed tireless, striding confidently along the battlement, sweeping the area with his spyglass and organising the team. He disappeared occasionally. I suspected he was visiting the other team leaders gathered around the Square, ensuring the continuing quiet.

It was most plain to me, however, that, should Bengel and the Colère de Dieu launch an attack on any of the other posts in Westminster, we would be certain to know of it immediately.

Joseph was quiet through the night, but he remained alert, likely refusing to concede any weakness to his lately adversary, Agent Key. He spoke to me rarely, merely grunting single syllable replies when I attempted light conversation, though I was certain this was due more to the amount of energy a proper conversation would require and less to a disinclination to initiate our usually enjoyable discourse.

I was slightly concerned for his health, as he had hardly been in top shape upon entering into this endeavour, but he appeared in marvellously robust well-being, at least for the moment. As darkness fully descended and the stars glittered overhead in the night sky, however, he joined me on the floor of the battlement, leaning with a heavy sigh against the wall beside me.

"I am beginning to think this is entirely futile, Astrid," he commented tiredly. I could read fatigue in his entire aspect.

I smiled. "Take a rest, Joseph. It has been a long and trying ordeal."

He frowned. "I refuse to admit defeat so quickly, Mrs Darby. If the man who murdered my mentor is intending to pay us a visit, I will wait as long as I must. I have every intention of confronting him." He sighed. "I regret I was not able to do the same with Thorne."

I waved my hand dismissively. "Thorne was but a pawn in this grand game. He was merely the weakest entry point into the project. He was unaware of the scale of the conspiracy. I don't believe he ever intended for it to go as far as it has."

Joseph's expression was dubious. "Be that as it may, he had every opportunity to alert his superiors or the authorities to the trouble. Instead, he chose to take the money and cooperate with a terrorist."

"He claimed to fear for the safety of his family," I offered fairly.

"I am most confident the Ministry of Defence is fully capable of protecting one family, should their acquaintances present a danger." His malachite eyes flicked to Asher, and his scowl deepened. "Despite my personally lamentable experience with them."

I smiled. "Perhaps. Thorne will receive the punishment he so rightly deserves. In the meantime, we must focus our attention on the issue at hand, which is, I am most aggrieved to say, quite dire indeed."

"I am in accord. In truth, though I assisted in its creation, I have only a theoretical knowledge of the scale of destruction of which the Eye is capable."

I glanced at him sharply. "You don't know what will happen if it's discharged?"

"Well, we couldn't exactly discharge a directed energy beam in a small concrete laboratory, could we? Besides, it was never completed while I was in attendance. I arrived to work the day of Cross' murder quite believing it to still be under construction."

I considered this. "And it was, from Thorne's account. It did not function upon Bengel's receipt. Do you think there is the slightest possibility Cobb was unable to complete the project?"

Joseph shook his head sadly. "I regret to say, I do not. Though he was a fraud and a traitor, he was most talented. Were he to lay hands upon the designs, he would have no trouble deciphering them and applying the construct. I am convinced the Eye is fully operational." He sighed deeply, resting his head against the stone wall. "It is most unfortunate; I had been anticipating the first discharge of the Eye to be a happy day indeed. Instead, I may be forced to witness my greatest accomplishment wielded in the hands of a murderous terrorist."

I slipped my hand into his, sighing heavily. "We shall endeavour to prevent such an event," I told him gently. "I am confident we have arrived in time to circumvent the potential catastrophe."

"Unless he has taken the Eye to France and is, at this very moment, destroying any number of government facilities."

"Ah, Asher believes that to be a highly unlikely scenario. Why risk travelling with the apparatus when so many potential targets remain within the very city? No, I am certain, should they choose to attack it will be at the very heart of the British Empire."

Joseph groaned softly, pressing his free hand to his eyes. "If Sebastian had suspected that his brilliant invention would, as opposed to defending our nation, be the force that threatened its very heart, he would have never conceived the idea. And if he had, he would have destroyed it immediately. Though it is a dreadful thing to say, it is almost better he is not able to witness what his triumph may achieve."

"Sometimes men with the noblest of intentions are more dangerous than the evilest of men." Joseph did not reply to this. I suspected he was suffering deeply. He closed his eyes, leaning back against the wall uncomfortably.

I turned my attention to the team, allowing him a moment of quiet. The deep night rendered the observation difficult. Though several torches lit the Abbey in the evening, it was impossible to make out more than dancing shadow upon the men's faces. By the position of their shoulders, however, it was quite apparent they were not only weary but resentful of the hitherto fruitless vigil.

Though I was slightly piqued by the lack of urgency in their aspect, I could understand the feeling. Unlike Joseph and me, who had been involved in the drama from the beginning, they had little idea with what they dealt. They were in no position to comprehend the truly frightful nature of the threat we faced.

Despite the painful accommodations, I dozed briefly, and when again I became aware of our surroundings, the sky was a deep lavender, signalling the soon rising sun. Joseph stirred slightly beside me, but I did not attempt to rouse him; if I had been in need of a rest, surely he was doubly in need.

I glanced around at the agents and found Asher immediately, his shoulders stiff and tense as he peered out over the Square with his hands on his hips.

"Still no sign of him?" I asked softly, and Asher spun to face me.

His gaze flicked across Joseph and me. He scowled deeply.

"No." His voice was clipped. He did not linger in conversation. I eased my hand from Joseph, whose fingers were clenched tightly around mine as if we had both fallen asleep clutching each other. Asher ignored me as I rose to stand silently beside him.

"He could hit any team from here to France," an agent I remembered was called Bennett grumbled, propped against the railing with a lofty bearing that signalled the waning interest of the team. "How long are we going to continue this?"

Asher was suddenly ablaze. I felt an odd, lingering affection that signalled an obvious continuing need for rest.

"As long as we must. The House of Parliament is Vaurien's most likely target. The Colère de Dieu is in possession of a terrible weapon that could, by all accounts, obliterate the entirety of the Palace with one fell swoop. I suggest you cease your complaints and return your attention to the task at hand. You should consider yourself most fortunate he has not already laid attack."

Bennett stiffened insolently, but he did not comment further, instead stalking quickly away to murmur quietly to his peers.

I turned my gaze to Asher. "You are quite right," I told him bracingly. "I only wonder why Bengel has not yet attacked."

Asher shook his head irritably. "I have no ideas as to why they have not used the weapon." His eyes darted around as if to ensure we were not overheard. "Honestly, Astrid, I am beginning to wonder myself if he means to attack at all. They could merely be planning to use the Eye as a means to extort the government somehow."

"I am most confident in your initial assumption. You have been investigating this organisation for several months; I am certain you are the most qualified to speak for their intentions. They will use the Eye, sooner or later. We shall wait days if we must."

I was not, in fact, entirely keen on the idea of waiting days for what would only become an increasingly unlikely event in the continuing absence of any life in the Square, but the arrival of tea and pastries upon daybreak improved the overall mood of the party. I roused Joseph gently from his awkward slumber. He moaned softly when he caught the scent of breakfast.

"Nothing new?" he asked hoarsely as I lowered myself beside him, sipping my sweet, black tea almost reverently.

"Not as yet. I am confident there will soon be a change," I replied blithely, though I was confident of no such thing. I was, however, determined to complete the task for which I was hired, and, having no more likely leads, I was content for the moment to wait out the vigil. I had, after all, faced much greater adversity than a stiff back and increasingly ill-tempered company.

Joseph eyed me sceptically, but he did not belabour the point. "I suppose all we are able to do is wait."

"Yes, a most undemanding task, yet nearly impossible for most people to endure. I suspect Asher will face a mutiny if there is no activity soon."

Joseph's eyes found Asher as he paced tautly before us, peering into his spyglass every few moments. I suspected, despite his continuing steadfastness, that Asher had not slept a wink since the vigil began.

"How do you know Agent Key?"

I was startled by the non sequitur, but I smiled serenely. "Oh, in my line of work, one makes all sorts of contacts. It was only a matter of time before the Ministry of Defence took notice of me. We have worked together a number of times before."

"I say, Astrid, deception does not become you."

I gazed at him disapprovingly. "I beg your pardon, Dr Ramsey, I am not a woman who engages in idle deception."

He raised his eyebrows in amazement. "Astrid, I have witnessed you deceive so many people since the inception of our relationship that I must protest that your assertion is, in itself, highly deceptive."

"Well, I am most affronted, Dr Ramsey."

"You are avoiding the question."

"As is my right as a woman. It is enough to say that my association with Asher Key ended a number of years ago and not under entirely amiable circumstances. It was with extreme hesitation and only out of obvious necessity that I involved him in our adventure."

"As it is apparent you do not wish to discuss these circumstances with me, I shall have to remain content with your discretion." His mouth was tight, however. I suspected he was, quite apart from content, wounded by my reticence.

In an attempt to lighten the suddenly tense atmosphere, I patted his arm gently, but he rose abruptly, striding towards the railing. I sighed, watching him peer out over the quiet grounds.

Well, I reasoned, I had quite enough to be getting on with at the moment to concern myself with the fragile egos of men. Despite the ostensibly tranquil morning, there was, in fact, still a highly dangerous terrorist in possession of a death ray who could attack at any moment. Perhaps, then, my attention was best put to the task of spotting him.

I turned it once again to the Palace. I wondered briefly how my young cousin and capable associates were fairing in the quiet morning, but I was most confident their watch was as unproductive, if not quite as hostile, as ours. Surely, should there have been a change among any of the other teams, Asher would be the very first to know.

There was little of interest to view along the deserted thoroughfares, and the early morning fog rendered the grounds ghostly and surreal. I was certain Bengel would be easily recognisable, alone in the square. I was confident the sketch I had examined would be sufficient to render him quite obvious.

However, I suddenly realised that I, having been utterly preoccupied by other matters, had absolutely no idea what the Eye of Ra actually looked like. I had, of course, having been married for several years to an impassioned and quite mad scientist, seen a number of similar apparati either in miniature or in design, but I had, as yet, to even ask in passing how one might identify the Eye of Ra.

Joseph was pacing on the other side of the balcony, in close proximity to Asher's own well-worn path. The men did not speak, but their eyes made contact as they strode sharply past each other like two large jungle cats sizing up their opponent. I sighed and shook my head, sensing electricity in the air like the coming of a lightning storm. Truly, men are exceedingly foolish, but there was nothing else for it.

"Joseph," I called brightly, and their attention snapped to me simultaneously. I had the sudden, uneasy sensation that I had just rendered myself prey. "It has recently come to my attention that I have most grievously failed in obtaining an actual description of the item in question. I have, quite correctly I am sure, been labouring under the assumption that I shall find it quite easily recognisable. Perhaps, however, it is advisable to request a thorough depiction of the weapon."

Both Joseph and Asher seemed momentarily distracted by my words. "I say," Asher remarked. "It had not occurred to me to obtain a description. I, too, had been under the impression it would be a simple task to recognise our quarry."

"It would," Joseph replied grudgingly. "I can assure you, it is most easily distinguished from an average weapon. It is unlikely there will be another foe anywhere near who might possess a weapon for which you might mistake it."

"All the same," I added in a careful voice, "perhaps it is best to pass the description along, in case there is some question."

Joseph sighed wearily and nodded, starting towards me. I was uncertain who struck first, but as he passed Asher, the two men collided violently. I groaned in exasperation and strode forward, pressing the palms of my hands to the two men's chests, attempting to force their angry, snarling faces apart.

"Gentleman!" I exclaimed. "This is most juvenile."

"Tell him that," Joseph growled, but he allowed me to propel him several steps away from Asher. "He is the one who shoved me."

"I beg your pardon, doctor, I did no such thing." Asher's voice was arctic, despite the deep scarlet flush on his cheeks. "Perhaps you should be more aware of where you walk."

"Enough," I ordered coldly. "Honestly, you are behaving like two prepubescent schoolboys. Tensions are quite high enough without this thoroughly undignified belligerence. Just endeavour to stay out of each other's ways."

They continued to glare silently at each other, but Joseph did not resist as I led him safely out of the Asher's path. Joseph pressed his hand to his forehead, leaning tiredly against the wall.

"I beg your pardon, Astrid. That was highly inappropriate. I am wholly ashamed."

"Not at all," I replied dismissively, leaning beside him. "This is a trying time for all of us. No vigil would be complete without an ill-time and ill-mannered battle of wills."

He chuckled wryly then turned serious, apprehensive eyes upon me. "Do you believe they truly mean to use my invention to destroy the British government?"

"It appears to be their intention, if Asher's judgment is to be trusted. I daresay he is rarely wrong in situations such as these. He has quite the aptitude for estimating the ambitions of others."

I had not noticed Asher approach until he spoke in a low, sombre voice. "Just so, doctor. And the Colère de Dieu is the most dangerous terrorist organisation with which I have ever contended. They have no demands, so we possess no means to negotiate with them. Their goal is only complete, meaningless destruction and chaos. They will surely use any means within their control to achieve them. They will absolutely use your invention to threaten us."

Joseph straightened, but, despite my wariness, he did not lash out at Asher. Instead, he pressed the heels of his hands to his eyes, exhaling in a soft, rueful growl. "I never should have built that thing. I should have known better. I should have anticipated the danger it posed."

Asher was unmoved by Joseph's sudden compunction. "Yes, you should have. You should have been aware of the implications before you helped build the most destructive weapon on the planet!"

Joseph bridled, snapping his shoulders back and facing Asher coldly. "If your government had not commissioned the weapon in the first place, I would never have had reason to build it."

"I am concerned with the defence of this nation, not its downfall," Asher countered dangerously. I made no move to interject myself into the discourse; in my experience, men often needed only to find expression for their hostilities in order to resolve them. "It was you who allowed the Eye to fall into the wrong hands."

"Asher!" I exclaimed, quite despite my initial intent. "Joseph had nothing to do with that. He could not possibly have foreseen the conspiracy against him and the trouble we now face."

Asher glared at me, but I returned his gaze steadily, refusing to quell under his ire.

Joseph, tense as a whip, scowled between us. "I pray Bengel does attack," he growled. "He murdered my friend and mentor. I am anxious to exact my reprisal."

Asher's eyes snapped to him. "Leave the punishment to the Ministry, doctor. We can hardly afford a reckless civilian mucking up an operation at this crucial juncture."

I sighed, recognizing the row, now underway, was unlikely to dissolve any time soon; I had a relatively thorough understanding of both men. I was certain neither was apt to compromise. They were both perfectly capable of continuing their inane quarrel quite without my attendance.

As I passed, I noticed the team watching the tense interaction with varying degrees of interest, though no one seemed inclined to interfere. I rolled my eyes; men, honestly. Schoolyard brawlers, all of them.

I resolutely tuned out their rising voices, leaning idly over the stone wall. Daylight had completely overtaken the Square, and sunlight glinted off the glass and metal of the looming structures. Big Ben, towering majestically over the

198

square, struck eight in the morning.

Did terrorists, I wondered, prefer to strike in the early morning, or were they, as their nature suggested, partial to the darker hours of the day? I supposed it depended entirely on the disposition of the terrorist involved. I had no personal experience with Luther Bengel or the Colère de Dieu.

I peered through my old, battered spyglass over St Margaret's, and a sudden, brief flash of light from one of the turrets caught my eye. As Joseph had warned, I suspected, one of the Ministry's ludicrously polished spyglasses had caught the sunlight, assuring any hostile onlookers of their persistent presence. I wondered absently if the other agents were fairing any better in the breaking day.

My instincts, however, were overcoming my weary mind, and I frowned, returning my attention to the turret. There had not, I remembered, been a team assigned to St Margaret's. In fact, Asher had been most adamant that the teams remain spread apart. I turned my attention back towards the flash of light. It was not the glint of a spy glass that had caught my eye.

There was a man upon the otherwise unoccupied turret. His actions were quite dissimilar to those of the languishing agents whose keenness for the vigil seemed to be steadily waning. He was crouched in such a way as to suggest he was leaning over something, adjusting or tinkering with it: whatever had initially captured my attention, I shouldn't wonder.

Leaning tenuously over the battlement wall in order to obtain an unobstructed view, I noticed the man roll his shoulders as if the suit he wore, while perfectly tailored, was slightly ill-fitting and causing him discomfort. His aspect was long-suffering, as if the task which he performed was distasteful; this was, I considered, not entirely unlike the agents with whom I was working.

However, he was thick with the muscular form of a man well-suited to a life of labour, and though his head was as bald as a newborn child's, his bearing suggested a young man of virility. He carried with him an aura of such obvious and certain menace that I was immediately convinced of his identity without having to glimpse his face.

"Asher!" I shouted urgently, but I did not pause to determine if he had noticed the call. Descending the battlement steps rapidly, I raced across the short distance between the buildings.

The turret upon which the man was positioned presented a clear view of the Palace, but it was inaccessible from the outside. Though it was an optimal location from which to launch an attack, it afforded few avenues of escape. Was

Bengel, I wondered, exceedingly foolish or exceedingly brave? Most likely and by all accounts, I decided, he was probably simply completely mad.

St Margaret's was a beautiful, monolithic structure, but I wasted no time in admiring the ivory pillars or intricate stained glass as I sprinted hastily through its cathedral. I came up on the irreverent interloper just as he had completed his ministrations upon the object that had been hidden during my initial observation. As Joseph had predicted, it was, in fact, quite easily distinguished from an ordinary weapon.

The Eye of Ra did not, as I had expected, possess a convoluted tangle of wires, dials and gauges with which I associated complicated scientific instruments. In fact, the apparatus, mounted on a small, stout tripod, merely resembled a much larger version of Nathaniel's clever pistol, though the barrel was longer and straight, rather than tapered, and the trigger guard was reversed, atop the ovular chamber in which I assumed Cross and Joseph had housed the power supply. The trigger itself was a fat, padded lever that appeared to require a certain application of force to engage.

I had little time to linger over my disappointment at finding this revolutionary weapon so commonplace in light of the current circumstances. Bengel had yet to notice my approach. As he swivelled the Eye to target the Palace's Central Lobby, I stepped, most irresponsibly to be sure, into his view. As I did so, I reached hastily for my own pistol but found my person quite unarmed. In retrospect, I considered, it might have been more prudent to ascertain the whereabouts of my weapon prior to this foolhardy confrontation.

Well, no matter, and no help for it now. I had faced down dangerous, violent criminals with little more than my wits and cleverness plenty of times in the past; I was confident I could do so again with equally successful results.

To my great astonishment, the terrorist did not strike upon my appearance. Quite the contrary; he spun towards me, and, taking in my appearance, began to laugh delightedly.

I blinked, nonplussed, but I did not allow the man to catch me out for long. I squared my shoulders, peering composedly into his pale eyes. At my cool reception, his laughter faded, but his smile remained, resembling the grinning countenance of a shark preparing to attack. The scar on his face, the confirmation of his identity, was neither dashing nor endearing as it had appeared in his sketch; it was gruesome and horrifying, a ragged, ugly mark that disfigured his otherwise even features from brow to chin. I was most disinclined to learn how one would obtain such a scar.

"Ah. Astrid Darby." His accent was thick, his voice slightly guttural, as if he were speaking through a particularly painful neck wound. I sighed; truly, men like this were born to terrorism. I was almost disappointed by the inevitability of the man. I was not, however, foolish enough to discredit his aptitude for the occupation. "I have been expecting you."

I smiled gaily. "Have you? I am gratified by your confidence in my abilities. I do hope I did not disappoint."

He chuckled. "No indeed. You are as foolish as I'd supposed. I am impressed, however, that you were able to outrun our people three times."

"Oh, I am particularly adept at saving my own skin, Mr Bengel. I value your acknowledgement."

Bengel inclined his head, his eyes twinkling in amusement. "Please do not assume I am not regretful in informing you that your luck has, at last, run out. I am, as it happens, particularly adept at murder."

If there was any moment in which I needed Asher Key more, I could not think of it. My eyes darted around me. I was suddenly aware that I had not fully appreciated the peril in which I had placed myself. How, I had a fleeting moment to wonder, had I expected this confrontation to transpire? Had I expected the man would simply step away from the apparatus, having been caught red-handed in the act? Had I been so thoroughly and foolishly confident of my own ability to talk him out of his course? More likely, the tribulations of the previous days and the lack of sleep had simply rendered me incapable of rational higher thought. Had I been functioning on my customary plane of extreme cleverness, I would not have been so keen to expedite this meeting.

Oh, Astrid, you always were likely to be the instrument of your own demise.

Well, I considered vaguely, better me than someone else. My questing eyes found no item that might come to my aid. I dove sideways against the battlement wall, briefly considering leaping from the balcony but knowing it would do little to save my life at so late a juncture. Bengel swivelled the wide barrel of the Eye directly towards me. Well, at least he was no longer aiming at the Palace, I thought wryly in the brief pause. It would remain intact, at any rate.

He yanked forcefully on the lever that functioned as the trigger. I closed my eyes in resignation.

I did not know how a death ray was meant to sound. Nathaniel's pistol, when discharged, made a soft, swift whooshing sound, which, Nathaniel assured me, sounded like a billion tiny particles suddenly changing direction and rushing through the small barrel of the weapon. This was, he explained, how the clever little dingus functioned. I had, therefore, expected the much larger version to sound precisely the same, merely proportionately much louder.

What I had not expected was for the Eye to sound almost exactly like a gunshot.

For a silent, disoriented moment, I lay in paralysed incomprehension on the hard, rough ground. "Astrid?"

The acrid smell of gun powder tickled my nostrils. I glanced up, utterly flummoxed, at Joseph, who stood in the doorway, a look of equal astonishment on his face. In his hand, he still held a smoking gun aloft, as if he could hardly believe he had fired it. Between us, Luther Bengel lay, pitched over the Eye, having fallen forward across the grip, tilting the muzzle away from my miraculously unscathed person and towards the brilliant blue sky.

"Joseph!" Relief flooded through me as I became aware of the situation, and I rose swiftly to my feet, launching myself into his arms. "I am utterly delighted to discover I am not, as I had thoroughly anticipated, quite dead."

He exhaled a bark of nearly hysterical laughter. "No, I am very relieved to assure you that you are not."

I turned to peer down at my erstwhile adversary, so easily dispatched after a journey so fraught with peril and terrifying revelations, and felt almost regretful that the chase had ended so smartly. "But why did the Eye fail to discharge?"

Joseph shook his head. "I cannot say. Perhaps it doesn't work. Perhaps it never did."

"Or perhaps your doctor disabled it permanently. Tore out its very heart."

"Or Phineas was unable to decipher Sebastian's designs after all. He was rather cryptic." He laughed a bitter, humourless laugh. "Sebastian died for nothing; for a weapon that never worked."

I reached for him, but the noise we heard then sounded precisely as I had assumed a very large death ray would sound. The loud, sudden whoosh was nearly deafening in the quiet of the Square. Joseph reacted instantly, as if the noise were an innate operant trigger, pressing me swiftly and painfully to the stone floor. He needn't have bothered, however.

In the distance, the clock tower of Westminster Place exploded in a burst of sparks and rubble, showering the Palace below with splintered wood and twisted metal.

"Well," I said uncomfortably. "That is most unfortunate."

"Was that—was that Big Ben?"

"Oy!" Asher burst onto the battlement, arriving at long last and infinite moments too late, receiving the scene with amazement.

"Good of you to offer assistance, Agent Key," Joseph said wryly, wrapping a bracing arm around my shoulders. "However, as you can see, we have the situation well in hand."

"What in the bloody hell just happened here?"

I turned a brilliant smile upon him. "As you can see, Asher, Astrid Darby has, once again, gotten your man." I strode forward, gesturing expansively towards Bengel.

"Astrid! You destroyed Big Ben!" Asher exclaimed, his face a deep, angry crimson. He jabbed a finger towards the ruined tower, then back at me with a look of utter incredulity.

I frowned disapprovingly at him. "Oh, Asher, what's a small bit of collateral damage in the face of preventing the complete destruction of Westminster Palace and, with it, the utter devastation of the entire British Empire?"

"Perhaps you are in need of some perspective," Joseph added blithely.

"Perspective," Asher repeated in a low, dangerous growl. He started towards Joseph, but I stepped smartly into his path. Completely sidetracked, he gripped my shoulders, shaking them roughly. "You should have waited for me! What were you thinking confronting him on your own?"

I peered curiously up into his eyes. His chest rose and fell rapidly with his shallow breaths, and his cobalt eyes blazed with a wild, panicked expression I had never seen in them before. I smiled gently, understanding at last, and patted his arm bracingly.

"Come now, Ash," I said softly. "Don't fret. Everything is all right now."

His voice was low and tight. "Astrid, everything is not all right." He released me abruptly and spun, gesturing violently. "You and your mad scientist friend demolished Big Ben. One of our nation's most beloved landmarks. Destroyed. I mean..." He squeezed the bridge of his nose, taking several long, deep breaths. "Who's going to pay for this?"

I smiled, avoiding Bengel's limp form as I strode forward to finally claim the long, perilous journey's prize. Ignoring the two men's incredulous expressions,

I bent and lifted the Eye carefully from its tripod.

"Oh, it's a bit heavy. Well, if you two strapping gentlemen would be so obliging and assist me in returning the apparatus to my employer, I believe we can sort everything out."

* * *

Dear Mr Cole,

I was most aggrieved to hear of the ill fortune befalling your esteemed organisation proceeding the startling public outcry regarding the regrettable temporary misplacement of the Eye of Ra and subsequent destruction of a beloved national landmark at the hands of a malicious terrorist. The prompt payment for services rendered upon my successful return of your apparatus was highly appreciated.

However, due to the unforeseeably complicated and perilous nature of this assignment, I am, most reluctantly, obliged to request recompense for additional expenses incurred in the successful resolution of my obligation to your organisation. Please see subsequent pages for itemised catalogue of said expenses. I am gratified by your thorough attention in this matter and shall confidently expect your timely reimbursement.

Yours sincerely with all due respect,

Astrid Darby

P.S. Your prompt payment is highly appreciated in the amount of: £3706

See Items below:

Travel (including but not limited to Airship, Train, Carriage let including driver and/or horse, Wagon acquisition): £500

Lodging: £10

Meals: £20

Miscellaneous (see appendix): £3176

Appendix

Clothing (including disguises and damages caused by smoke, fire, tumbling from trains and wear and tear associated with frontier travel): £25

Bribes: £1

Fines resulting from alleged obstruction of justice and failure to report a serious and deadly threat to national security: 150£

Big Ben: £3000

THE END

Read Book Two in the exciting Astrid Darby Adventures

Astrid Darby and the Laughing Coffin

Available now from DC Dreams

www.diogenesclubpress.com

ABOUT THE AUTHOR

Eleanor Prophet is an author, columnist, editor, lady of leisure and amateur sleuth. Her most popular works include the Astrid Darby Adventures. When she isn't writing books, short stories, essays and articles of questionable veracity, she is typically enjoying the attentions of Mr Prophet, a dashing international man of mystery and intrigue. Her favourite activities include larking about, rule-breaking, mischief-making and getting to the bottom of things. She often receives fascinating, comical and occasionally disturbing mail to her desk and publishes on her blog for the public's information, entertainment and frequent outrage.

Read Ellie's Blog at:

www.ellieprophet.wordpress.com

www.ingramcontent.com/pod-product-compliance
Lightning Source LLC
Chambersburg PA
CBHW061221170626
46809CB00007B/2546